ALSO BY
DONNA ALWARD

JEWELL COVE SERIES
The House on Blackberry Hill
Treasure on Lilac Lane
Summer on Lovers' Island

DARLING, VT SERIES
Somebody Like You

Someone to Love

Donna Alward

St. Martin's Paperbacks

This is a work of fiction. All of the characters, organizations, and events
portrayed in this novel are either products of the author's imagination or
are used fictitiously.

SOMEONE TO LOVE

Copyright © 2017 by Donna Alward.

All rights reserved.

For information address St. Martin's Press, 175 Fifth Avenue, New York,
NY 10010.

ISBN: 978-1-250-09266-3

Our books may be purchased in bulk for promotional, educational, or
business use. Please contact your local bookseller or the Macmillan
Corporate and Premium Sales Department at 1-800-221-7945, ext. 5442,
or by e-mail at MacmillanSpecialMarkets@macmillan.com.

Printed in the United States of America

St. Martin's Paperbacks edition / March 2017

St. Martin's Paperbacks are published by St. Martin's Press, 175 Fifth
Avenue, New York, NY 10010.

10 9 8 7 6 5 4 3 2 1

CHAPTER 1

Bright July sunshine soaked through Willow Dunaway's bamboo T-shirt as she took a bite of her veggie wrap. The lunch rush at The Purple Pig Café was over, and she'd snuck out for twenty minutes or so just to enjoy a bit of fresh air and a snack. The "Green," as the locals called it, was a park that ran alongside Fisher's Creek. The town kept the grass neatly clipped, flower beds watered and weeded, and had installed several benches both in the sun and in the shade of trees. Willow loved it. Sure, it was more manicured than wild and natural, but it was still calm and restful. Even when, like today, the tourists came to take their turn on the Kissing Bridge that spanned the creek, guaranteeing that their love would last forever. It was a cute, if somewhat silly, concept that played a major part in the town's economy.

Willow had been back in Darling, Vermont, for just over a year. After six years in Florida, she'd come back to northern climes and had to adjust to the change in seasons. She'd stayed through the cold winter, deep snow, frigid temperatures, and the ski season that brought downhillers to the inns and bed-and-breakfasts in town. Through the pale green of early spring, when the snow melted, tiny sprigs of grass poked up through the earth, testing to see if winter was truly over, and crocuses and snowdrops carpeted front yards with the first bursts of color. Through the warm, lazy summer beside the lake and a bright, cozy autumn filled with colors and the scent of fallen leaves in the air.

She'd liked living in Florida. And it had served its purpose. She'd had to get away—from memories, mostly. Someplace neutral where she could sort out her thoughts and feelings and get her feet beneath herself again. Clearwater had done that for her. But in the end, Darling had beckoned her back. And when she'd checked realty listings and noticed the café up for sale, she'd known it was time to come home. Now, a year later, some of the new-business pressure had eased as the café was a resounding success. For the first time in many, many years, Willow felt everything was just as it should be.

She took another bite of her wrap and watched a young couple trot along the path to the stone bridge, the town's number one tourist attraction. Willow had heard at least three versions of how the Kissing Bridge got its name, but there was one consistency in every single story: when a couple kissed on the bridge, it was said that their love would last forever. She thought it was cute, and she smiled a little as the pair reached the top of the arch, looked out over the sparkling creek, and then kissed.

On a less sentimental side, no one could deny the revenue the Kissing Bridge brought to Darling. Whether it was a simple kiss, a proposal, or posing for wedding pictures, the bridge was a huge draw. Heck, her best friend had just been married there a month ago. Laurel and Aiden had surprised everyone with the impromptu ceremony disguised as a publicity photo shoot for the town's new tourism campaign. Now the two of them were cozied up together in Laurel's house, acting like newlyweds. Willow missed seeing her friend, but she wouldn't begrudge Laurel this happiness for the world. She'd earned it.

The bridge kept The Purple Pig busy, too. Willow put the lid back on the container she'd used for the wrap and dropped it into her tote bag. She really should get back. There was supper prep that needed doing.

The couple on the bridge kissed again and stood with their arms around each other for a while. Willow watched for a few stolen seconds, feeling a wistfulness open up inside her. She hadn't had a real relationship in so long. She'd tried, once, in Clearwater. He'd been in her yoga class. An ex-soldier with a soft spot for animals and meditation. At first he'd seemed perfect. But then Willow had discovered that he carried even more baggage than she did. Instead of healing wounds, they'd ended up bringing each other down. Walking away had been the right, if painful, decision.

Life was good now. She had the business. She had good friends. She was at peace with a lot of things from her past, and those she wasn't, she'd at least accepted. She should feel perfectly happy. Not like there was something missing.

It was past two thirty, so she shouldered her bag and stood up, knowing her assistant manager, Emily, could use the help making sure things were ready for the supper rush. She'd just taken a step when a soccer ball came out of nowhere, bouncing between her feet.

She looked up and saw a boy, maybe five years old, running at her full tilt. "Whoa," she ordered, laughing. "Slow down, buddy."

"Sorry, lady." Brown eyes flashed up at her, full of boyish charm. He looked familiar somehow. Maybe he'd come into the café before or something.

"No worries," she replied, giving it a light kick with the side of her foot. "Here you go." He trapped it—rather expertly for such a small boy, she thought—beneath the toe of his sneaker.

The kid squinted against the sun as he looked at her. "How come your hair is pink?"

She laughed again, enchanted by his honesty. It wasn't the first time she'd been asked that question since she'd added the pink stripe. "Oh, I felt like doing something fun with it." She squatted down in front of him. "Do you like it?"

"It's all right, I guess. 'Cept I like green." He peered at her closer. "And you have a thing in your nose."

God, the little guy was charming. Dark auburn hair with just a hint of curl and eyes that were guaranteed to break a girl's heart someday. She pointed toward her nose. "My stud? It's a real diamond."

"No way."

"Way."

"Cool."

"Connor!"

The boy's head shot up as a masculine voice called his name. "That's my dad," he said, biting his lip. "Sorry."

"It's okay. Have fun."

He smiled and turned around, only his dad was walking toward them with purposeful steps. Another boy, a little younger, raced behind, trying to keep up.

Willow stood and tried hard not to gawk. He was tall—over six feet for sure, and in jeans and a plain T-shirt she could tell he was in good shape. When he looked at her it was as if she'd suddenly taken a blow to her chest, pushing out all the air so she couldn't breathe. Even with the stern look on his face he was stunning in a rough way. Strong jaw, seriously blue eyes, and auburn hair, a little on the long side, unruly with a bit of natural curl. It wasn't hard to imagine him in shorts and cleats, sweaty from playing soccer. Or in a kilt, like one of those highlanders in the books she'd been reading lately.

She had to get a grip.

"Connor, it's time to go. Next time I tell you, you listen, rather than kicking the ball in the other direction, you hear?"

Alas, Willow thought with disappointment, there wasn't a hint of a Scottish brogue in his terse voice. The boy's face fell at his father's sharp tone . . . Had it really been necessary for him to be so snappish? Any lingering romantic notions fizzled completely as she realized he was assessing her. From the look on his face, he didn't like what he saw.

Wait. He seemed familiar. He . . . that was it. He was one of Aiden and Hannah's brothers. But which one? She frowned. She and Aiden were the same age. He had a younger brother . . . Rory. Hannah was a few years older than Willow. And there were the twins and then . . . that meant this was the older brother. Try as she might, she couldn't remember his name. What she did remember, however, was Laurel and Aiden's wedding reception. She'd caught the bouquet. He'd caught the garter. And he'd slipped it onto her calf in one of the most awkward, uncomfortable moments of her life.

As soon as the elastic had snapped onto her leg, he'd extricated himself from the embarrassing situation. *More like run away,* a little voice in her head chided. As fast as he could manage it.

"Connor," he said, only slightly softer, "take the ball and your brother and go put your stuff in the backpack."

"Yes, Dad," Connor said, the earlier ebullience gone from his voice. "Come on, Ronan." He held out his hand and the other boy took it. Willow watched them and couldn't help the little smile that curved her lips. The brothers were cute, and it was clear that the younger one idolized the older. He had similar hair and eyes, but he looked up at his big brother like he ruled the world.

"They're very cute," she said, hoping the pleasant tone would ease the stern look on the dad's face.

"They're very energetic. And stubborn."

"Aw, don't be too hard on them." She tried smiling again. "It's a beautiful day on the Green. You can't blame them for wanting to play a little longer."

He was quiet for a moment. She saw his gaze slide over the pink streak in her blond hair, and a tiny lift of his eyebrow telegraphed his disapproval. She resisted the urge to roll her eyes. People put color in their hair all the time.

"I'm Willow," she said, holding out her hand, determined to be polite.

"Of course you are," he replied, and he shook her hand. Briefly. "Laurel's . . . friend."

Willow bristled at the dismissive way he said "friend." She kind of wished he hadn't opened his mouth. The fantasy of him being . . . well, different, was pretty much gone. Instead she got the impression that he didn't know how to smile.

So she made her smile bigger and said, "And you're one of Aiden's brothers, right?"

"Ethan Gallagher."

That's right. Ethan. "I knew you looked familiar. It's the Gallagher hair and eyes."

His stern expression didn't change.

"Come on, it's a compliment. Hannah's gorgeous."

He sighed, then looked over his shoulder to check on the boys. "And she knows it, too. I'd better get back."

Wow. Would it have killed him to say thank you? "Me, too. I'd better get back to work."

"At The Purple Pig," he said.

She frowned. She was sure he hadn't been in before when she'd been working. "How did you know that?"

"It's on your shirt?"

His tone was dry and condescending, and he voiced it as a question so that the word "duh" echoed in her head. She'd forgotten she was wearing the T-shirt that the employees wore in lieu of a uniform. Her shirt today was lilac with a darker purple pig embroidered on the left chest. He could have pointed it out without being so rude. Aiden and Hannah were warm, friendly people. Ethan, it seemed, was cold and pretty unapproachable.

"Oh. Right." She was annoyed to realize that a stranger could make her feel small and a bit stupid, and so she couldn't resist coming back with a bright smile. Just because he was unfriendly didn't mean she had to lower herself to his level. "You should bring the boys in for a treat sometime."

His lips finally curved, but his smile was patronizing and not warm, as if he were saying, "Yeah, right." He wouldn't be the first to roll their eyes at the café's philosophy: local, organic, and fair trade food. Willow felt heat rise in her cheeks. It had been a long, long time since she'd allowed anyone to make her feel inferior, but Ethan Gallagher had managed it in a few short sentences and one down-the-nose look.

"The Pig isn't really my style," he said.

Yep. She was starting to feel sorry for his kids. Hopefully they had a kind and gentle mother who at least smiled once in a while. Something else twigged in her mind, from her conversations with Hannah and Laurel. Something about Ethan's wife. She really needed to start paying better attention.

"You'd better get back to your boys." Willow stepped back, done with trying to be nice. "Enjoy the afternoon."

She turned her back on him and walked away, her sandals crunching on the fine crushed gravel of the pathway. Her brows pulled together as she frowned. Resemblance aside, it was hard to believe that man was Hannah Gallagher's brother. Willow was pretty sure she couldn't have done a single thing to offend Ethan, but there'd been no warmth whatsoever in his manner.

She left the Green and walked the block and a half back to the café along Main Street, shaking off the encounter and taking deep breaths. There was a reason she'd come back here. Darling was, simply, *home*. The little shops, the small-town vibe of familiarity, the personal touches to the storefronts that showed care and pride. The buildings in the town center were more often than not constructed of reassuring red brick, with lots of white trim and colonial design. Color was added in the form of shutters and doors, and one of Willow's favorites was at the florist's, where the red door boasted a heart-shaped window, and the trim around it was painted with vines and leaves.

The Purple Pig stood out from several other businesses. The building itself was newer, a three-unit row-house constructed in much the same colonial style, but with siding instead of brick, and two large storefront windows. The Pig's siding was a muted shade of pink, with a white awning over the front door and the logo—a fat, curly-tailed, happy purple pig—painted on the bay window in the front.

It added a sense of whimsy to the street, to Willow's mind. As she approached it, thoughts of Ethan Stick-Up-His-Butt Gallagher faded away. Running the café was like her particular talents and philosophies finally all blended together into one perfect job.

A little bell dinged overhead as she stepped inside to the aromas she loved: cinnamon, chocolate, tea, bread. There were two kinds of soup on special today, and a variety of sandwiches, all handmade to order from fresh, organic ingredients. She planned the menus on a simple principle: nourishing the mind, body, and soul.

She stowed her tote in the office and put her apron on, returning to the front to help her part-time employee, Steven. Willow and her assistant manager, Emily, both agreed he was doing great, so she was going to increase his hours to full time in August. He could use the money for college and he was a fast learner. Plus he was a fantastic up-seller. If someone came in for a scone, he'd sell a bowl of soup with it. A sandwich? Have a tea and cookie to round it out. She wasn't sure how he did it, but customers had a hard time saying no to him. It showed in his tips, too.

He was currently making a turkey and cranberry sandwich for a customer, so Willow went to the next person waiting and took her order. It was Shelley Burke, a former nurse who spent a good deal of her time volunteering around town. Willow slid a blueberry scone into a bag and handed it over the counter along with a cup of licorice mint tea. "Here you go, Mrs. Burke. What are you up to today?"

"I just finished at the food bank." She smiled widely. "And tomorrow's book club."

"That sounds like fun."

"It is. We even talk about the book sometimes." Willow laughed.

Shelley took the food and drink and frowned a little. "I wish you could join us, Willow. Maybe for next month's meeting?"

"We're right in the middle of tourist season. It's hard to get away." She genuinely felt disappointment at having to say no. The café kept her so busy that she didn't have much time for anything purely social, and a book club sounded like fun. The kind of thing you did when living in a small town. Then she had an idea. "But if you want to hold it here, I can set up a little area for you in the corner, and you can have tea and treats. Then maybe I can sneak in for some of the discussion. Just let me know what the new book is." Maybe that was something they could look into. Shouldn't a café be a gathering place too? And for more than the occasional Chamber of Commerce meeting.

"I'll ask the girls." Shelley smiled. "Thanks for the offer."

"See you soon," Willow replied, and she slipped the change Shelley had left on the counter into the tip jar.

Emily came through the swinging doors of the kitchen to the front of the café, two trays of baked goods in her hands. "Brownies and cookies coming through."

"Those smell delicious," Willow said, sliding open the display case.

"Black-bean brownies and honey-oat trail-mix cookies. The apple muffins are coming out shortly." Emily stood and brushed her hands down her apron.

Willow looked at Emily, and wondered yet again what it might be like if she joined the business as more of a partner rather than assistant manager. "Are you happy here, Em?"

"Are you kidding? I love it."

"I know the pay isn't great."

"It's the food service industry. I wasn't expecting to get rich." She laughed. "Good thing. Not that I'm asking for a raise or anything . . ." Her eyes widened and a blush crept into her cheeks.

Willow laughed. "That's not what I was getting at. After the fall rush, we should sit down and talk. Think about expansion. Think about whether or not you want to join the business in a more permanent way."

Emily's face broke into a smile. "Oh my gosh. I'd love that. And I'm flattered. I have a bunch of ideas for the menu, and if we had more space . . ."

"Slow down," Willow said, laughing again. "Let's get through the next few months first. We work really well together, you know? I'm sure we can come up with some great plans."

They always had another rush between five and six, when the commuters came home and stopped off for a quick meal. Em, who'd worked the breakfast and lunch crowd, left at five, after ensuring the kitchen was prepped for the evening. Willow and Steven handled the dwindling crowd.

Hannah Gallagher came through the door, her

crown of red hair and bright smile announcing her entrance.

Willow smiled back. Hannah was wearing jeans and red wedges, with a short-sleeved cobalt-blue top that suited her Irish coloring and gave Willow a bit of style envy. Since seeing Ethan this afternoon, Willow saw the resemblance and also marveled at the disparity between brother and sister.

Willow finished wrapping up the roasted vegetable and goat cheese panini she was making, then turned to greet Hannah at the counter. "Hey, stranger. Did you come for dinner? Emily made a tomato basil soup this afternoon that's to die for. We might have some left."

Hannah grinned. "Of course I came for dinner. I haven't eaten in . . ." She checked her watch. "At least two hours."

Willow was always teasing Hannah about her metabolism. Hannah had announced a few months ago that her newest "thing" was training for a triathlon. She had the running and biking down cold, and now that summer was in full swing, she'd added swimming to her schedule. Plus she was a realtor two doors away. It was an odd day when Willow didn't see her at least once.

"You want me to surprise you?" Willow asked.

"Of course. You always make the nicest things."

"Go sit down. I'll bring it out. I might even be able to take a quick break and have a tea with you."

Hannah sat at the one vacant table left and Willow went to the kitchen. "Hey, Steven? I'm going to grab a cup of tea with Hannah."

"No problem," Steven replied, pushing the start button on the dishwasher. "I've got this."

Willow grabbed a green tea, then took out a flax tortilla and filled it with free-range chicken, spinach, feta, and a few of the roasted vegetables. Knowing Hannah's emphasis on protein, Willow also filled a bowl with her special bean salad and sprinkled a little fresh parsley from the herb garden on top. It smelled so good when she was done that her stomach was growling with hunger as she took the tray to the table.

"I could eat a horse," Hannah said, as Willow sat down.

"Sorry. No horse here. But good fuel."

"I know." Hannah took a bite of her wrap and closed her eyes for a minute. "What is that?" she asked, licking her lips.

"It's the marinade for the roasted vegetables. If I use those, I don't need to add any extra dressing. Olive oil with a little garlic, lemon, and oregano."

The combination was her basic go-to for just about everything, including the bean salad. And the easiest thing in the world to whip up or modify.

After a second bite, Hannah pinned Willow with a sharp look. "You're really making quite a splash here, you know. Especially with the Kissing Bridge bringing in so much traffic. Couples from all over the world come here to say I love you and all that crap."

"I hope so," Willow replied. "And gee. Aren't you the sentimental one."

Hannah laughed.

"I've worked in the service industry for a long time. This place has the added benefit of, well, matching my life philosophy. I was just talking to Em today about expansion."

Hannah pointed a finger at her. "If that's true, come see me. We can look at leasing more space." She raised an eyebrow. "Or if you want to take on any investors."

Willow didn't know what to say. On one hand, it all seemed very exciting. On the other, she tried to keep her life calm, peaceful. There were days that running the café tested her tranquility. What would happen if things got out of hand? She'd already seen her best friend, Laurel, work crazy hours trying to get her garden center up and running. The last thing Willow wanted was to become a workaholic.

Like her mom.

"You know my thoughts on eating clean," Hannah said, breaking into Willow's thoughts. "It'd be a fabulous opportunity. Of course, my folks aren't quite as crazy about it as you and I are, but I grew up having a vegetable garden and fruit trees and stuff. Way better than processed. Speaking of, Sunday's the weekly family dinner. I think you should come."

"Sunday?" Willow had met Hannah's parents at Aiden and Laurel's wedding. They were nice enough, but like Hannah, they were all a bit "larger than life," with big personalities. The idea of being a guest at a family dinner made her a bit nervous. It would be all of the Gallaghers together in one place. Including Ethan. Mr. Friendly.

"Yes, Sunday," Hannah replied, wiping her lips with a napkin. "It's my birthday. Mom wanted to throw a party but . . ." Hannah shuddered. "I'm a bit old for that nonsense. So I got around her by promising I would bring a friend to dinner. She kind of hoped it would be a friend of the opposite sex, but I'm not into picking up random guys off the street, you know?"

Willow laughed. Hannah was assertive, professional, a real take-charge kind of woman. But Willow knew from their conversations, and ones she'd had with

Laurel, that the matriarch of the Gallagher family had the ability to put all the children directly under her thumb. Willow was glad she'd already met Moira. If Willow was any judge, Moira Gallagher was big-hearted and had a great sense of humor. She also commanded a great deal of respect from her kids.

"Please," Hannah pleaded. "It's all the birthday present I need. Save me."

Willow laughed. "Wow. You make it sound so fun, how could I possibly refuse?"

"Thank you," Hannah breathed the words like a benediction.

"That wasn't a yes. I was being sarcastic."

"Too bad. You said it and now it's out there. You're in. I'll pick you up at five. Dinner's at six." She pointed her fork at the plate of bean salad. "And bring this. My youngest brother Rory will go crazy for it. Besides, I think Mom is making a big baked ham and I'm trying to avoid extra salt." She puffed up her cheeks.

"Everyone's going to be there?" Willow's nervousness returned. She was fine behind a counter, when she had a job to do. A purpose. There was a reason she always kept busy. There was a comfort zone thing and making small talk wasn't exactly it.

"Yep. My parents, three brothers, two sisters, two nephews, one set of grandparents, and you and me."

"Awesome," Willow muttered under her breath.

"I'm not letting you back out now. Besides, if I pick you up, I have an excuse to bug out early. We can always say you have to get up early to open the café."

"This is sounding better and better." She hesitated. "Three brothers? And nephews? That means Ethan is going to be there, right?"

Hannah lifted her chin. "Of course." Her eyes narrowed. "I didn't realize you two knew each other. I mean, other than crossing paths at the wedding."

Willow felt her cheeks heat beneath Hannah's direct gaze. "Actually, I ran into him by accident today. On the Green."

"Really? He must have had the boys out. Connor is crazy about soccer since Ethan signed him up this spring."

"Sounds right. A soccer ball went astray and landed at my feet. The oldest one . . . Connor? He's a cutie."

"He's full of it, for sure." Hannah grinned. "Like his dad."

"Is Ethan always so crabby?" Willow asked, and Hannah choked on her food.

She gasped for air for a few seconds and then answered. "Oh my God, you nearly killed me." She patted the middle of her chest. "Ethan wasn't always so grouchy. But the rest of the family is fun, I promise. Ethan'll come around. And he's much mellower around the boys. I don't know what he'd do without them."

"He was kind of rude," Willow admitted. "He must have a patient wife."

A shadow passed over Hannah's face, and her voice quieted. "I forget sometimes that you haven't been back here for long. Ethan's a widower, Willow. Lisa died a year and a half ago. Being a single dad . . . well, it's taken a toll on him."

Willow put down her tea and felt ten kinds of stupid. "Oh, Han, I had no idea. I mean, I know a lot of people by name by now, but not, well, not a lot of personal details. I'm sorry. That's terrible. It must have happened just before I moved back."

"I should have said something ages ago, since you and I started hanging out."

Willow shook her head. "You're not a gossip, and I appreciate that. I'm sure it's not easy to talk about."

"No. We all help out when we can with the boys. Ethan's shift work makes for an extra challenge. But there're lots of us to lend a hand." Her smile came back. "You'll see. He's really a great guy. He just dotes on the boys, making sure they don't miss out on anything, even though he works shift work with the fire department." She finished her wrap and wiped her mouth with her napkin.

Willow thought back to their meeting. It shouldn't have made any difference in regards to his behavior, but it did anyway. Those adorable boys had lost their mother. He'd lost his wife. His heart must be utterly broken. And yet he'd been out on the Green with them today, playing soccer. She had no idea what it was like to have a parent do something like that.

"Fine," she agreed. "Just this once I will enter the lion's den of the ginormous Gallagher family. And I want a code word that I can use that means I have an escape route."

"No problem." Hannah's eyes sparkled. "Trust me, you're going to have a great time. Besides, there'll be cake."

"How could I possibly turn down cake?" Willow answered, getting up from the table.

"That's sarcasm again, right?" Hannah's smile was so wicked that Willow couldn't help but laugh.

"Hey, Hannah?" She stopped, holding the dirty dishes in her hands. She hadn't forgotten Han's enthusiasm about the business. "The landlord's not in a hurry to rent out the space next door, is he?"

"Not right away, no. Is that what you're thinking? Making this place bigger?" Hannah was also the property manager for the building, which was why they'd become such good friends to begin with. They seemed to be in each other's orbit quite often.

"It's something to think about. I just . . . well, if someone wants to lease it, is it too much to ask to come see me first?"

"Of course not. It might help if you had a business plan, too."

"I was planning on sitting down later in the fall and working on that," Willow admitted.

"I can't promise anything. But I'll mention it."

"Thanks, Han."

"No problem." Hannah reached inside her purse and took out a twenty. "Here. For supper."

"I'll get you your change."

"Don't worry about it. Just throw one of those black-bean brownie things in a bag for me for later. And I'd love a raspberry tea to go."

Willow laughed. "You're a bottomless pit," she said, reaching for a take-out cup for the tea.

"One day it's going to catch up with me," Hannah acknowledged. "But not today."

After Hannah was gone back to work, Willow put her apron back on and went out front. She served coffee and sweets and made the odd sandwich, but her thoughts kept slipping to earlier that afternoon. It was hard to reconcile the irascible Ethan with what Hannah had told her about him being mellow around his kids. Her initial impression had been based on his raw physicality, but that flicker of awareness had been snuffed out by his, well, cold behavior. Seeing his stern face had stirred memories she tried not to think about that often. Willow's mother had brought her up alone, but there'd been no fun and games in the park. She'd always been too busy to be bothered. Willow had always felt like she was an inconvenience.

His wife had died. That gave a man an excuse to be grouchy, didn't it? And Hannah knew him better than anyone, probably. Her face had softened, talking about him and how he loved his kids.

Willow's heart ached for him. He had to be hurting so much. She knew what it was like to feel you'd lost everything.

On Sunday, she decided, she would be the epitome of kindness and tolerance. No matter how condescending he was. In her experience, a good dose of kindness went a long, long way.

Chapter 2

Willow clutched the covered bowl close against her middle, wondering why on earth she'd accepted an invitation to a family dinner when the only member of the Gallagher family she knew well at all was Hannah. Of course, her best friend, Laurel, was also a Gallagher now, but the wedding was so recent that it didn't exactly count as "knowing the family."

Hannah was the oldest daughter in a family of six children. Six kids in an Irish family. Rowdiness came built in. Willow, on the other hand, was used to being alone, with things peaceful and quiet.

The noise from the backyard was punctuated with some comical and inventive PG cussing, and as they turned the corner Willow saw a large man with rusty hair and a huge grin holding a small boy upside down by his feet. The boy was giggling so hard he could barely breathe. "Grampa! Put me down!"

"I don't think so, me boy. Not until you tell me who put you up to it." John Gallagher gave the feet a shake and the boy belly-laughed so hard Willow couldn't help but smile. Clearly they were both enjoying the shocking form of extortion. An excited retriever bounced in circles around them, enjoying the game.

"It was Dad." He finally gave it up and the man eased the boy down onto the carpet of grass.

"Of course it was. And he's too big for me to hang by his feet." He helped the boy stand up. Connor's impish eyes were filled with the same merriment as the other day when he'd commented on her nose ring.

"Sorry, Grampa. Dad said to put it in your glass or he'd hold back my allowance."

"And what did you put in his glass, Connor?" Hannah stepped forward, leaving Willow slightly behind.

Connor grinned wickedly. "Just a worm, Aunt Hannah. From the garden."

Gross, Willow thought. Boys and their pranks. And his dad had put him up to it? Nice guy. *Blech*. That sort of immature prank definitely didn't fit with the impression he'd made the other day. Maybe he did know how to cut loose once in a while.

"Hannah, darlin'." Her father came forward and kissed her cheek. "You're looking pretty as ever."

"Whatever you're scheming for revenge on Ethan, forget it. I'm out. You'll have to use your double agent here." She gestured at Connor. "Don't try flattery on me, old man."

He laughed, a big hearty laugh that made Willow smile on the inside.

"Oh, and you've brought a guest." He noticed Willow over Hannah's shoulder, and his blue eyes twinkled at her. "I'm John Gallagher. Hannah's dad. Welcome."

"I remember from the wedding. Thanks for having me," she said politely, charmed and yet slightly intimidated.

Connor dashed off in the direction of the house, while at the same time the back door opened and a procession of people came out to the deck carrying a variety of dishes and talking in loud voices.

"My family," Hannah said, with a sideways grin. "I did warn you it'd be loud."

Willow nodded and smiled. "That's okay. I'll just sneak in under the radar."

To be honest, despite the shyness, she was kind of enjoying the "big happy family" vibe going on. It wasn't like anything she'd had growing up, but things had been a little different after she'd moved to Florida. She'd met families in Clearwater who'd maintained that sort of closeness, and they'd included her quite often on different occasions. It was there that she'd learned what families were supposed to be like.

"Hey, guys, you remember Willow, right? She was Laurel's maid of honor." Hannah led her toward the steps of the deck.

"Hi, Willow." A female voice floated on the air. "I'm Claire."

"And I'm Caitlyn," came another voice that sounded identical. When Willow looked up, she saw they sounded identical because they looked identical. "But everyone calls me Cait."

"I'm totally jealous of all the red hair." She smiled at the girls as she climbed the steps. Hannah's hair was darker, more of a reddish mahogany, but Claire and Cait were closer to strawberry blond.

Hannah grinned. "We've all got Dad's red hair, in some shade or another. Except for Rory. He's got his mama's curly locks."

"I'm Rory," came a deeper voice, carrying a big

platter loaded with sliced ham. "The youngest boy. I'm the nice one."

Willow laughed. Rory had blue eyes that twinkled and his dark hair curled around his collar a bit and gave him a roguish look.

Aiden and Ethan came through the doors, their hands full of dishes, and Willow could definitely see their father's influence in their looks. Both were gingers, though Aiden was more on the light auburn side while Ethan's was a duller shade, a mix of red and light brown. Not a dramatic red like Hannah's, or the strawberry blond of the girls, but something more understated. And very attractive. Hmm.

"Is Laurel stuck at work, Aiden? I thought she was coming."

Aiden shook his head. "She wanted to, but Jordan ended up going home sick so now she's short-staffed. She might stop over for cake after she closes the garden center. She'll be sorry she missed you."

Behind everyone came Hannah's mom, her nearly-black hair streaked with a few grays, Ronan on one hip and Connor holding her hand.

"Mom," Hannah called out, "You remember Willow, don't you?"

"Hi, Mrs. Gallagher. Thanks for including me."

"Of course! And you have to call me Moira." She led Connor to his chair and let go of his hand as he climbed up. "We're glad you could come to Hannah's party."

"It's not a party, Mom," Hannah said as Willow followed her around the table to a couple of empty chairs.

"Of course it is! You're only twenty-nine once." She laughed and winked at Willow. "Most of us try to be twenty-nine a few times, but you can't fool time."

Willow awkwardly held out the bowl of bean salad she'd been cradling in her arm. "I brought something," she said, feeling totally conspicuous as several sets of eyes turned her way. "It's Hannah's favorite from the café."

"Willow's a fantastic cook," Hannah said. "I eat at the café more than I should because it's so tasty."

Moira took the bowl from Willow's hands. "Thank you, this is lovely. Have a seat, Willow, wherever you can find one." She grinned. "Our family dinners are generally a bit unruly. You take what you can get, kind of like musical chairs."

Willow found a chair near the end of a patio table that was pushed against another to form one big dining area. As she sat down, Ethan gave a brief nod that was barely a courtesy. And it was just her luck that she'd chosen the only empty seat at the table, which was directly across from him.

"Ah, the instigator," she said, trying to lighten things.

"Instigator?" he looked up, his brows pulling together. When he looked directly at her, she realized how blue his eyes were, like the sky on a clear winter's day. And sad. She reminded herself of her vow to be positive, and smiled at him.

"The worm." She leaned over and whispered it. "Your son gave you up."

He smiled . . . if she could call it a smile. His lips curved up a little, but it looked like it pained him.

Willow sat back in her chair. Those poor boys. She wondered if they ever had any fun. Hannah's description didn't seem to fit at all. Right now she highly doubted that he'd had anything to do with the worm in the glass.

"I thought Gram and Gramp were coming?" Hannah asked, reaching for her water glass.

"They're going to try to make it for cake," John replied. "Apparently they decided to play another nine holes."

"Of course they did," Rory said, chuckling. He looked at Willow. "Our grandparents are big golfers. As soon as the club opened for the season, they dusted off their clubs and started up again."

Claire nodded. "Well, they finally started using a cart rather than walking the entire course."

"Only when they do eighteen instead of nine," Rory said. He looked at Willow and his eyes twinkled at her. "I hope I'm that spry when I'm in my seventies."

"Rory, put your bedroom eyes away," Hannah instructed.

His face went blank with surprise. "What'd I do?"

Everyone laughed . . . including Willow, who wasn't quite sure what to make of everything. Even the wedding hadn't been this chaotic, but it had been a casual barbecue, not a big family meal. It gave her a definite pang of loneliness, and real regret that she'd never had any brothers or sisters or even grandparents to share in this kind of banter. She tried to live a life of gratitude, but right now she was feeling left out—an odd sensation considering she was anything but alone.

The chatter grew to a deafening level, but then John took over the situation and everyone quieted.

"Okay, you circus, let's say grace."

Everyone bowed their heads. Once more Willow was surprised. People still said grace these days? She peeked over at Ethan. He'd bowed his head slightly and his sandy lashes lay on his cheeks as he closed his eyes.

Further down the table, the boys shut their eyes so tightly they squinted, and Willow hid a smile as she bowed her head, too.

"Dear God, thank you for bringing us all together, and for Hannah, who is nearly thirty and still hasn't brought home a husband. Maybe you can help in that regard. Bless our boys, and our grandsons, and our other daughters. Thank you for bringing us a guest tonight and bless Moira for cooking this great-smelling meal. Amen."

When heads were raised, Willow caught Hannah glaring at her dad. "Really? You pulled the 'you're not married' thing into *grace*?"

John reached for the ham platter and arched an eyebrow at his daughter. "You ever hear of divine intervention?"

That started some good-natured ribbing around the table, and Willow was able to sit back and remain an observer, which suited her just fine for the time being. Dishes were circulated, and she put a little of everything on her plate: a small slice of baked ham, though she didn't tend to eat much pork these days, and a spoonful of creamy mashed potatoes, along with honeyed carrots and minted peas. She looked around at everyone else and noticed that other than Hannah, no one had taken much bean salad, and she wondered if it wasn't quite "traditional" enough for Hannah's family. When it came to her, she added a good spoonful to her plate and then rounded it all off with Caesar salad.

If there was cake later she was going to be very, very full.

She looked up and caught Ethan watching her.

"Your kids are really cute," she said, attempting a

smile. You couldn't go wrong complimenting one's children, could you?

"Thanks." He looked down the table at where they sat on either side of their grandmother. "They really love being here."

"It looks like your parents enjoy having them."

"Good thing. They're here a lot."

There was a bitterness in his voice Willow couldn't mistake. She didn't know how to reply, either. So she looked down at her plate and speared a golden circle of carrot.

"Sorry," he offered after a moment. "I have to work tonight. I feel guilty a lot of the time, relying on my family to watch the boys so much."

Ah, so that was it. "I'm sure they don't mind." Hannah had said that they all helped out. "That's what families are for, right?" Not like she'd know. Her singular experience with family was looking after herself. Some single moms did a great job raising their kids, but hers hadn't. Hers hadn't been home long enough to worry about it.

"They say they don't mind." He looked beside him at Claire. She was busy talking to Hannah about apartment listings in town and wasn't paying any attention to Ethan. "I do, though."

She smiled, and this time it was genuine. "It's not a bad thing to feel responsible for your kids. Sometimes, though, you just have to accept that life isn't perfect and do what you can, you know?"

His blue gaze bored into her again. "I'm more of a find-a-solution guy."

She shrugged. "Well, in my experience, people tend to be one of two things. Either they're really oblivious, or they overthink things. You don't strike me as the oblivious type."

"Meaning I overthink?" His voice was sharp and his gaze hard. "Maybe I do. I mean, I'm responsible for two little boys who lost their mother. I'm a fireman, so I can't really zone out during the job or someone could get killed. I guess I'm okay with being an over-thinker."

Oh God. She'd totally just put her foot into her mouth. "Sorry," she said quietly. "I didn't mean it to sound like a criticism." She zipped her lip and focused on her dinner plate, confounded by a slight stinging behind her eyes. What the heck? How did Ethan Gallagher have the ability to make her feel so small and inadequate? She'd dealt with those sorts of feelings years ago.

After a few moments of awkward silence, she exhaled slowly and lifted her chin, determined to move past the moment. She watched, curious, as he took a bite of potato.

He looked up, and his blue gaze locked with hers. "This is a bit philosophical for dinner, don't you think?"

She smiled weakly. "We did get off on the wrong foot, didn't we?" Her throat tightened. "Hannah told me about your wife. I'm sorry for your loss."

"What do you do for fun, Willow?"

The question was totally a deflection off himself and put the focus on her. It was the kind of move that said, *talking about my wife is off limits*. There was something about the way he said *Willow*, too, that rode on her nerves just a little bit. Like her name was something to laugh at. She was trying, for Pete's sake. It wasn't her fault he seemed to take everything personally. "That change of subject wasn't subtle at all," she pointed out.

He did smile then, a genuine one, and she blinked at the transformation in his face. Holy bananas, he had a great smile. Why didn't he use it more often?

"I wasn't trying to be subtle," he said.

Her lips twitched as relief rushed through her. Maybe she was forgiven? "Touché. Okay, what do I do for fun? Not that I have a lot of spare time, with the café and all, but I like to garden. Laurel's been great at getting me into some new things, like edible flowers. And I'm big on yoga and meditation. I'm staying in the apartment above the café, and it has a great south-facing window. I've made it into a yoga corner." A bit more relaxed now, she scooped up some peas. "What about you? What do you do for fun?"

"Not much. When I'm not working, I spend my time with the boys."

"And is that fun?"

He hesitated, looked at her intently. "Yes, I suppose it is."

"Like playing soccer the other day? Because you didn't look like you were having much fun then."

He picked up his knife and cut a piece of ham. "I'd worked the night shift, and hadn't slept. I picked up the boys instead, and took them to the Green. By the time I saw you, I had a monster headache."

"Oh."

"Hannah's told you all about my situation, I suppose."

"Briefly. And I *am* sorry, Ethan."

"Thanks."

She didn't know what to say to him after that, and it seemed they'd brokered a very tenuous peace, so she made a point of participating in the dinner conversations around the table. It was easy to see that Aiden was the joker of the group, Rory was steady and calm, and the twins were the youngest and got teased the most. Connor sat up and ate heartily, clearly enjoying the ham and potatoes and carrots, though he only picked at a few peas. Ronan, on the other hand, was younger, and after he'd eaten a bit he got down from his booster seat and went over to his dad, crawling up on his lap. She watched surreptitiously as Ethan curled his arm around the boy and settled him securely, finishing his meal one-handed.

Ronan, she thought, was probably three, though judging from his size, she thought he might be getting close to four. He rested his cheek against Ethan's shirt, against his father's broad, hard chest. Clearly he felt safe there, and Willow's heart melted a little as Ethan worked at cutting a piece of ham with the side of his fork since he didn't have a free hand for a knife. He could have insisted that Ronan return to his seat, or shifted him so he had both hands. But he didn't. He held his son close even though it was inconvenient.

Hannah leaned over and murmured in Willow's ear. "Ronan's a sweetheart. Connor's all go-go-go, but Ronan's a snuggler."

"I can tell," Willow said, smiling a little. It was a bittersweet feeling, knowing the little boy had lost his mother. What had she been like? Did the boys remember her?

"So how do you like being back in Darling, Willow?" John's voice rose above the rest of the chatter. "I understand from Hannah that you went to school with this bunch."

She turned away from the sight of Ethan and his son. "I like it a lot." She considered her answer, because she didn't talk about the past much. "I think sometimes you don't really appreciate home until you've been away from it for a while. And I love running the café. That's a dream come true."

"Where were you before?" This question came from Moira.

"Florida." She smiled. "In Clearwater, not far from the beach."

Rory wiped his mouth with his napkin. "And what did you do there?"

She put down her fork. "Well, I did a bit of everything, I suppose." She was very conscious that she hadn't gone to college or gained some sort of degree. "I waitressed, and I picked up hours at an ice cream parlor on the waterfront in the summers, and I volunteered a lot." She smiled, missing it a bit. "And I taught a yoga class once a week."

Claire sat up. "You do yoga?"

She nodded, focusing on Claire though she was constantly aware that Ethan's eyes were on her. "I have since I was a teenager. I started holding classes a few years ago, once I got my certification."

"I suppose you're really bendy," Rory commented, which earned him an elbow from Caitlyn. Willow just laughed. Rory was charming, but definitely not her type. He was a little *too* charming for her taste. She tended to gravitate toward men with a little more . . . depth.

And she noticed Ethan didn't join in the laughter at Rory's suggestive comment, either. For some reason she felt warm all over.

"I focus on meditation a lot," she admitted, happy

to share. Practicing mindfulness had literally saved her life, and she couldn't imagine her day without practice, both spiritual and physical. "I know some people joke about me being zen, but finding inner peace is life changing."

The table went a little more quiet, and she wondered briefly if she'd overshared. Ethan stared at his plate, pushing a pea around with his fork.

"I took a few classes once and really liked it," Claire said, starting up the conversation again. "But all the classes I'd like to take here are during the day, when I'm at work or school. The only ones offered in the evenings are yin or hot."

"Princess here doesn't like to get too sweaty," Aiden commented, and Claire gave him a dirty look.

Willow nodded. "Yin is nice. Personally, I'm more of a flow person. You should come by sometime. We can do something together."

"Maybe I will." She smiled, but Willow was certain Claire wouldn't take her up on it. Taking a few yoga classes at a studio wasn't the same as a one-on-one yoga session in someone's home.

Aiden and Rory started in teasing the twins again, and Willow looked at Hannah. "Is it always like this?" She laughed, enjoying the ribbing that was happening between the siblings.

Ethan spoke up. "Don't worry. When the chips are down, we have each other's backs."

Willow looked over at him, and saw that a tiny smile tipped up his lips just a bit. So the ogre did know how to smile.

"We sure do," Caitlyn said, and Aiden nodded.

The table quieted after Ethan spoke, until Moira

pushed away and started gathering plates. "All right, let's make room for cake."

Everyone got up to help, but when Willow pushed out her chair, Hannah stopped her with a hand on her shoulder. "Not you. You're a guest." With a smile Hannah took Willow's plate and stacked it on her own. She reached across and took Ethan's, too. "I'll bring you your piece," she said softly. "You have your hands full."

Ronan had nodded off in the warmth of his father's arms. His dark head drooped against Ethan's shirt, his lips relaxed in sleep.

"Thanks, Han." His voice was warm and low, and slid over Willow's nerve endings like melted butter.

"Extra scoop of ice cream?"

He smiled up at her. "You know it."

Willow looked over at him. When he forgot to be grouchy, his face relaxed into something far more pleasing. Almost . . . gentle. The silence stretched out until he finally spoke.

"So. Yoga and meditation. Sounds pretty touchy-feely."

She chuckled. "Maybe. It grounds me, though. Keeps me calm, gives me peace."

"Oh yeah? Some deep breathing and chanting keeps you calm in the middle of a muffin crisis? Inner peace in the face of a kitchen emergency? Sounds more like avoiding the real world to me."

"Maybe that's because the real world's been unkind to you. It can be hard to grasp the concept of inner peace when you're going through hard times." She smiled to soften the deeply personal words. It was clear Ethan did not like talking about his pain, but Willow knew talking about the things that hurt the most was the only way to move past them. "You could benefit from some 'deep breathing and chanting,' as you called it."

He gave a dry laugh. "Seriously, Willow. What would you know about it? Look at you, with your—what—hand-painted shirt and pink hair and nose ring and . . . you probably will go home and cleanse your aura or something. Maybe all that inner peace is easy to achieve when your life hasn't been torn apart."

He kept his voice down; the clatter of dishes could be heard through the screen door. But there was a harshness to his words that bit into her, making her both sympathetic and defensive. She tried to see it from his perspective. From the outside, Willow knew it probably looked as if she had it all together. His words said far more about his view of himself rather than his opinion of her. It made her feel even more sorry for him, rather than angry.

"You don't know anything about my life," she said, gently correcting him. "My lifestyle isn't for everyone, nor do I expect it to be. But I've had my share of hard times, Ethan. And for all your protests, I don't think I've met anyone in my life more in need of some serenity than you."

She got up from the table, her stomach churning a little bit from nerves. She hated conflict, and rarely had to deal with it. But Ethan had lashed out and despite trying to understand, his judgment still stung. She wasn't sure why. She didn't even like him.

But it was maybe because she recognized his pain, felt sorry for him, understood what it was like to feel like your life was totally out of your control. Compassion, she realized. That was what she felt for Ethan, even though he'd barely been civil both times they'd met. Knowing his history and seeing the way he snuggled his son made her compassionate.

No matter how much he criticized her, that capacity for compassion was something she was proud of. She wasn't about to let him take it away. It had taken a lot of work for her to get to a place of not just self-acceptance, but self-love.

"I'm going to check on the cake," she said quietly, and went toward the house. She took a deep, cleansing breath before opening the sliding door, then stepped inside with a smile on her face. "What can I do to help?"

CHAPTER 3

The house had cleared out and Ethan was helping his mom dry the last of the dishes before he had to put the boys to bed and head to work.

He felt a bit like an ass. He hadn't exactly been friendly to Hannah's guest, even though Willow had been nothing but pleasant. She seemed to know how to push his buttons, and that irritated him. He'd been downright rude, which was unlike him. It was just . . . He sighed heavily. He looked at her and saw what he wished he had. She was happy. Not just on the surface. He could tell she was really, truly happy, and he had all but forgotten how that felt.

And he'd taken it out on her by making fun of her and a "muffin crisis." "Dick move, Gallagher," he muttered to himself.

As penance, he'd told his siblings that he'd stay to help with the cleanup since the boys were staying overnight anyway.

Again.

"Did you say something, dear?"

Moira had heard his muttering, and he tried a smile. "Just saying thanks, Mom, for keeping the boys tonight."

"Don't be silly. We love having the boys here. What's family for, anyway?"

Ethan hung up the dish towel. He tried not to clench his teeth as he retrieved Connor's worn backpack and reached inside for his son's day camp schedule. Each afternoon a note was sent home with updates on what was upcoming or needed for the following day. It was almost as bad as school. When Ethan had been in kindergarten, there'd been no such things like agendas and homework. But Connor's spiral-bound, school-issued notebook had a note from the teacher most nights and a parent was supposed to sign it. The teacher collected them each day and put a check mark beside each signature or an "x" if it was left blank.

It bugged him that he saw his mother's signature at least as often as his own, if not more. Ethan had his own house. The boys had their own rooms. But right now they spent as much time at his parents' place as they did at home. They liked it because Waffle, the family Golden Retriever, lived here, and Grandma was a good cook, and Grampa took them on what he called "nature walks."

How could he compete with that? He'd signed Connor up for soccer, and he tried to take them to the park or even just kick the ball around in the backyard as often as he could. He still felt like a failure. It seemed like he was always telling the boys "in a minute" or "we'll do it later."

"Mom, you and Pop are great with them, and I appreciate it more than I can say. But I hate having to rely on you so much."

"You could always get married again." When Ethan opened his mouth to protest, she held up a hand and smiled, a teasing glint in her eye. "I know, I know. And I'm teasing, Ethan. All I'm saying is that being a single parent is a tough gig. Your job doesn't make it any easier." She rinsed out the sink with a nozzle.

It was true. He loved being a firefighter, but the shift work was killer. It hadn't been so bad when Lisa had been alive . . .

It seemed like his whole life had been condensed into two distinct sections: *Before Lisa's Death* and *After Lisa's Death*. And damned if he didn't resent the hell out of it. Before her death they'd been ridiculously happy. They had two beautiful boys, he worked as a firefighter, and she planned on staying home until they were both in school and she would go back to work part-time. All that had changed the day the diagnosis had come down. A year of limbo had followed, with treatments and prayers and hopes that they'd be able to reclaim their lives . . . and then the heavy, heavy weight of inevitability. She wasn't going to get well. After limbo came grief. And there's where he was stuck. Just trying to get from day to day.

"I know. But I love my job. So what should I do? Quit? Hire a full-time nanny?" He'd considered that solution, actually, but the idea of someone else living in his house, looking after his kids . . . it was too much like someone stepping into Lisa's place, and the idea made something twist painfully in his gut. And he had no doubt he would need someone to live in, because of his night shifts.

Goddammit.

"Don't be silly," she repeated. "Like I said, that's what family is for. And we're all happy to help out. For goodness' sake, your sisters love the boys. It's good for them to be close. We'll just keep on as we have been."

Moira took her cup of tea and went to the kitchen table, pulling out a chair and sitting down with a sigh, as if waiting for him to join her. The boys were in the den with their grandfather, probably playing with dinky cars. He could hear their laughter from the kitchen.

This was not how it was supposed to be. Not how he and Lisa had planned it.

He took his mug of coffee and joined her at the table. He was thirty-two. Six years ago he'd married the woman he loved. They'd had a five-year plan and it hadn't looked anything like this. He had to stop thinking this way. Nothing would change what had happened and he had to accept his new reality. And unless he actually did hire a nanny, accepting his family's help was necessary. He needed to get over himself and simply be grateful. He remembered Willow after dinner, helping to clear the dessert plates. She hadn't been able to finish her piece of cake and he'd watched as she snuck the leftovers to Connor and Ronan. They'd looked up at her as if she hung the moon and she'd smiled and whispered something he couldn't hear. Even though he'd been testy toward her, that same serene smile had graced her face.

But there was more than just envy of her happiness. He'd noticed her. Really noticed her, down to her pink stripe of hair and little diamond nose ring, and the compact body he now envisioned twisting into some complicated yoga pose. The awareness had caught him by surprise, and he didn't like it.

"What's your schedule for the rest of the week?" Moira asked, sipping her tea.

"Night shift today and tomorrow, then two days off, then days starting Thursday." Night shift was the worst as far as caring for the boys. Sometimes they slept here, in Ethan and Aiden's old room and the twin beds that were still there with the same blue plaid bedspreads. Sometimes one of his sisters came over to his house and stayed over, then took Ronan and Connor to school and day care so Ethan could sleep.

"Well, I'm making that pasta bake you like for tomorrow night. You can eat before you have to go to work, and the boys can stay here again."

Only Claire and Cait still lived in the big house in the summer, and Ethan figured any day now they'd look at getting their own place together. Tonight they'd gone back to Hannah's to give her her birthday present and to hang out for a while for some girlie time. He figured Willow probably got invited to that, too. He tried to imagine her letting her hair down and having a few glasses of wine and watching a movie or getting a manicure. The image didn't quite gel. He expected she'd be more apt to sit cross-legged in front of a Buddha and "om" or something.

And why his thoughts kept shifting back to her, he had no idea. He wasn't interested. Not like *that*.

"Well," he said, standing, putting his hands on his hips and stretching out his back, "I should get the boys into bed and then head into work. I don't want them to be up late and I still like tucking them in."

His mother's face softened. "Aw, honey. I know it's hard right now. I know how much you hate accepting help, too. It's that damned pride of yours, so much like your father's. But it's going to get better, I promise. You just need to find a new normal."

"Mom, I gotta say, it pretty much feels like things are never going to be normal again."

She smiled sadly. "It just takes time, sweetie. In the meantime, give yourself a break. Lean on your family. That's what we're here for and we all know you'd do exactly the same for us. Right?"

He nodded, his throat tight. "Right."

He went to gather the boys and get them tucked into bed. As he kissed their freshly-washed faces and tucked the blankets around them, he knew that his mom believed everything that she'd said.

But deep down, he wasn't buying it. How could things be normal when it felt like half of you was missing?

Wednesday was his day off and in the afternoon Ethan picked up the boys early. He'd promised he'd take them out for a treat after day care and then to the playground across the bridge, because they loved the swing sets there best. Once he'd buckled them into their booster seats in the back, they headed toward Main Street.

"So what'll it be, boys? Ice cream? Pie at the bakery? Slushies?"

Connor shifted in his seat so he was looking up at his dad in the front. "The lady from Aunt Hannah's party, the one with the pink hair? She works somewhere where they make cookies with weird chocolate chips in them. And brownies out of beans." He made a face. "Yuck. But the cookies sounded yummy. Can we go there, Dad?"

The Purple Pig. Ethan tried not to roll his eyes. Granted, he'd tasted her bean salad the other night and it had been delicious, much to his surprise. But the café wasn't his speed at all. It was . . . rabbit food, meant more for the seasonal tourists who couldn't survive without their almond milk lattes.

"Yeah," Ronan piped up. "The Purpo Pig."

"You remember that?" Ethan asked, looking at him in the rearview mirror.

Ronan's dark head bobbed up and down. Connor laughed. "Ronan remembers everything. Right, Ronan?"

Ronan nodded. "Connor farted in his sleep last night."

Ethan laughed before he could stop himself. There were times that the boys just came out with stuff he didn't expect. It was a joy, and sometimes bittersweet, but he didn't know what he'd do without them. "Ronan," he chided, but his heart wasn't in it.

The boys giggled and the sound eased the ache in Ethan's heart. It was impossible to be glum when your kids were indulging in big belly laughs in the backseat.

"I guess we can go there, if that's what you want."

"Yeah!" Connor made a fist of victory. "I want the biggest cookie. I ate my lunch at recess."

"Why?"

"Cuz I was hungry," he said, as if it were the stupidest question in the world.

"Do I need to pack you a bigger lunch?"

Connor shook his head. "Naw. Danny McBride dared me to put my whole sandwich in my mouth so I did."

"What about the rest of your lunch?" He eased through the stop sign, looking for a parking spot along the street.

"Then I was thirsty so I drank my juice box. And Grandma packed me raisins." The humorous tone was missing from his voice and Ethan smiled to himself. He knew Connor hated raisins unless they were in oatmeal cookies.

"What did you do with the raisins?"

"Gave them to Ronan."

Ronan nodded vigorously. "I like raisins."

Ethan pulled into a spot about three spaces down from the café. "Hey, maybe when we're done we'll pop in and see Aunt Hannah if she's in the office."

"Aunt Hannah keeps chocolate kisses in her desk," Connor said. "She said that it's . . . I forget the word. Something-control."

Ethan put the car in park. "Portion control?"

"Yeah. That."

Ethan chuckled. Hannah was so into her training right now, but everyone had a vice. He'd get some mileage out of this one.

"All right, boys. Good manners now."

Ronan held his hand, but Connor put his hands in his jeans pockets. Ethan reached for the door handle and let out a breath. Maybe Willow wasn't even working right now. Maybe it would just be someone he didn't know behind the counter, they'd get a quick bite and get out.

The bell above the door chimed and he looked up to find Willow's blue eyes settled on him.

His chest tightened in a strange way, but Ronan was tugging on his hand, anxious to get to the glass display case. Willow smiled—a small, sweet smile—and the tightness squeezed.

What the heck was that about?

"Well, hello," she said as they approached the counter. "What a nice surprise."

Ethan tried to smile, but his face felt tight as he looked at her. She looked so relaxed and comfortable and pleasant. It was damned intimidating. Other than his sisters, he'd avoided conversations with the women of Darling since Lisa died. He'd quickly learned that they either ended up looking sad and pitying, or worse, prospective. He was definitely out of practice in the art of everyday conversation.

"The boys had their pick of a treat today. They wanted to come here."

He realized he'd put it all on the boys, making it sound like he would have rather gone somewhere else. Which was, well, the truth, but he could have been more tactful. Tact wasn't exactly his finest skill.

But Willow didn't seem to even notice. Instead she looked over the counter at the boys. "You did? Awesome! Why don't you come back here and pick a treat?" She looked up at Ethan. "Any allergies to be aware of?"

"No," he answered. "Though Connor isn't fond of raisins."

"What?" She raised her eyebrows and looked at Connor. "But raisins are delicious! And full of good stuff. I think they're nature's candy."

Ethan tried not to roll his eyes.

"I like them in cookies," Connor admitted.

"Oh, well then. That's okay." Willow grinned. She turned her head and Ethan saw the nose ring wink in the light, and the pink stripe that ran along the side of her head since her hair was pulled back in a braid. She looked about twenty.

She moved to the end of the counter and waved them in. "Come on, boys. You can come back here and pick something out. It'll be our secret."

Ethan had to admit, his boys seemed smitten. And she was genuinely nice, that was clear. Too nice, maybe. Or maybe he was just a big old crab. Thinking it just made him crabbier.

He stood back and watched as the boys picked a sweet from the refrigerated display. Willow got them each a little plate and when they came back around he saw that Ronan had a huge chocolate chip cookie and Connor had two plates. One held a square of blueberry cake and the other a fudgy looking brownie with thick icing on the top.

He remembered what Connor had said about the beans and hoped to God that the blueberry cake was for him.

"Daddy, look! I got you a brownie cuz chocolate's your favorite."

Shoot. "Gee, thanks Connor."

Connor beamed up at him.

Ethan reached for his wallet. "Boys, why don't you go find a table and I'll be right over with something to drink."

"Okay, Daddy."

He looked at Willow. She seemed far too pleased with herself, as if she could read his mind. Right then and there he determined that he'd eat every bit of that brownie if it killed him.

"Milk," he said quietly. "A glass of milk for each of them, if I could."

"And for you? Did you want a coffee or tea, Ethan?"

He focused on pulling bills out of his wallet. "A coffee with milk, please."

When she told him the tally, his jaw nearly dropped and his head came up. "How much did you say?"

It was the better part of twenty dollars. He supposed because they were a specialty market, they could charge through the nose. He added a five to the bills he'd already taken out and handed them over. "Thanks," he said.

"I'll bring your drinks out. You go sit with the boys."

He nodded and went to the table, where Connor and Ronan were already munching on their food. It surprised him that Connor had gone for the blueberry cake, instead of the cookie he'd been talking about. His boy was growing up . . . too fast.

He was poised to take his first bite of brownie when Willow came out with a tray of drinks. She put two small glasses of milk before the boys, and carefully set Ethan's coffee in front of him. "So, how is it? Do you like the carob chips, Ronan?"

His mouth was full so he nodded, his brown eyes sparkling. She laughed lightly and looked at Connor.

"Good cake." He waved with his fork. "Almost as good as my mommy's."

Ethan froze. Connor had been Ronan's age when Lisa died. How could he possibly remember what his mother's cake had been like? Was he making it up? Pretending? Trying to hold on to fading memories or creating his own reality? Funny how a simple observation made Ethan question whether he'd paid enough attention to his son's grieving process.

More than that, though, the simple words had brought forth a memory. Blueberry cake had been Lisa's favorite, usually with a warm, lemony sauce for the top, and she asked for it every August for her birthday.

There would be no more birthdays.

"Are you okay, Ethan?" Willow's voice was soft and her hand touched his shoulder.

He swallowed tightly. "Sorry, yes, I'm fine. Just getting ready to dig into this brownie." He forced the memory away and picked up his fork.

"Are you sure?" She squeezed lightly, and his throat tightened.

"I'm sure." To prove it, he valiantly stabbed the brownie with his fork and guided the piece to his mouth. He would eat it. He would pretend to like it, the boys would finish their snack, and they'd go to the playground as planned.

He put it in his mouth, steeling himself against the taste, determined not to show his dislike, and then he stopped in surprise.

It was delicious. Really, really delicious.

He looked up at her. "This is *beans*?"

She grinned. "Yessir. Black beans, and organic cocoa, free-range eggs . . ."

"It's moist. And rich."

"You're surprised."

"Well, yeah."

She smiled at him, a big smile that seemed to warm the whole room. He found himself smiling back. The boys continued to eat, totally unconcerned, but for Ethan it seemed like an important moment. He didn't like being bad-tempered. It wasn't who he was, deep down. She'd prompted an honest-to-goodness smile from him, and it felt awesome.

"Did you think all 'healthy' food was tasteless and dry?" Her lips twitched.

"Well . . ." He chuckled. "Hannah always raves about the food here. I should have had more faith, maybe."

Business was slow so she pulled up a chair. "So," she said quietly. "Your boys are sweet, Ethan. And they have manners. You're doing a good job with them."

He didn't really care about her opinion, so it didn't make sense that the compliment touched him. But it did.

"Thanks. I try. If I didn't have my family . . ."

"Your family seems pretty great, too."

"They are." He took a sip of coffee and then put down his mug. "How about yours?"

She smiled again. Lord, the woman smiled all the time. How on earth did she manage that?

"Oh, I'm pretty much on my own. My mom moved away when I was twenty, and lives in Connecticut. I'm not used to a big family like yours. But I have Laurel. We both moved back here after years away, and now we're best friends. She and Hannah keep me from being too much of a hermit." She winked at him. "Hannah more recently. I miss Laurel, but between the business and being a newlywed . . . I understand."

He nodded. "Yeah. We don't see Aiden very much either, lately. The lovebirds are holed up in their nest."

The observation made her cheeks color prettily. He looked away, took a napkin, and wiped Ronan's hands, then handed him his milk. In no time flat the little boy had an adorable milk mustache.

"So you're really committed to this place," he said.

She nodded. "It's like a dream come true. I love it. I love the work, and the people, and what it stands for."

"And what about down the road? Do you think you'll open another, or expand or something?"

She shrugged. "I don't know. I'll figure that out when the time comes. There are some possibilities, but nothing's really in the works yet. I kind of like letting life happen, and not planning everything out. It feels like more of an adventure that way."

Ethan frowned. It was strange. He'd always planned out his life, what he wanted to do and a time frame to do it in. Become a firefighter. Get married by twenty-five. Kids before thirty. Check, check, check.

Live happily ever after. Maybe that was where he'd gone wrong. Maybe he'd planned so much that he'd considered everything a done deal. And then God or fate or whatever decided *nope! You're a little too smug, Gallagher. Real life doesn't have guarantees.*

"Doesn't it bother you? Not having a plan?"

"Not really. I just trust that things will work out as they're meant to. Right now I'm enjoying where I am. This is a beautiful town, it's summer, and I have a dream job. Life doesn't get much better."

She made it sound so simple.

"Dad," whispered Connor. "I need to go."

Willow smiled. "I'll show you were the bathroom is, Connor."

"You can go alone?" Ethan asked.

"I'm not a baby, Dad."

Willow met his gaze. "It's a private bathroom. He'll be the only one there, and you can see it from the table. But I'll wait for him if you like."

"It'll be okay," he said, knowing he couldn't baby them forever. He leaned over to Connor and whispered in his ear. "Don't make a mess, and wash your hands."

Connor rolled his eyes. "Yes, Dad."

When they left together, he noticed that Connor took Willow's hand, in a way that he'd refused to when they'd been walking to the café together.

His sons missed having a mother. Perhaps Connor more than Ronan, because Connor actually still had memories. His offhand comment today reminded Ethan of that.

But Willow wasn't the kind of female figure he imagined them having in their lives. He imagined someone more mature and . . . well, less flighty.

Kids needed structure and stability. Someone like

Willow would have them meditating somewhere and eating organic kale, or putting stripes in their hair and taking them for tattoos. He sure couldn't imagine her being a PTA mom baking cookies for a class event or volunteering for field trips or being field-side watching soccer games.

It was a shame, then, that he couldn't get the shape of her lips out of his mind. Or the way her eyes seemed to see right through the walls he'd built around himself.

Connor came back to the table by himself, his hands still damp from washing them, and Willow was back behind the counter, serving a customer. Ethan finished his brownie, Ronan washed down the last of his carob-chip cookie with his milk, and Connor managed all but a few bites of his blueberry cake. Ethan stacked the plates and glasses and took them back to the counter.

"Oh," she said, taking them from his hands and putting them in a dishpan. "Thanks, Ethan."

"Thank you, Willow. The boys enjoyed it."

"Just the boys?" she asked, lifting one eyebrow. "Seems to me you finished every last crumb." Her eyes sparkled at him.

She was surprising. Just so real and honest. And so not in the same place he was. But the brownie had been good and the whole thing had been nicer than he'd expected. He also appreciated how easy she was to talk to. Even when he was being a gruff jerk, she just smiled that serene smile and didn't try to pry into his feelings. Not a lot of people would have done that. He knew that for a fact. He still got the long looks and quiet voices from people around town. He wished people would stop tiptoeing around him about it.

Lisa was gone. She wasn't coming back.

"I concede the point to the brownie-baker. It was delicious."

She rested her hips against the back counter. "Wow. High praise. Thanks."

"You made them?"

"At nine this morning." She crossed her arms in front of her. "I'm usually down here by six, six-thirty, and get the baking going for the day. Muffins and scones first, and then the sweeter stuff."

"Dad, come on. I want to go on the swings." Ronan tugged at his hand again, and Connor waited impatiently, shifting from foot to foot.

"Better go," he said, stepping away.

Willow looked at the kids. "Have fun, guys. Come back again soon."

They waved at her, looking happy. Once they were outside, Connor piped up, "I like Willow. And she said that earring in her nose doesn't even hurt."

Ethan let out a big breath. "Don't get any ideas," he warned.

"Ew, only girls get things pierced."

Ethan didn't correct him; Connor would figure it out soon enough. Though he wouldn't be disappointed if his boys kept themselves pierce-free.

More than that, though, was that he couldn't get Willow off his mind. She was the exact opposite of what Lisa had been like. And yet there'd been a moment when she'd put her hand on his shoulder and squeezed that he felt something. A . . . communion of sorts. Like she understood. How could she, though?

They walked over to the park and Ethan sat on a bench while the boys ran for the slide. All around him were moms with their kids, watching them play, shouting out cautions and warnings.

Connor went down the slide and then waited at the bottom, ready to help his little brother with the landing.

They were his world. Them and no one else. And if he did ever marry again, he'd be damned sure it was a woman his sons deserved. One that would stay.

CHAPTER 4

Willow took the time to settle into Pigeon pose, one of her favorites. She brought her right knee forward out of Downward Facing Dog, keeping her shin parallel with the front of the mat as she stretched her left leg behind her. The pose opened her hips and she inhaled deeply, her ribs expanding as she arched her back. A few more moments and she leaned forward, collapsing over her front leg with a long exhale, sinking into the stretch.

Her practice this morning wasn't her usual routine. She'd started with an invigorating flow practice and then had found she needed more quiet in her mind, and she'd switched to holding her poses longer, paying more attention to her breath. She wasn't holding on to stress so much as distraction.

She gently unfolded and repeated the pose on the opposite side. This hip was a little stiffer, and she eased into it slowly. Soft music played in the background, with the sound of a waterfall behind it, and she opened her eyes and focused on the light green lotus flower painted on her wall.

Inhale. Hold. Exhale. Release.

She unwound herself and moved into Savasana, flat on her back in a prone position. Her body melted into the mat and she envisioned the remaining tension in her muscles exiting through her fingertips and feet. She deepened her breath and remained there for a while, until she was so relaxed she was in a quasi-sleep state.

The sound of a car alarm down the street pulled her back into the present, and she released a calm sigh. Nothing restored her like a good yoga practice. This morning her mind had been too busy. Now she was centered and ready to face the day.

After a shower and a breakfast of yogurt and fresh berries, Willow made her way downstairs to the café. Emily was already there, taking the first pans of muffins out of the oven. Steven was there too, filling napkin dispensers, readying the coffee machines, and taking care of anything to do with the front end. He'd already scrubbed the floor and it was nearly dry. She'd bet any money he'd cleaned the washrooms, too. He'd admitted on day one that he was an early riser, so she often put him on the schedule to open. Tina and Mary would be in later.

"Morning, boss," Emily said, going back into the kitchen. "I'm going to put some steel cut oats on for the breakfast menu today. That okay?"

"Sounds perfect." Even though it was July, the day was cool and a bit gray, with a fine drizzle. They'd go through more soup than sandwiches today, and lots of coffee. She made a mental note to add a third soup if the weather didn't clear by ten or so.

The minutes flew until she unlocked the door and

turned over the open sign. Then the morning passed in a blur. Instead of the rain slowing business, it seemed as if everyone in Darling was looking to warm up with a cup of coffee or tea and some sort of carb. Scones, muffins, coffee cake . . . it all disappeared like lightning, and Willow did nothing but bake while Em and Steven waited on customers. No one had time for a break until nine-thirty, and even then it was five minutes for each of them to catch their breath and grab something to drink to keep them going. Then the coffee-break rush started at ten and they were in the thick of it again.

She loved every minute.

The pace wasn't very zen, but that didn't matter. There was something comforting about the smells, and Willow loved the hands-on task of baking, of nourishing. She liked the sound of someone wishing someone else a good morning; the odd laugh, or even the weary customer who ended up leaving with a smile. She took a few precious seconds to look out over the packed coffee shop, and her heart was full. This . . . this was her family. This town had welcomed her back, even with her quirkiness that was so different from the Type A teenager she'd been. Not all of those characteristics had disappeared, and she liked to think they served her well as a business owner. But she liked to feel as if she'd balanced her inner perfectionist with acceptance and calm.

The most important thing she'd learned during her time away was that taking care of other people was the best way to take care of herself. When she focused on others, and tried to make their day better, her day got better, too. Call it karma, call it whatever, but she knew that giving of herself made it possible to receive good things in return. She was a nurturer at heart, which was a huge surprise considering her upbringing.

Hannah popped in, though Willow didn't bother to check the clock. She didn't have time to stop to chat for long, but Hannah scooted around the counter and darted into the kitchen for a moment anyway. Only Hannah would do such a thing and look utterly comfortable about it.

"Holy cats. Look at the mess in here."

Willow laughed and efficiently rolled out cheese scone dough, then cut them in triangles with a metal cutter. Her hands flew as she placed them on a metal sheet and then put them in the oven.

"Busy day," Willow offered. "A little bit of rain and the tourists want coffee and carbs and to stay inside."

"I guess. I've got to get back, but I wanted to tell you that I spoke to Billy."

Billy Robertson was the owner of the building, and he rented the space to both Hannah and Willow.

"About the space in between us?"

"Yep. He agreed to let me know if anyone else offers. He likes having you as a tenant. He said your sugar-free cookies are the only sweets his wife will let him eat."

Willow laughed and wiped her hands on a towel. "Well, that's good."

Hannah's face was all business, though. "I meant what I said about expansion. That's prime real estate and you're already crowded in here. If it's the money, we can talk about that, too. I can help."

Laurel had said the same thing about funding an expansion, even though Willow knew Laurel had her hands full with the garden center and keeping her business in the black. "I'll keep it in mind. Promise." In fact she had been thinking about it, a lot. It was part of the reason why she'd been a little edgier than normal lately.

She didn't want to grow too fast, or too big, and add additional stress to her life. She'd worked very hard to find inner acceptance and a balance of doing what she loved and having enough quiet time to keep herself on an even keel. To double the size of the café would mean hiring a full-time baker and more staff, not to mention more overhead. More everything, including risk.

"Let me think about it, Han." She put her hands on her hips. "It's a big step. I don't want to rush into anything. Right now I have time to do some things I enjoy. I don't want to end up married to my business, and if The Purple Pig expands, that could happen."

Hannah shook her head. "Nah. You're the most well-balanced person I know. But agreed, you shouldn't rush into anything. If you want, we can run some numbers sometime . . ."

Hannah looked so hopeful that Willow laughed again. "You're wasted doing real estate, you know."

"That's what you think. I love the wheel and deal and I do my share of number crunching. Anyway, I'll scoot and let you get back to work."

Before she could dart out the door, Willow called out to her. "Hey, Hannah?"

"Hmm?"

"Ethan was in here with the boys. Connor mentioned his mom, and Ethan clammed up."

"Yeah. It's been really hard for him. They were longtime sweethearts."

Willow's heart ached for him, and his cute little boys. "What was she like?"

Hannah smiled, and Willow saw sadness in it. It looked like the family had loved Ethan's wife, too.

"Lisa was perfect for him. She was sweet but no pushover, and she ran a tight ship. Always organized, always taking the boys on little outings, making sure they did things as a family. For a long time it seemed as though she had limitless energy. Maybe that's when we first realized something was wrong. She lost that crazy spark."

"Connor mentioned blueberry cake."

Hannah laughed. "She was a good cook. Ethan didn't eat nearly as much of mom's cooking as he does now. And she always made me feel like I was all thumbs. She knew how to knit and sew and all that stuff."

It sounded like Lisa Gallagher had been an absolute paragon. For some reason, the glowing description annoyed Willow. She figured it was because she was so flawed and it made her feel inferior.

Those feelings didn't happen very often, not anymore. But today they snuck in and tapped her on the shoulder.

"Thanks for telling me," she murmured. "Now scoot. I've got muffins to make."

Hannah disappeared, but Willow's fingers rested on the edge of the counter and she frowned. Why did it matter about Lisa? It wasn't as if she even liked Ethan.

Except she sort of did. And if it wasn't exactly "like," it was an understanding of what it was like to deal with daily pain and hide it from the world. Her teen years had been fraught with struggle, and it had taken years and a lot of therapy to deal with the eating disorder she'd hidden from everyone. She was a strong person now. A whole person. But when she looked at

Ethan, she saw a man who had a part of himself missing, and she knew how that felt.

She remembered how he'd looked, taking the boys out of the café to go to the park and her heart softened. He was there for them. And she knew his family was supportive, but she'd bet a million dollars that he'd never allow himself to be a burden on his family.

Which meant there was no one there for him.

And lonely was a terrible place to live.

CHAPTER 5

Ethan sat on the back of the ambulance, the smell of smoke clinging to him like a second skin, and wiped his forearm across his sweaty forehead. His other arm rested by his side, the pain at a minimum as long as he kept still.

From his perch waiting for the paramedics to care for the people with smoke inhalation, he could see the other firefighters milling about near what remained of the old food bank. The red brick building was stained black from where the fire had broken out just a few hours earlier, which thankfully had been contained before anyone was seriously injured. Now, there was just paperwork, cleanup, and the assessment of the attached homeless shelter for possible smoke and structural damage.

Christine Palmer, one of the paramedics, made her way over to the ambulance. "What happened to you?" she asked, frowning. "You doing okay? You didn't mention being hurt earlier."

"Shelving unit came down. I guess my reflexes are

slowing." He sent her a grin, but inside he was feeling rather grim.

"Right arm?"

"Yep. My guess is it's broken, but I'll need an X-ray. Figured if you had room, I could hitch a ride to the hospital." His injury wasn't serious, though if he were honest, it hurt like a sonofabitch. Still, he could wait until the ambulance wasn't needed. Right now he was just wondering what the hell he'd do if he couldn't work for a while.

"There's nothing major here," Christine replied. "I don't think there'll be a problem with giving you a lift. You doing okay for pain?"

He nodded. "Yeah. Though if you happened to give me a sling or something, I think the support would be welcome."

In no time she had him trussed up in a sling and the shooting pains lessened. Of all the goddamn things to happen today. His mother would have a fit, even though he hadn't been in any mortal danger. It was a stupid steel shelving unit. She wouldn't see it that way. And now he'd be off work.

"Hey, Christine? What time is it?"

"Nearly ten."

Shit. He was supposed to be home by eight thirty this morning. Hannah had come over to stay with the boys last night, but they'd be up now and she would need to go to work. It wasn't unheard of for him to be late, but he was going to be a while longer still. "You got a phone I can borrow?"

She took out her cell, opened her lock screen, then handed it over. "I'll be back in a few minutes and we'll get going."

He'd been right. Hannah was worried and wondering

where he was, and late for work. When he explained what happened, however, her tone changed and he closed his eyes, making assurances that he was fine. "Can you stay with the boys? I don't want Mom to know yet. I'd rather get checked out and have it all looked after before I talk to her. It was just a stupid shelf, but she's going to freak out."

"But . . . what am I supposed to do with the boys?"

"Can you take them with you today? Their day camp is over, and I didn't book them into day care today because I was supposed to be home."

"To my office?"

He sighed. "I know it's a lot to ask. I'm sorry, Han. I can find someone else. Just give me a few minutes."

Christine came back, along with Greg, the other paramedic. "Hey," she said to Ethan. "We're ready to roll."

"Who's that?" asked Hannah.

"The paramedics. They're ready to take me to the hospital."

There was a moment of silence. "Okay," she said, her voice steadier. "Don't worry about the boys. I'll take them with me and figure something out. I'm just glad you're okay, Ethan."

"Thank you, Hannah." His shoulders sagged in relief. "I'll be in touch."

He clicked off the phone and then boosted himself up into the back, using his good arm for balance.

Now that his job was done and the adrenaline was fading, his mind started to wander, the pain a sharp reminder of what could have been. Despite what he'd told Hannah, today had him shaken. For a few seconds in that burning building, he'd been on the edge of a "what if" moment. What if the shelf had pinned him down? What if he'd been hurt worse than a broken arm? What if one day he went into a fire and didn't come out?

He handed the phone to Christine and stared at the opposite side of the ambulance.

The potential for something to go wrong was always there, but today, after a close call . . . it felt more pronounced than usual. It highlighted the fact that he was all the boys had. He couldn't afford to be distracted.

It was quarter past eleven when Willow looked up and saw Hannah come into the café, with Connor and Ronan holding her hands.

She looked frazzled.

"Well, hello, Auntie Hannah. Hi, boys. Have you come in for a treat?"

Connor bobbed his head up and down. "I want a brownie like my dad got the other day."

"Good choice. What about you, Ronan?"

Ronan was a little more shy, but he gave a little smile and said simply, "Cookie."

Hannah gave him a nudge. "What do you say, boys?"

"Please," they said together, and Willow melted a bit. Heavens, they were sweet.

Hannah took them to a table, but then came back to Willow at the counter. "I told them I was getting their stuff. Truth is, Willow, I'm at my wits' end. Ethan is at the hospital and I stayed at his place to watch the boys during his night shift last night, but now I have to go to a showing and I've had the kids in my office for the last forty-five minutes and I'm losing my mind."

Willow's hand paused over the tray of brownies. "What do you mean, Ethan's at the hospital?"

"Something to do with his call this morning. Said

he hurt his arm or something and they were taking him to the hospital to get checked out. I agreed to keep the boys because Ethan wants to spare Mom any worry until after he knows what's up. But trying to work with those two orangutans around?" She sighed heavily.

Willow was still stuck on the fact that Ethan had been hurt, presumably fighting a fire this morning. There'd been talk for the last few hours that something had burned just by town limits, where the properties turned more industrial.

She wondered what had happened to him, and if he was all right.

It was sunny today, and slow. Instead of coffee, most people beat the late July heat by heading to the ice cream shop down the street. Willow looked at the boys and then at Hannah. "Leave them with me for an hour or so. I can blast off from here and watch them while you're doing your showing. Would that help?"

Hannah's eyes lit up. "Are you serious? You'd do that?"

"Of course I would. They can have lunch here, and we'll walk over to the park or something. Just call me when you're back."

"You're a lifesaver."

"Yeah, yeah. Give me five minutes to tie up a few loose ends and I'll be right there." She frowned for a moment. "Are you sure Ethan won't mind?"

Hannah shrugged. "Nah. It's only for a few hours. He knows you."

Barely, Willow wanted to answer, but she kept her mouth shut. Hannah was a good friend and would return the favor anytime Willow asked.

While the boys ate their snack and Hannah drank a latte, Willow checked supplies and left instructions in the kitchen. To be honest, she was looking forward to the afternoon. She didn't often allow herself to play hooky, and the idea of spending some time at the park or around town, even with two little boys, sounded perfect.

She packed a small cooler with fresh buns and cheese, added some carrot and celery sticks, and a couple of the bananas they had set aside for making banana bread. There was no reason why they couldn't have a picnic at the park.

Then Hannah was gone and Willow was left with Connor and Ronan, and she realized she was a bit nervous after all. These were Ethan's children. Ethan was not her biggest fan, and she wasn't used to being around small kids for any length of time. She hoped it all went well, because if it didn't, she was sure Ethan would have something to say about it.

"So," she said, sitting down at their table. "Looks like it's the three of us for a few hours. What would you like to do?"

"Ice cream!" shouted Connor.

"Park!" Ronan's sweeter voice called out, and she laughed.

"Okay. Let's say we do the park. I have a little picnic we can have after you've played a while, how's that? And maybe, just maybe, if you have room for ice cream, we can get some later."

"A picnic?" Connor's eyes sharpened, staring at her little insulated bag. "What's in there?"

"A surprise," she decreed. "Want to go? I bet you like the swings best, don't you, Connor?"

"You can give me an underduck."

She hadn't heard that term in nearly two decades. "We'll see."

"Ronan likes the slide. And the dinosaur."

They got up from the table and she held out her hands. Each boy took one, and her heart gave a little pang at the sweet, trusting gesture. A surge of protectiveness ran through her. Kids were so innocent. So at the mercy of the adults in their lives. She refused to look back at her own childhood, but the idea that Connor or Ronan had already lost some of that innocence because of their mother's death made her sad.

There was nothing she could do about that, so she decided that they would just have fun today.

The park was predictably busy. It was mid-day, and the sky was a perfect, clear blue without a single cloud. Mothers with strollers, toddlers, and school-age children all fought for space on walking paths and around the playground equipment.

There was a wait for the swings and the slide was hot on bare legs; both Connor and Ronan bent their knees and slid down as best they could on their cotton-covered bums, but after two or three turns, decided they wanted to do something else. The dinosaur turned out to be some spring-loaded triceratops that Ronan could sit on and rock back and forth, while Connor took a turn on a dragon. It wasn't long before they were bored, though, since it was still impossible to get a swing and Ronan was too scared to climb the jungle gym. If they'd had a soccer ball they might have played, but they hadn't brought much with them to Hannah's office.

The picnic didn't last long, either. She'd thrown some towelettes in the picnic bag to wash off dirty hands, and they chomped on buns and cheese and carrots—neither liked the celery—and shared a banana. Then they flopped down on their backs, their little bellies full, and stared at the clouds for a few minutes. It was all quite idyllic, really, until a bumblebee settled on Ronan's arm and he flipped out, shaking his arm and wailing at the top of his lungs.

Willow's heart rate went bonkers as she leapt to his side. "Ronan, he's gone, honey. Shhh. It's okay. Did he sting you?"

"N . . . no but he was on me and . . ." He didn't say much, but his little body shuddered. Clearly he was not a fan of bees.

"He didn't hurt you. He probably just sat on you because you smell so sweet."

"Gross," said Connor.

"Not helpful, Connor." She gave him a sideways glance and a teasing smile, and Connor smiled back. For a five-year-old, he was quick to pick up on tone. That probably had to do with the crazy Gallagher family's Irish humor.

"Sorry."

Ronan sent him a dirty look. "That's cuz you stink, Connor."

Willow burst out laughing. She couldn't help it. And once she laughed, Connor laughed, and so did Ronan. Disaster averted.

They put away the picnic and Willow wondered what to do next. "Do you boys like flowers? We could look at the gardens."

"I like flowers, Wi . . . Miss . . ."

Oh, she could really learn to love Ronan. Connor was sharp but Ronan was as sweet as candy floss.

"You can call me Willow, like the tree," she said.

"Wil-low," he said carefully.

There was no handholding this time, and they walked along the path, Willow hoping the entire time that they didn't ask to go into the creek. She didn't have a change of clothes for them, and she wasn't sure how swift the current ran in the narrow waterway. It had been years since she'd dipped her toes in there. Back in high school, the lake had been the place to go, not the creek. Not that she'd been able to go that much. Her mom had been strict, and any social events she'd gone to she'd had to sneak out. And boy, had that backfired. All the straight A's in the world hadn't protected her from getting in trouble.

Ronan definitely liked the flower gardens and got a bit whiny when she told him they weren't for picking. The hard set of his lips warned her that an explosion might be forthcoming, so she formulated a new plan. They'd walked far enough down the Green that they were probably only a quarter of a mile from Laurel's Ladybug Garden Center. Behind the center, Laurel had planted a large bed of mixed wildflowers for bees and butterflies. Willow was pretty sure that Laurel would let the boys pick a few blossoms. Maybe they could make a bouquet for Hannah or for their grandmother. Besides, Laurel was married to Connor and Ronan's uncle, Aiden. It would be almost like being with family.

"Do you guys want to go see your aunt Laurel? You could look at all her flowers, too."

"Aunt Laurel!" shouted Ronan. Then quieter, "Willow, I need to pee."

Oh Lord. "Can you hold it until we get to the garden center, do you think?" She didn't want to be responsible for Ronan peeing in the bushes on the Green, though she doubted he'd be the first boy to do so.

"I guess so." He looked up at her, eyes wide. "Is it a long walk?"

She squatted down and tapped her shoulder. "You

hang on to my neck and I'll piggyback you. How's that?" The picnic bag was across her shoulder and practically empty, so it didn't get in the way. Ever trusting, Ronan locked his hands around her neck and she stood, hitching his little legs with her arms. "Connor, you're okay to walk?"

"Is there ice cream in it for me?"

She laughed. "You drive a hard bargain. Ice cream after flowers."

"Then I can walk."

Connor did a good job keeping up, and Ronan seemed to enjoy the piggyback, though after the first hundred yards or so, Willow was regretting carrying him. The posture was awkward and his little, sweaty body was plastered against her shirt. When they got to the Ladybug, Laurel came out to greet them. "Well, look who we have here?"

"Hi, Aunt Laurel." Connor squinted up at her. "This's Willow."

"I know. Willow's my best friend."

"She is?" There was a distinct sound of wonder in his voice. Willow grinned and knelt down again, letting Ronan off her back. She rolled her shoulders a few times, trying to unstick her shirt from her skin.

"Yep. She's nice, isn't she?"

Ronan shifted from foot to foot.

"Um, Ronan needs to use the bathroom."

Laurel grinned. "No problem. Come with me, tiger," she said, holding out her hand. "Bathroom's right over here."

They disappeared for a moment, and Willow was very glad Laurel was helping Ronan with bathroom duties. She knew nothing about kids, other than she found them entertaining. When they came back, Laurel showed them to the flower garden, then they walked together and the boys picked out flowers and Laurel snipped them with little scissors.

"How did you end up with the boys?" Laurel asked.

"Hannah was keeping them, but she had a showing and I offered to watch them for a few hours."

Laurel nodded solemnly, looked at the boys, and kept her voice low. "I heard about Ethan and the fire."

"Is he okay? Hannah didn't tell me much of anything."

"Broken arm. Not a bad break, but they're putting him in a cast and he'll be off work for a while." She shrugged. "Maybe it'll be good for him. He works a lot, and he needs to slow down and enjoy the summer with the boys, you know?"

Willow was surprisingly relieved that Ethan hadn't suffered any painful burns or anything too serious. For his sake, and for the boys, too. The last thing they needed was for their lives to be turned upside down again.

"Aunt Laurel, what's this flower?" Connor had his fingers on a magenta-colored blossom.

"Coneflower," she said. "The butterflies love it. So do—"

"Don't say bees," Willow warned quickly and quietly. "We already had one meltdown at the park."

"—I," Laurel finished, before turning to Willow with a grin. "You know, you're kind of a natural at this. When Aiden and I start a family, you're going to be a fabulous aunt."

Something triggered inside of Willow. Happiness for her friend, certainly, but other feelings she hadn't had in a very long time. Hadn't she just been thinking lately that she was perfectly content? Talk of babies brought back too many horrible memories. And none that she could talk about.

"Are you okay?" Laurel asked.

"Of course." Willow smiled. "Is this an imminent event?"

Laurel blushed. "Not really. We're still in the honeymoon phase."

"I know. I feel like I haven't seen you in forever." It was true, but she added just enough innuendo to her tone that Laurel's blush deepened.

She looked over at the boys. Ronan was whispering in Connor's ear, and Connor was nodding. What were they up to? Connor came running over to Laurel. "Aunt Laurel, will you help us cut some more flowers now?"

"Sure."

"May I help?" Willow asked.

Connor frowned, a little wrinkle forming just about his cute little nose. "Just Aunt Laurel."

Willow tried not to be hurt. After all, they did know Laurel better, and they were just little boys. As Laurel and the boys snipped flowers, Willow took the time to walk through the rows of flowering shrubs and trees. Many of the shrubs had bloomed ages ago, in the spring, and now sported healthy foliage. The trees, too, though a couple of fruit trees remained and one apple tree even had two tiny apples on it. She took a deep breath and sat on a bench near a concrete birdbath, letting the sun soak into her face. Connor and Ronan's voices reached her and she smiled.

Peace. That was what she'd needed today. She deepened her breath. Listened to her exhale, long and slow.

In her subconscious she heard voices, and cars going

by on the main road. The slam of a car door, dull and heavy. The sweet song of a finch and a flutter of wings.

"What the actual hell are you doing here with my children?"

She opened her eyes, her peace shattered, and faced a very angry Ethan Gallagher.

CHAPTER 6

"Ethan. You're not at the hospital."

His eyes snapped at her, and his nostrils flared just a little at her obvious observation.

"Don't you answer your phone? I've been looking all over for you. Hannah said you'd gone to the park."

"We did . . ." She faltered a little in the face of his ire. "We had a picnic and played for a while. Ronan wanted to pick flowers and use the bathroom. We weren't far, and with Laurel here . . ."

"You should have called. Or texted."

"Hannah said . . ."

"Hannah said she'd look after the boys. I'm not thrilled with her, either. She had no right to leave them with you."

Willow frowned now, getting over the shock of seeing him standing over her like some avenging god. "She was trying to help you out, and I was trying to help her." Her gaze fell from his face to his arm, now in a navy-blue cast and held across his ribs in a sling. She lowered her voice. "Is it bad?"

He stared at her. "It's broken. That's enough, isn't it?" His lips thinned. "It's my dominant arm, too."

"I'm glad you weren't hurt worse," she offered. "And I'm sorry I didn't answer my phone. It's in the cooler, because we had a picnic. The boys were just going to pick some flowers and then I was going to take them back to the café to wait for Hannah." She swallowed. "They're great kids, Ethan. And precious. I know that. They were safe with me, I promise."

His throat bobbed as he swallowed. "Flowers," he scoffed, though his voice had softened. "What were you planning on doing, showing them how to make daisy chains?"

She got it. He didn't like her pink streak in her hair or her nose ring or the food she ate or much about her. She was not his type. But it wound her up when someone was so . . . derisive. Dismissive. "Is there something wrong with daisy chains?"

"For boys?"

She rolled her eyes. "Why not?"

"I am not getting into this with you. I'm going to take the boys home. Thanks for watching them."

It did not sound much like gratitude.

"Boys! Come on, let's go home!"

Both Connor and Ronan looked up at the sound of their father's voice. "Daddy!" Connor came pelting down the path, clutching a handful of flowers, while Laurel and Ronan followed behind. Ronan also had flowers in his hand, albeit a smaller bouquet.

Connor stopped short at the sight of his dad.

Willow watched the emotions cross the little boy's face. There was shock, then fear, then a guardedness that made her heart hurt.

"Daddy?"

Ethan erased the scowl from his face and replaced it with a smile for his son. "Hey, dude. Look what I got today."

"Did you break it?"

Ethan nodded. "Yeah. Like the cast?" He rapped on it gently with his knuckles and it sounded hollow.

Connor's eyes were huge. "Does it hurt? Are you going to be okay?"

Something passed across Ethan's face, just for a moment. It looked like pain, but not the physical kind. Rather the kind of pain that burrows right into the soul. She knew why the question hurt so much. It didn't take a brain surgeon to figure out that Ethan worried about the after-effects of Lisa's death on his sons.

"Of course I'm going to be okay. A shelf got knocked over and hit me just the right way, that's all. I'll be good as new."

Relief wreathed Connor's face. "Okay." He held out his hand. "I picked these for Aunt Hannah, but you can have them if you want."

Ethan smiled. "You can give them to Aunt Hannah. She loves flowers."

Laurel and Ronan had joined them. Willow stayed on the bench, out of the family drama. It wasn't her place. Apparently she'd done enough damage for one day.

Ronan came over and held up his flowers, a mixture of daisies and black-eyed Susans and cosmos. "For Wil-low," he said, his deliberate pronunciation of her name sounding quite adorable.

"You picked these for me?"

He nodded, then climbed up on the bench and into her lap.

She took the flowers into her hand and looked up at Laurel and Ethan, quite startled at Ronan's easy acceptance of her. Laurel's eyes looked suspiciously misty, while Ethan seemed uncertain, and still angry.

She cradled Ronan close, loving the smell of his slightly sweaty head mixed with whatever fabric softener was used in their laundry. "Thank you, Ronan. They're beautiful."

He looked up and grinned. "Now do we get ice cream?"

She laughed. "You charmer. Did Connor put you up to that?"

He giggled. So did Connor. And even Ethan's expression seemed to have softened a little.

She hugged him and laughed. "How about ice cream at my place? I keep some in my freezer for emergencies."

"Mmm," Ronan answered. "Ice cream 'mergency."

Willow had temporarily forgotten about Ethan, and now she looked up at him. "But it has to be okay with your dad. He might really want to get home."

"Please, Daddy? Please can we go for ice cream?"

Laurel grinned at everyone. Clearly she was enjoying this little scene. Willow would have to talk to her about that later.

Ethan sighed. "I have to pick up a prescription at the drugstore. I guess it'll be all right. For a few minutes."

"We'll meet you back there, then," Willow said.

"I've got the truck."

"Hannah has the car seats."

"Damn."

Connor looked up at his dad. "You said a swear."

A muscle ticked in Ethan's jaw.

"Seriously, we can walk back, can't we, boys?" Willow hefted Ronan onto her arm—heavens he was heavy—and stood. "It's not that far, and there's ice cream at the end. Meet us in half an hour or so?"

"I guess."

"Okay, then. Come on, boys, bring your flowers. We'll put them in water at my place and have some ice cream."

"Probably some soy garbage," Ethan muttered, barely under his breath. Willow heard him and shook her head. Then she put Ronan down, took his free hand, and straightened with a bright smile. "Thanks for the flowers, Laurel. See you soon, Ethan."

"Bye, Aunt Laurel! Bye, Daddy! See you soon!"

They marched their way to the sidewalk and headed to Willow's through the afternoon heat.

His arm ached and so did his heart.

Ethan sat on the vinyl seat at the pharmacy waiting area, flipping through a magazine but not actually seeing any of the pages. Why it was taking so long, he had no idea. He just wanted to pick up the boys and go home and be quiet. Theoretically he probably shouldn't even be driving, though he did have finger mobility with his cast.

He already depended on people for things far too much. This was only going to make things harder. Still, it could have been a lot worse.

He flipped through another magazine, the irritation from the garden center still humming through him. What had Hannah been thinking, letting Willow keep the boys? As far as he knew, she had no experience with kids and his boys barely knew her. And when he couldn't get a hold of her on her phone . . .

Ethan's hands clenched the magazine's glossy pages.

It wasn't Hannah's call to make—they were *his* children. It wasn't unreasonable to expect that he should have some idea where they were, or who they were with. Especially after a day like today. He appreciated his family's help, but he also didn't necessarily enjoy the "raising kids by committee" thing that frequently happened. Complaining would only make him seem ungrateful.

That certainly hadn't kept him from complaining to Willow, however, he realized with a sigh.

Seeing Ronan curl up on her lap had done something to him, though. It had opened up a wound so painful and deep he'd caught his breath. Sometimes he forgot because he was used to seeing his boys with their grandmother or aunts, but seeing Ronan cuddled in her arms was a painful reminder that their mother was gone. And that they should have a mother. Sure, he loved them more than anything, but it wasn't the same as having a mom. Ronan had even picked flowers for her, and she'd been touched. He could tell.

She was different, that was for sure. Bold, unique. Willow didn't bow down to criticism and certainly wasn't afraid to speak her mind and be pleasant as a sunny day while doing it. Incapable of not being herself, Willow was the definition of "free spirit," and that self-assuredness—that inner tranquility, New-Age zen—grated on him for some reason. But there was a sweetness to her that shone through every time they met. He wondered if he also resented her for that, since he was so unhappy and grouchy. She was a ray of sunshine that refused to go behind a cloud.

The pharmacist called his name and he picked up the painkillers they'd prescribed for the first few days. He probably wouldn't even take them; he was in charge of two small kids, after all. But he figured he'd better get them all the same, and take one at night if the pain got bad. He'd bruised his shoulder quite a bit, too. He caught his breath as he tucked the bottle into his pocket, then headed back to his SUV.

Willow lived in the space above the café, so he parked nearby and walked around to the back of the building and the stairs that climbed to a small landing on the second floor. Her exterior door was painted a robin's egg blue, a contrast to the purply-pink exterior with the darker purple trim. It damned near hurt his eyes, and he thought, rather nastily, that he wouldn't be surprised to see unicorns and rainbows.

He knocked on the door.

Connor answered, a ring of chocolate around his mouth.

"Daddy! You have *got* to see Willow's chair!"

He stepped inside and hesitated, surprised by her living space. It was so . . . open. Gleaming hardwood floors, white and pale green walls, a small kitchen and a few doors beyond the big room. Part of the space served as a living room—Willow had minimal furniture—and the rest housed a small . . . well, shrine, was the best word he could think of, with a Buddha and some candles and a little indoor fountain that created a constant trickle. In the corner was the chair that Connor was so excited about. It hung suspended from a frame, and he watched as Connor climbed into it next to his brother, who'd been holding his bowl of ice cream.

Ronan had an identical ring of chocolate around his mouth.

"Want some ice cream?"

He spun to see Willow approaching from one of the

doorways, a wet cloth in her hand. She held it up. "We had a little mishap," she explained.

"Sorry if they're making a mess . . ."

"Don't be silly. Kids are supposed to be a bit messy." She went over to the kids and did a quick wipe of Ronan's knee and elbow, then let them get back to their treat. "I've got more. It's homemade."

"It is?"

She grinned. "I like ice cream. I like chocolate. It's actually not that hard to make."

"It's not one of those nondairy, sugar-free things, is it?"

Her eyebrow lifted and one side of her mouth took on an impish curl. "I know what you think of me, Ethan. I'm not what you're used to. I have a nose ring and some pink hair and make brownies out of black beans. Did you know I'm not even a vegetarian?"

He didn't know what to say. Now that he thought of it, she'd eaten the ham at his mom's place on Hannah's birthday. He wasn't used to someone calling him out so bluntly, and yet so pleasantly.

"I choose to eat as naturally as I can, that's all. I like all sorts of stuff. I like to keep an open mind and try new things. So the ice cream is made from organic cream, organic sugar, real vanilla bean, organic cocoa. No strange or funny ingredients."

"Try it, Daddy! It's yummy!"

"How can I say no?" He watched as she turned to go into her little kitchen and got out another bowl and a metal tub from the freezer. As she scooped some into a bowl, he looked around. The place suited her. It was plain, but also peaceful and cozy in a strange sort of way. A minute later she was back, and handed him the bowl and spoon.

"Go have a seat. You're managing with one arm. I'll get you a tray to put your bowl on."

Her sofa was actually a plush futon. She brought over a folding table and set it up before him. "Thanks."

"No problem." She looked over at the boys, and he was surprised to hear her use a firm voice with them. "Boys, no swinging. Remember what I told you."

The motion of the hanging chair stopped to a lazy drift. "Sorry, Wil-low."

The way Ronan said her name hit Ethan right in the heartstrings. He bent his head and tried some of the ice cream. It was delicious. More than delicious; it was decadent.

She sat down beside him. "So, does it meet your expectations?"

He nodded and met her gaze. "More than. I can't deny that you're an amazing cook, Willow." He swallowed a little of his pride. The truth was, she'd come through for him today even though he hadn't given her a reason to. At the very least he owed her some gratitude. "Thank you for watching them today. I can see you're really good with them. I need to apologize for what I said earlier."

When she looked him square in the eyes, his heart did a little thump. Her eyes were a clear, beautiful blue, and for a moment he was reminded of grassy fields and puffy clouds and blue skies.

"They're your children," she said softly. "The most important thing in the world to you. There's nothing to apologize for, Ethan. It's all water under the bridge now."

"I was rude."

She laughed softly. "Well, yes. Though I would say . . . surly."

He swallowed tightly, uncomfortable with how her laugh made him feel. "I've judged you. Or . . . misjudged you, I guess. I *keep* misjudging you."

"I'm used to it. Here's the thing. What most people judge me for are the things I actually like most about myself. It's probably easier for me to brush off, you know?"

"You're always so calm."

She sat back against the cushion and her eyes twinkled at him. "No, I'm not. I try to be, though. I like myself better when I'm not freaking out. Negativity is really, really draining." She grinned. "A friend of mine back in Florida called it being a *bucket filler* rather than a *bucket spiller.* I prefer to add rather than deplete."

He thought about that for a moment. Since Lisa's death, he'd really struggled. That was natural, but grief and stress—about his job, about being a single parent—had definitely worn him down. It wasn't that he was tired, like the sleep-deprived kind of tired. He was just, as she said, drained. Weary.

"I came for ice cream and feel like I'm getting a therapy session."

Her smile was wide. "Oh, I'm glad."

Before he could ask her what she meant, she popped up off the futon and went to wipe hands and faces again. Once the boys were clean, they hopped down from the chair and went to Ethan to examine his cast and ask him all sorts of questions. After they'd touched his fingers and the hard cast, Connor looked up at his dad, his expression sober. "You're sure you aren't going to go away like Mommy?"

"I'm sure, Connor. Sometimes accidents happen, and people go to the doctor and get better and are good as new." He looked at Willow for backup, since he wasn't too sure about how to answer and she seemed to always know the right thing to say. "Ask Willow if you don't believe me."

Willow sat on the floor and crossed her legs, folding her hands in her lap. "It's true. I'm really sorry for what happened to your mom, you guys. I know it must make you and your daddy very sad. But know what?" She paused, and stared down at her hands for a moment, and when she looked up, there was something in her eyes that hit Ethan—maybe under her calm Willow did have secrets and pain of her own. "Lots of people get sick, or have accidents, and they're just fine. They just need time to heal. Your dad's arm is going to be all better in about a month." She smiled at them. "Doctors and nurses can do amazing things."

Connor frowned. "Then why couldn't they save my mommy?"

Ethan winced. It wasn't the first time he'd been asked that question, but the answer was always the same. "I don't know, pal. I just don't."

Willow's eyes looked suspiciously soft. "Know what, Connor?"

Connor shrugged.

"It's perfectly okay to wonder. It means you love your mom very much." Ethan didn't miss how she used the present tense of love—Connor's feelings were still there even if Lisa wasn't. "When I get sad about something, know what I do?"

He shook his head.

"I sit down in a favorite spot, and I listen to everything around me. Sometimes I close my eyes. For example, maybe I'll sit out on my balcony and listen to the breeze in the trees, and the birds singing, and a couple of squirrels arguing in the branches. Maybe I'll sit with a bowl of ice cream and really enjoy how wonderful it tastes. And I'll think about all the good things in the right now, and it makes me feel better."

Ethan got a lump in his throat. Connor had climbed onto his knee, but all his attention was on Willow.

"If I were going to do that for this afternoon, I'd think about ice cream, and the flowers that Ronan picked for me, and the sound of you and Ronan laughing, and how you looked in the garden with your aunt Laurel. See? You made *my* day special. How about that?"

Connor nodded. Ronan's eyelids were starting to look a little heavy, and Ethan knew he should get them home. He was tired, too. He'd been up all night and add to that the fire at dawn and the stress of the day . . . He was drained.

"Okay, boys, we should let Willow get back to the café. I'm sure she's got work to do."

She hopped up from her spot on the floor and took away his bowl. He stood and rolled his shoulders, then reached into his pocket for his keys. Fatigue was starting to hit him now, and he suspected that dinner would be something like grilled cheese and that he'd hit the sack at the same time as the boys.

"I'll walk you down," she said. She hefted Ronan into her arms and they made their way down the back stairs and to the truck parked on the street. They spied Hannah through her office window, and gave a wave. She popped out of her office to get the car seats out of her car, and they got the boys strapped into the back.

Hannah was helping, and Ethan saw Willow back away, as if she were going to sneak off. But then Hannah's cell phone rang and she gave a quick wave and disappeared, leaving them alone again.

"Hannah never seems to slow down," Willow said, chuckling.

"She's all go and panic, and you're all slow down and calm. Hard to believe you're friends."

"She just finds her peace in a different way."

He shook her head. "You're right, you know. I don't know what to make of you. But I do need to thank you. For taking care of the boys and for what you said up there."

"They're sweet boys," she replied. "Busy, but awfully, awfully sweet. You must be doing an okay job. Don't be too hard on yourself."

Easy for her to say.

She poked her head into the open window. "Bye, guys. Come visit me again soon, okay?"

Connor nodded. Ronan was clearly exhausted; he'd popped his thumb into his mouth. Ethan figured he'd be asleep before they hit the one traffic light in Darling.

"Ethan?"

He looked into her eyes.

"What burned today? I never did hear."

He sighed. "The food bank. Thankfully the only damage to the shelter was a little melted siding. Easy fix. But the food bank . . . at the very least it'll have to be gutted and redone, if it's even salvageable."

Her face fell. "Oh. That's terrible. I'm glad everyone is okay . . . present company notwithstanding."

He smiled a little and jiggled his elbow in the sling. "Aw, this'll be fine. It's more of an inconvenience than anything. Doing things with one arm isn't going to be fun. And neither is facing my mother. She worries. Particularly about me. I hate adding to it."

"You've got a wonderful family."

And he was aware that she didn't. She was alone here in Darling, despite it being her hometown. She was lucky to have friends like Laurel and Hannah. "You're welcome to join us anytime." It wasn't pity that prompted his reply; it was simply the knowledge that he knew what it was like to be lonely.

He smiled a little bit, and she smiled back, and the moment drew out. A hint of color blossomed on her cheeks, and he was sure she didn't realize it but she bit down on her lower lip just a bit, making the soft flesh plump slightly. Tension settled low in his belly. Had he finally flapped the unflappable Willow Dunaway? As their gazes held, he realized she wasn't the only one shaken from the intimate moment.

He cleared his throat. "Right, well, I'd better get these two home. Thanks again, Willow."

"You're welcome," she said quietly.

When he got in the truck, a glance in the rearview mirror showed Ronan perilously close to dozing off and Connor looking like he'd follow if given a chance.

The burden of being a single father didn't weigh on him so badly just now. He put the truck in gear and pulled away from the curb. And when he looked in the mirror again, he could see her still standing there, her arms wrapped around herself.

CHAPTER 7

Telling his mother went just about as well as Ethan had expected. Moira was waiting for him at his house, full of concern and unsolicited criticism about the danger he put himself in each day when he had two little boys to worry about. It gave him a headache, in addition to the dull ache in his arm. It would be better once the inflammation went down. Rather than listen to the speech over and over, he took advantage of the child-care and went to bed. He'd been up nearly twenty-four hours, and he was exhausted.

He woke near midnight, and tiptoed into the bathroom to find some ibuprofen. The house was silent, but a quick check showed the spare room occupied by his mom. He closed his eyes and sighed. Did all single fathers need this much help?

He crept downstairs and opened the fridge, looking for something to eat since he'd skipped dinner. There was leftover homemade macaroni and cheese, one of the boys' favorites, and he took out the container and ate it cold, just to fill the hunger hole. He stared out the window at the backyard as he held the bowl in the crook of his elbow and speared more pasta with his fork. Earlier this summer, the yard had been rather plain. He'd kept the grass neat and tidy, but Lisa had always put out flowers in little beds and planters. This year Laurel had stepped in and added some colorful touches, but it wasn't the same. Now, at midnight, the flowers were just dark lumps in the pale moonlight.

Nothing was the same. Maybe it was time he accepted it, and stopped wishing it was different. What he had left now were memories, but he couldn't feel her anymore. Not like before. It scared him a little to realize that his grief had shifted to something new that was even more difficult: emptiness.

Thank God for the boys.

By the time he finished his snack, the pain relief was kicking in. He headed back to bed, but lay awake a long time, staring at the thin lines of moonlight coming through his blinds.

He'd become accustomed to sleeping alone. He no longer imagined the weight of her body on the bed beside him. Her clothes were gone from the closet, donated to charity. The décor was the same, but it was as if . . . well, as if the personality that had filled the house was absent. He blinked back tears, wondering at the odd sensation of grieving for his actual grief. Because the absence of heartbreak had to mean he was moving on. It was a sad, complicated feeling.

He adjusted his position to get comfortable, and remembered Willow's words to Connor. *I'll think about all the good things in the right now, and it makes me feel better.*

Maybe he'd try that. Everyone kept telling him to count his blessings, but this was different. He tried to remember what Willow had said. Something about squirrels and flowers and ice cream . . .

He thought about his boys cuddled together in her swing-chair, faces smudged with chocolate ice cream. He thought about Ronan's innocent look of happiness as he handed Willow his bouquet of flowers, and the flitting wings of butterflies as they darted around the garden center. Willow's soft laugh and gentle manner, and how she'd stayed on the sidewalk and watched his truck pull away.

Right now, Willow was at the center of any good thing that had happened in the last twenty-four hours.

He closed his eyes. That was silly. He was just tired and worn out, that's all.

He was not going to lie awake and think about Willow Dunaway.

"So, did you hear?"

Aiden and Laurel stopped by on Saturday morning, bringing breakfast for everyone from the diner. Bacon, pancakes, hash browns, and sticky ketchup and maple syrup covered the table and streaked across two very happy faces. Laurel cut the boys' pancakes into smaller pieces, since Ethan found cutting anything with a knife and fork more than challenging right now.

"Hear what?"

Laurel was beaming. "What Willow and Hannah and I are up to. Or mostly Willow, anyway. Hannah's helping with the paperwork side and I'm the odd-jobs girl."

Ethan frowned. Just when he was finally able to stop thinking about Willow, her name popped up again. "No, I didn't hear."

"She's rented the vacant space next to the café and is offering it to the town as a temporary food bank."

Ethan put down his fork. "Are you serious?"

Laurel nodded. "Dead serious. Hannah told us last night when she stopped in for a new porch basket." Laurel grinned. "She killed the last one. Your sister does not have a green thumb, Ethan."

Aiden reached for more bacon. "I heard Willow watched the boys the other day. I got the impression that you guys didn't exactly hit it off at Hannah's birthday. You both looked like you'd rather be anywhere else."

"She's not my type," Ethan replied sourly, squirting ketchup on his fried potatoes. "She's a total earth child, you know." Guilt shot through him as he said it. Yes, Willow was a free spirit, but he didn't dislike her. Not really.

"No kidding." Aiden laughed. "She doesn't strike me as the soccer-mom type at all."

Oddly enough, after the other day with the boys, Ethan could see her doing that easily. He scowled and stabbed at a piece of pancake.

"Daddy, what's an earth child?"

Little ears. He sighed. "Nothing. Finish your pancakes and then you can have more juice."

A food bank. Why wasn't he surprised? He hadn't expected the news, but it sounded like something Willow would do. He wondered if she realized how much work there was to setting up something like that. Wouldn't she need some sort of zoning or permit from the town? Then there was stocking it, and volunteers . . .

And where would she find time to do that anyway? He was pretty sure that the café kept her pretty busy.

Laurel reached for the bacon and selected a crisp strip. "Anyway, Willow's already wrangled us into taking a shift next week. They're going to start stocking shelves so that they can have a pick-up day by next weekend."

"That's fast."

"That's what I said," Aiden remarked. "And then Hannah roped Rory and me into helping construct shelving. You're lucky your arm's busted. Otherwise she probably would have asked you, too."

"I'm in charge of scheduling the manpower," Laurel said proudly. "I asked George if he wanted to help out, and he's going to go over a few nights this week. He's pretty handy, you know."

Ethan nodded. George was a veteran who'd been living on the streets in Darling until this past spring. Now he worked for Laurel at the garden center. "I suppose it's a cause he believes in."

"Absolutely." Aiden's gaze met Ethan's. "E, I know you're limited with the cast and all, but it's got to be driving you crazy, being off work. Why don't you ask if there's something you can do to help?"

"I'm fine, Aiden. You don't need to dream up activities for me."

Laurel frowned. "Ethan, you just seem to isolate yourself so much. Without work to get you out of the house . . ."

Ethan got up from the table and went to the sink. He snagged a small towel and wet it, then squeezed it out as best he could since he couldn't actually wring it. Without saying a word, he went to the table and helped the boys wash their hands and faces, trying to get all the syrup. "Boys, go play outside for a while."

"But Daddy, I wanna watch cartoons."

"It's nice out. Go kick the ball around or something."

His tone made the order very clear, and Connor scuffed his feet as they made their way to the mat by the door to put on their shoes. After several frustrated sighs, Ethan went over and helped them tighten the Velcro straps across the top of the sneakers. Thank God he didn't have to try to tie shoes just yet. His could use his fingers, but everything was just so damned awkward.

Once they were outside, he turned back to Aiden and Laurel. "Look, I appreciate the breakfast. But I don't need you coming up with ways to keep me occupied. I'm a big boy."

Laurel got up and started cleaning off the table.

"For God's sake, I can clean up the mess, all right? I'm not an invalid."

She paused.

He felt instantly guilty for his sharp tone. "I'm sorry, Laurel. I don't mean to snap. I know everyone means well."

"Yes, we do," said Aiden. "Look, I know I've ribbed you a lot in the past, but the truth is, I worry about you. I know losing Lisa was devastating. How could it not be?" Aiden reached over and took Laurel's hand. "You've had to deal with your own grief, plus that of the boys, plus being a single dad. Seriously, we just want to see you smile again. That's not going to happen if you keep shutting yourself away from living, you know?"

Ethan sat in the chair. The sling kept his arm cradled close to his ribs; the swelling had gone down significantly, which helped immensely. The truth was, the afternoon he'd spent at Willow's was the closest he'd felt to actually living in a long time. There'd been no expectation, no agenda, no trying to prove anything. Just a simple bowl of ice cream and a little conversation.

It made it very difficult to keep thinking of her as a "free spirit." He was starting to think that she was one of the most grounded, stable people he'd ever met.

"I'll think about it, but that's all I'll commit to. I certainly can't build any shelves or do much physical labor."

The three of them cleared the table, then Laurel said she had to get to the garden center for work. After they were gone, Ethan checked on the kids. They were in the back corner, playing in the playhouse that Ethan and his father had built together when Ronan was born.

He was a firefighter. He was a dad. How hard would it be for him to be a man again?

The sound of hammering echoed through the walls as Willow packed a supply of food for the workers next door. The café was quiet for a Tuesday night, which meant that the sounds of drills, saws, and hammers added to the ambiance. She didn't mind. Everything was coming together as quickly as humanly possible.

But it was six thirty, and she'd promised to feed the workers, so she filled six bowls with today's Hearty Vegetable soup, added six ham-and-swiss sandwiches, and a plate of oatmeal cookies. There was more than she could carry, so she'd just determined to make two trips when Ethan Gallagher stepped through the door.

Her heart gave a leap of unexpected pleasure, then settled down again. But that leap was a sufficient warning. Ethan was not on the market, and neither was she, for that matter. She was content the way things were.

"Hungry?" he asked, a slightly crooked smile teasing his lips.

She looked down at the tray in her hands. "Oh. I was just taking it next door. Feeding the crew."

He lifted his arm and frowned. "I'm not much help. But I can get the doors for you."

"Thank you, Ethan." She hoped she wasn't blushing as he held the door open for her, then jogged ahead to the adjoined property and opened that door, too.

He followed her inside. It was coming together, she realized with delight. Sheets protected the floor as volunteers put together shelving, but already she could see a difference. The office space was divided into three sections. There was a reception area at the front, which right now consisted of a surplus desk from Hannah's real estate office and a steno chair that Hannah had found somewhere, plus a metal filing cabinet courtesy of Ethan's brother Rory, who'd unearthed it at the veterinary clinic. Beyond that area was a larger room, where stand-alone shelves already lined one wall. A third room was beyond that, originally intended for storage. Other shelves and tables would go there, to hold extra stock, boxes, and one industrial-sized cooler where Willow hoped to keep perishables.

"Wow. This is a pretty big space," he said, coming to stand beside her.

She tried to focus on the topic at hand and not the fact that she could feel the warmth of his body so close to her side. "I know. It's messy now, but it'll come together. We have a few more days. Stock starts arriving on Thursday night. We're hoping to have fifty hampers ready to go by Saturday morning."

"You're kidding."

"I wish." She smiled up at him. "Actually, no, I don't wish. It'll be better once everything is up and running. The volunteers from the former location will be handling a lot of the day-to-day bits. Shelley Burke's looked after a lot of that, and she's amazing." She put the tray on the desk. "Hey, guys," she called out. "Soup's on. I'll be back with sandwiches."

They went back to the café and picked up the rest of the food. Ethan managed to carry the plate of cookies, and once they left everything for the volunteers, she gave him the tour. There was so much hubbub there wasn't any chance for privacy, but that didn't stop her from being aware of him. Clearly he kept himself in shape for his job, because his chest was wide and spare, leading to strong, straight shoulders. The kind of chest a woman could lean on. Arms that would surround and protect.

"What brings you by, anyway?" she asked, as they left the storage room.

"Actually, I wanted to see if there was anything I can do to help. The boys are at soccer practice, and I don't have to pick them up until eight. I know it's only an hour, but . . . well, I need to get out of the house before I go crazy."

His eyes were so earnest. Her heart did that funny little beat thing again and she looked away. "I'm sure there's something for you. We can always use an extra . . . hand." She looked back at him again and gave him a silly smile, hoping he'd appreciate the levity.

"Funny." His voice was dry and she couldn't help the little zing of appreciation at his warm tone. Ethan Gallagher actually had a sense of humor. There was a world of difference between his acerbic "funny" and his previous, clearly grouchy pronouncements.

She leaned against the doorframe. "The shelves will be done by Thursday morning, and the donation bins from around town will start arriving. When that happens, everything will need to be sorted and stocked. You could help with that."

"I can see if Mom can watch the boys."

She pursed her lips. Granted, it was going to be busy, but everything was running on schedule and she knew that Shelley would be on hand to help organize and sort.

"Bring them," she suggested, putting her hand on his arm. "They can help. You're never too young to learn about helping other people, right?"

"You're sure they won't get in the way?"

"Maybe have a backup plan just in case?"

"I could bring them with me for the first hour or so, and then see if Mom or one of the girls could take them home. They've been nagging for a dip in the pool."

"Perfect."

They spent a few minutes moving some shelving units. She used both hands to lift her end, and Ethan braced his hand beneath a shelf and lifted, then let the end rest on his cast. "Doesn't that hurt?"

"Not a bit. These aren't heavy anyway, they're just awkward." They shuffle-stepped their way into the biggest room and found space against the wall for the first unit.

"We'll organize all the dry goods on the shelves. Canned vegetables, pasta, beans, peanut butter, that sort of thing. The church has loaned us some of their old banquet tables for the middle of the room, and we'll put things like potatoes and produce there."

"Fresh stuff?" Ethan wiped his hand on his jeans.

"I contacted my local produce suppliers, and they're going to help out a bit and add a bit extra to my shipments, particularly the less-than-perfect stuff that grocery stores and markets won't shelve. Laurel also knows a lot of gardeners in the area. Vegetables are just starting to come on now, and she's let people know that we'll accept their surplus."

"I don't know how you pulled this together on such short notice." Ethan shook his head, and his look of wonder made her feel warm inside. Was this actual approval from the Ethan Gallagher?

She shrugged. "I went to Hannah after you left the other day. She called the mayor, we had a meeting, contacted the board of the food bank, and it was a done deal. This is already zoned for commercial use, and our landlord offered us three months of free rent." She didn't mention that she'd had to sign a year lease in order to get the three months. She'd panic about that later. "I met with the coordinator, we devised a plan, and then we went about setting up local food drives and rounding up volunteers. Laurel helped with the shift scheduling. Donations, too. All the shelving materials have been donated, and they'll end up going to the old location once it's been gutted and renovated."

"And did you sleep at all?"

She laughed then. Truthfully, not as much as she should have. "Enough, I suppose. But I won't lie. I'll be glad once this settles down. The café usually keeps me plenty busy. I'm afraid my employees have all been putting in extra hours this week."

And the more hours they worked, the more she had to pay out in wages. But she wasn't going to think about that right now, either. She could only worry about one thing at a time. "Listen, Ethan, do you want to get some tea? These guys will be working for another few hours, and I'll have to close up here and next door, too. I could use fifteen minutes to sit down and have something to drink."

She watched as he pulled out his phone and checked the time. "I have some time. But not tea. Something else, maybe." He gave a shudder and she laughed again. She wasn't surprised that he wasn't the tea type.

Back at The Purple Pig, she made herself a soothing cup of jasmine tea and then poured Ethan a glass of tart lemonade. They took a table in the back corner, away from the other customers, and she sank into the seat gratefully. "Oh, that's nice."

"Is it possible you're working too hard?" Ethan lifted the glass and took a sip of his drink.

"More than possible." She smiled, took a deep breath in and out. "It's good, though, you know? A good cause."

"A necessary one," he replied. "Though I wish it weren't."

"I know. But some people, they just need a helping hand." She took her spoon and pressed her tea bag against her cup before removing it from the water and putting it on the side of her saucer. "Maybe it's Pollyanna of me, but I just think that if we focused more on helping each other, the world would be a happier place."

"It's a nice sentiment," he offered. "Not sure how realistic it is."

She sipped the fragrant tea. "I can't fix the whole world, Ethan. But maybe I can do something about my little corner of it. Imagine what would happen if we all did that? The world would be filled with happy little corners."

He sipped his drink again, and didn't reply.

She knew her views weren't for everyone, but they didn't have to be. If she had learned one thing over the past years, as she'd dealt with her own demons, it was that she didn't need anyone's approval but her own.

She lifted her cup and drank again, deeper this time. What she really needed wasn't tea, but some quiet time to do some deep breathing, maybe meditate. She recognized the antsy feeling that tightened her muscles. It could be caused by working too much, or too much stimulation and not enough quiet . . . or too much Ethan. Certainly she'd been thinking about him a lot lately, particularly when she was trying to quiet her mind. She'd let the other thoughts drift away, and thoughts of him kept drifting in. It was really quite annoying.

"I didn't really peg you as the tattoo type," he said, nodding at her arm.

Her stomach twisted into a knot. Her ink was rather personal, though its meaning was well known. "I only have the one," she remarked, keeping her voice light. "Though I've thought about getting another."

"A semicolon in a flower. That seems kind of a weird choice, don't you think?" He gave a little chuckle. "Did you study English or something?"

He didn't know. She wasn't sure why she was surprised. Not everyone understood the meaning behind the semicolon, she supposed. Did she want to explain? And if she did, did she want it to be here, sitting at her business, with the chatter of other customers around?

He put down his glass. "Did I say something wrong?"

"No, of course not."

"Yes, I did." He sighed. "Look, I know we got off on the wrong foot . . . I'm sorry for that. Forget I said anything, okay?" He checked the time again. "I should probably walk over to the soccer field anyway. I can catch the end of the boys' practice."

She made a snap decision. "I'll walk with you, if

you don't mind. I think I need to get some fresh air. I've been cooped up inside too much."

"Okay." He didn't look too sure, but now that she'd said it, the idea of walking along the riverbank and to the soccer field sounded perfect.

It wasn't yet dusk, but the sun had that late-day mellowness that seemed to soak into everything, warm and lazy. Next to sunrise, Willow liked this time of day best. Early morning held the brightness of a new day's potential, but sunset was restful and calm. The green of the grass was deeper, and everything held a gilded glow. She let out a deep breath and stretched her neck, tilting her head to first one shoulder, then the other.

They ambled along the sidewalk until the crosswalk on Main, then hit the footpath that followed the creek through the park. "I really needed this," she remarked. "Normally I stay pretty in tune with myself, but I've been so preoccupied with the food bank thing, I've pushed my normal routine aside."

"I pegged you as someone who goes with the flow. That you'd hate routine."

She looked up at him. It was very odd, thinking about walking in the park with a man—with Ethan. Not a date, but not entirely platonic, either. "Actually, I'm very regimented. That's part of what keeps me sane." She laughed lightly. "And yeah, it helps me go with the flow when I have to. That probably doesn't make any sense."

"Not really."

They sidestepped around a couple stopped on the edge of the path, then kept going and she picked up the thread of conversation once more. "I get up at the same time each morning. I start my day the same way—with some tea, a yoga practice, maybe a brief meditation."

"You must get up early."

She laughed. "Five. I'm downstairs in the café by six-thirty, to help get ready to open. I'll have something to eat then, usually some fruit or yogurt or something. The days differ depending on how busy we are, what is going on . . . but that routine helps me feel prepared to meet those challenges, you know?"

She half expected him to look at her like she was some aberration. Instead, his eyes glowed with approval. "You always seem so unflappable."

"Hah!" A laugh burst out of her mouth. "Oh, Ethan, I can be flapped very easily. That's why I'm so regimented. I . . ." She turned over her wrist and looked at her tattoo. "Ethan, are we becoming friends, do you think?"

His cheeks colored a little bit. "Uh, I guess we probably are. Kind of an odd combo, but there's nothing wrong with that."

"And you know what it's like to hurt a lot, right? Emotionally. I know you do because I've seen you whenever someone brings up your wife."

She watched him swallow, his Adam's apple bobbing as his gaze skittered away. "Yeah. I know what that's like."

They were nearly to the soccer field. She could see parents lined up by the chain-link fence; hear the cheers and the yelling from the players on the field. There were two separate games going on, the field divided in half, presumably because of the ages of the participants. She halted, not wanting anyone else to hear what she was about to say.

"You asked about my tattoo. It's a semicolon. You know what a semicolon does in a sentence, right? It creates a pause, but the sentence isn't over."

"Well, I think my mom the grammarian would probably have a different definition, but we can go with that."

She smiled, then met his gaze, her insides quaking. "When I was twenty, there was a pause in my life. I considered ending that pause with a period."

"A period . . ." He looked confused.

"A period marks The End."

Understanding dawned on his face. She saw it in how his eyes widened and his lips softened just a bit. She would not let her lip wobble. Instead she lifted her chin just a bit. "I decided that I didn't want the end. I wanted to go on. I was going to fight to go on, and I did. When you see someone with a semicolon tattoo, that's what it represents, Ethan. The fact that at some point, that person might not have gone on, but they chose to fight. Their story isn't over."

"Willow," he said softly.

Her lip did quiver a bit and she bit down on it, then drew a deep breath. "I'm good now. But yoga, meditation, they saved me, and that's why my semicolon is inside a lotus flower. I did a lot of work on me, because I finally decided I was worth it. Ironically, all that serenity you sense takes a lot of conscious effort."

"I had no idea."

"Everyone has a story. You have one. Laurel has one. The people coming to the food bank have a story. We're all just people trying to muddle through as best we can."

He moved his left hand, and she was shocked when he clasped her fingers. "Thank you for telling me," he said. "No one has trusted me with anything for a very long time."

"Surely your brothers—"

"No. Everyone thinks I can't handle it. Like I'm some fragile creature they need to smile around all the time."

"Oh, Ethan."

"I understand they're just trying to help. You're the first person to treat me like I'm nothing special in months."

She laughed, a thick, emotional sound, and pulled her fingers away from his, somewhat regretfully. "You don't want to be a special snowflake?"

He laughed too, and slid his hand into his pocket. "Sometimes I just want to be a man."

And there it was. That slow simmer of attraction again, hanging between them, like a branch laden with fruit ready to be picked. He was a man. Oh, what a man. Tall and strong and sometimes reticent and . . . what was it her mother used to say? Something about still waters running deep.

And he was still holding her hand. Her throat tightened as their eyes met and clung.

Oh boy.

"Dad! Dad! Did you see?" Connor came running over, looking adorable in his yellow soccer shirt and shorts with little black shin pads. "I scored a goal!"

"Way to go, tiger!" Ethan held Willow's gaze as Connor barreled against his legs, but he released her fingers and ruffled the boy's sweaty hair. "This might be cause for celebration. Ice cream? Just this once, before baths and bed?"

"Oh boy!"

"Go get your brother."

They watched him run off, straight for Ronan, who was a shorter version of his brother and wearing a red shirt instead of yellow. Ethan raised his hand and waved to one of the moms. "Mrs. Sanders," he explained. "She agreed to watch over the guys while I went to see you."

The boys came back, Connor dutifully dragging the small backpack with their water bottles. Ronan's head was equally sweaty. "Ice cream!" he shouted happily. "Connor said!"

"That's right. Just this once, though." Ethan looked over at Willow. "Join us? Or do you have to get back?"

"Come with us, Willow! Please?" Connor jumped up and down, his energy level still at its peak.

She should get back. There was so much to do. But she didn't quite want to walk away just yet. The evening was soft and full of promise, and the idea of ice cream with the boys—with Ethan—was too alluring to pass up.

"Of course I will," she responded, and ignored the voice in her head that said things were about to change.

CHAPTER 8

Five a.m., and Laurel, true to her word, was at Willow's door with yoga mat in hand. "Okay," she said, a little breathlessly. "I haven't been sleeping that well. I think I need to chill out."

Willow smiled. "You've come to the right place." She stepped back from the door and let Laurel inside. True enough, her friend seemed wound tighter than a spring. "Anything in particular going on?"

For a brief moment, Willow thought maybe Laurel was going to say something, but Laurel shook her head and toed off her sandals. "Just antsy, I guess. Maybe it's a full moon or something."

Her voice sounded a little too nonchalant, but Willow wouldn't press. People revealed things on their own time, when they were ready. Instead she grabbed her own mat, put out a few blocks and a bolster for Laurel, and started the soothing background music.

"You need to breathe deeply first," she said quietly, raising her arms and filling her diaphragm with air.

Dutifully, Laurel inhaled as deeply as possible, then blew it out.

"It's just that—"

"Not now," Willow said firmly. "After. Focus on mindfulness now. Listen to your breathing. Feel your chest rise and fall."

It took several minutes, but finally Laurel started to melt into the poses, her breathing deep and regular. Willow needed the practice herself; today was Thursday, she hadn't seen Ethan or the boys since Tuesday, but they'd been on her mind constantly. And she'd see them today, when they came to help organize the food bank.

Frustrated that she'd allowed her thoughts to wander away from the moment, she focused on a more challenging move. Grasshopper pose required focus and strength in the upper body and core. Willow pressed both hands on the floor, exhaled, and lifted both her legs perpendicular to her body, while being balanced on her hands. Laurel, meanwhile, modified it by doing the Baby Grasshopper, and kept one foot and both hands pressed on the floor, since she couldn't quite reach for her other foot.

"Show-off," Laurel muttered. Willow carefully came out of the pose, angled Laurel a sideways grin, and then led them both through a few cool-down poses.

She was sweaty. Laurel was, too, but the tension seemed to have melted out of her shoulders, and her face wasn't so tight. "Better?" Willow asked.

"Much," Laurel replied.

"It's unusual for you to come over for yoga this early." Willow went to the kitchen and put on the kettle for her morning cup of green tea, then grabbed two glasses, filled them with water, and went back to the

living room. "Normally you're an end-of-the-day practice girl."

Laurel took the water and drank half of it down,
then looked at Willow. "Oh, I suppose it won't hurt to
tell you. I know my secrets are safe with you."

Secrets?

"There's nothing official yet, but since the wedding,
Aiden and I . . ." Laurel paused, and her cheeks colored a bit. A smile spread across her face. "Well, we're
trying to have a baby. We decided we didn't want to
wait."

Willow put down her glass, a wave of surprise making her temporarily silent. A baby? They'd only been
married a little over a month! "Wow, that's fast,"
she said, but she couldn't help but smile back. How
could she not, when Laurel looked so happy? "So why
the sleeplessness?"

Laurel sighed. "Excitement? Overthinking? I keep
wondering if I already am, and what it will be like, and
what our lives will be like, and then what if I don't get
pregnant right away . . . my brain is a runaway train."

Willow put her hand on Laurel's forearm. "You're
sure it's not too fast? You just got married. I figured
you'd still be running around naked at this point."

Laurel's blush deepened. "Who says we're not?"
Then she giggled. "Oh God, Wil. If I'm not pregnant,
it's not from lack of trying."

Willow burst out laughing, and Laurel added her
sheepish grin.

"Are you late yet?"

"A few days, but that's not unusual. And I haven't
said a word to Aiden. One of us being wound up is bad
enough. He'll hover."

The kettle began to whistle, and Willow went to the

kitchen and poured the water over the leaves. "Well, it would make Aiden's mom happy. I hear she's very big on grandchildren."

Laurel came into the kitchen and sent Willow a sly look. "And how would you know that?"

Without missing a beat, she reached for a cup and replied, "Hannah gets a lot of pressure at home to settle down and start having babies."

"And is that your only source of information?"

"What do you mean?" She focused on the mug and carefully poured the tea.

"Rumor has it that you had ice cream with one of the Gallagher boys the other night."

"Actually, it was three of the Gallagher boys, and we got a cone after Connor and Ronan's soccer practice."

"And you say that as if it happens every day of the week. What the heck, Wil? You start seeing Ethan and you don't tell your best friend?"

Willow's jaw dropped. "Wait . . . seeing him? Oh, it's not like that. Not at all. I watched the boys for a few hours the day that Ethan was hurt, and now he's kind of at loose ends, being off work and all. He stopped in to ask if he could help with the food bank project, and I walked over to the soccer field with him. That's all."

"So you went for a walk to see his children play soccer?"

Oh, that made it sound like it was totally something it was not. "Honestly, Laurel, I've been managing the café and the project at the same time. I needed some fresh air and some time to decompress. I walked over. They were going to ice cream and asked if I wanted to go along. I like the boys, they're good kids. So I said yes. End of story."

Laurel drank the rest of her water and gave Willow a "sure it is" kind of look. Willow's serenity from her morning practice was now shot. Not just because of Laurel's insinuations, but because they weren't totally unfounded. They'd gotten off to a rocky start, but she couldn't deny there was something about Ethan that intrigued her. It didn't hurt that he was ruggedly gorgeous. Redheads usually weren't her thing, but his coppery hair only seemed to highlight the blue of his eyes. And then there was the way he treated his boys. They were his whole world.

"You probably want to shower," Laurel said, "And I have to get back and get ready to be at the garden center by eight. Can we please set aside some time to get together soon, just us? I miss that."

"You mean when you're not chasing Aiden around in his birthday suit? Because I don't think I want to witness that."

Laurel giggled. "Touché." Then her expression sobered. "Look, I know I gave you a hard time about Ethan, but honestly, think about it. He's withdrawn a lot since Lisa's death, but he's a good guy. The Gallagher brothers . . . they know how to treat a woman right." Then she rolled her eyes. "Well, except maybe Rory. He's still in the 'plaything' stage."

"Get going and worry about your own romantic life. This interfering can't be good for your uterus."

"Not a word," Laurel cautioned, and Willow made a motion as if zipping her lips.

"Love you." Laurel's face softened and she gave Willow a quick kiss on the cheek. "And I'll be by on

Saturday for my volunteer shift." She zoomed out the door, leaving silence in her wake.

Willow checked the time and panicked, then headed for the shower. She got under the spray while the water was still cool, not wanting to waste time. Besides, the sooner she got to work, the sooner she could focus on something else. Or someone else.

The new food bank wasn't quite bedlam, but it was close. Willow took a deep breath and consulted quickly with Shelley, the previous coordinator, to get new instructions. Shelley was old hat at this, and knew just how to organize incoming donations. These were only the first deliveries. More food drives were expected to happen on Saturday, and then they'd go through this again.

Right now Willow was writing labels on recipe cards and pasting them on the shelves. Canned vegetables, soup, pasta, canned fruit, cereal . . . All had their own shelves. Tomorrow morning the first of the fresh food would arrive: lettuces, tomatoes, beans, cucumbers, late-season strawberries.

By two, the initial rush had calmed and food was sorted and put in front of the appropriate shelving. It was perfect timing when Ethan walked in with the boys. He was wearing faded jeans and a gray-blue T-shirt, and his arm wasn't in the sling anymore. It hung by his side, still encased in the cast. Connor and Ronan looked adorable. They were dressed in shorts and T-shirts with sandals on their feet. When they stepped inside the reception area, their eyes got huge.

"Hi, guys!" Willow stepped forward to greet them.

"Hi, Wil-low." Ronan still said her name in that cute stilted fashion, and it made her smile.

"Hi, Ronan." She looked at Connor. "Have you grown since I saw you last?"

He beamed.

Then she looked up at Ethan, and heat flooded into her cheeks. "Hello," she said, softer.

"Hi." He smiled, a small, faint smile, but it was more than she was used to seeing on his face. "We came to work." He slid his gaze away and down at the duo at his feet. "Didn't we, boys?"

Connor nodded. "Willow, what's a food bank? I thought a bank was where you keep money."

She smiled. "Well, sometimes people don't have enough money to buy food for themselves or their families. People donate extra food, and we keep it here, and when someone needs help, they can come get some groceries for free."

"Free?"

"That's right. You and me, we're pretty lucky, aren't we? We have lots to eat, and a nice warm house to live in, too. But not everyone is that lucky, so it's our job to give them a hand."

Connor's eyes never left her face. "That's nice, isn't it?"

Her heart melted a bit. "Yes, it is. And you're nice, because you're going to help us get everything ready. It's a very grown-up, responsible thing to do."

She looked at Ethan, trying to ignore the fluttering she felt when he watched her so closely. "I have just the job for them, and we'll be close by if they need direction."

Willow led them into the biggest room, where the bulk of the shelving held nonperishables. A few volunteers were stocking the shelves, and she led the boys right to a laundry hamper that was loaded with canned vegetables.

She showed them how to stock the cans on the shelves, and watched as Ethan gave Connor a little step stool to stand on to reach the third shelf. His T-shirt stretched across his shoulders as he lifted and moved the basket for the boys, and Willow reminded herself that dealing with attraction was not on the day's agenda.

Ronan handed her the cans and she started a little row on each shelf: a row for peas, green beans, corn, tomatoes. It took very little time before they were digging around in the hamper for different kinds of veggies.

"That's cute," Ethan said. They watched as Connor lined up a can of peas precisely with the one before, the label facing out.

"I thought sorting and stacking might be something they could do. I've got some for you, too." There was a rolling bin full of cereals a few feet away. "You're on cereal duty. I'm going to do peanut butters and jams and those sorts of things. If you run out, let me know. There's more in the back to be sorted."

"You're not going to work with me?"

That was just what she needed . . . to be in even closer proximity to him. "You're a big boy. I thought you could figure it out on your own."

They worked for an hour, with only a few interruptions to settle small squabbles. Willow finished the vegetables when the boys started to get bored, and moved them to another spot where they could stock sweets like pudding cups and granola bars. That got them excited, and Willow heard them chattering on about their favorite treats and what Riley so-and-so took his lunch, and what snack time was like at the day care.

Ethan's bin was empty, so they wheeled it into the back room and Willow started filling it with pasta, rice, and potato flakes. She spun around to wheel the bin and came chest to chest with Ethan, who was preparing to do the same.

"Sorry," she murmured, but the word came out all breathless. There were no windows in this room, and the dim light added an artificial intimacy to the situation.

His left hand had grabbed her arm as she'd stumbled against him, and she felt his fingers tighten there for a moment. Her gaze was drawn to his by an unseen force, and the intensity in his made her weak in the knees.

When was the last time someone had looked at her this way? The combination of attraction and complication was seductively dangerous. She hadn't been wrong, then, the other night on the Green. That moment when their eyes met, and she hadn't been able to look away. It hadn't been just her. He was feeling it, too. And, she suspected, he didn't like it any more than she did. The pull between them had trouble written all over it.

They were too different. Too damaged. He had kids. She was a free spirit who, despite liking his children, hadn't really thought much about settling down and having a family. In fact, she'd tried very hard *not* to think about it.

And yet his fingers tightened on her arm and she wet her lips with her tongue. The swirl of nerves in her abdomen intensified as his gaze followed the movement, and fixed on her mouth.

So much for serenity.

He leaned closer, and she was sure that there was

confusion and something else tangled up in his eyes, something that drew her in and made her breath catch. Closer, closer . . . another few inches and his mouth would be touching hers. Her lashes began to flutter closed . . .

A scream interrupted the moment, and they both backed away as if slapped. "That's Ronan," Ethan said, turning to the door and hurrying to the main room. Willow rushed behind him, her heart pounding both from the almost-kiss that had just happened and the adrenaline shot from hearing the child scream.

Ronan was sitting on the floor howling, holding his foot in his hands. Connor was beside him, red in the face, his brow puckered. "I didn't mean to!" he insisted, stomping his foot a little. "Be quiet, Ronan!"

"What happened?" Ethan knelt in front of Ronan.

"We were just putting cans on—"

Ethan held up a finger, silencing Connor. "Ronan? What happened?"

There was a big, shaky intake of breath, and then Ronan looked up, two giant tears welling in his eyes. "T'matoes," he said hatefully. "Connor dropped it on my t-t-toes."

"I didn't mean to!" Connor insisted again, his voice a miserable ball of frustration.

"Let me see," Ethan said, holding out his hand. Willow watched as he carefully examined Ronan's toe. There was a smear of blood across the top of his big toe and when Ethan touched it, the little boy howled again.

"Owwww!"

Willow saw Ethan sigh. He was limited in what he could do because of his cast. "Can I help?" she asked.

Ethan stood and leaned closer. "He's cracked the

toenail, and I don't want it to catch on anything. It needs to be trimmed, but I doubt he'll sit still for me to do it."

Willow's stomach turned a bit. The last thing she wanted to do was hurt a little boy, even if it meant helping. But Ethan couldn't do it. She set her jaw. "I've got nail clippers and a first-aid kit upstairs. I can go get it."

The other volunteers had come to the door, wondering what all the commotion was about. Willow smiled at them. "We had a rogue can of tomatoes take on a little toe. The tomatoes won. No biggie. Sorry for the disruption."

"Is he okay?" Shelley asked, coming forward.

"You're okay, aren't you buddy?" Willow tried to inject positivity in her voice. She looked back at Shelley. "I'm going to bandage it up and he'll be good as new. Though maybe ready for a nap."

"We're ahead of schedule here, Willow, and appreciate everything you've done. Really, providing the space and organizing all this is more than enough. Why don't you look after this little guy and take a few hours' rest? You deserve it."

Willow was a little uncertain. "Are you sure? I don't want to leave you in the lurch."

"Of course I'm sure. And I know where to find you if I need anything. Go." She smiled warmly and leaned closer to Willow's ear. "Besides, if I had the option of stocking shelves or spending an hour or two with Ethan Gallagher, I know what I'd choose."

Willow hoped she wasn't blushing, but figured she was when her cheeks felt hot. It didn't help that she was still reeling from that moment out back. What on earth was wrong with her?

She turned back to Ethan. "Come on upstairs. You and Connor can have a drink and we'll get Ronan's toe like new." She knelt down in front of Ronan. "Is that okay? Will you let me bandage your toe for you?"

His little lip quivered. "It'll hurt."

"I will be as gentle as I can, sweetie. That way it can heal faster and you'll be all better."

"Can I have ice cream?"

She grinned. "You drive a tough bargain."

He smiled a little and held out his arms. Touched, she helped him up and then lifted him into her arms. He was heavy, but not too much for her to manage. Ethan and Connor held the door for her as they went out, and then again when they climbed the back stairs to Willow's apartment.

Once inside, she put Ethan and Connor to work getting out the last of her batch of ice cream while she put Ronan down on the futon and went for the first-aid box.

"Ronan, I'm going to have to use my nail trimmers to trim your nail a bit."

"No!" He pulled his foot away from her hand.

She looked him in the eye. "Do you trust me?"

He shook his head, and she smiled.

"If I don't trim it, it'll catch on things and hurt a lot worse. I promise I'll be gentle." She crossed her heart. "Just be brave for me and this'll be all better before you know it."

She felt Ethan's eyes on her, but she ignored them and focused on Ronan. She lifted his foot in her palm and felt the tension in his leg. There wasn't much blood; it was easy to see where the nail had split. As carefully as she could, she snipped away the nail, avoiding lifting along the split and causing more pain. Ronan was stiff as a board and whimpering, but he held steady, thank goodness.

"There. The worst part is over." She dropped his foot to her knee and reached for the antiseptic. "Now we're just going to put on a bandage and you're all set."

"That stings!" He pulled away again, and Willow restrained herself from sighing. He was just scared, as any three-year-old would be.

She leaned forward. "I'll tell you a secret. This kind doesn't sting. And I spray it on so I don't even have to touch your toe. It's like *magic*."

She sprayed the toe, then made quick work of wrapping it with clean gauze and then a bandage. "Oh my goodness! Look how big your toe is now!"

Ronan giggled.

"Good job, buddy," Ethan said from behind them. The sound of his voice sent ripples along Willow's nerve endings. Here he was, with his kids, in her apartment again. Her sanctuary was invaded, and she didn't actually mind in the least. That was what bothered her most of all. It felt *right*.

Ethan handed Ronan a small bowl of ice cream. "You did some great first aid," he commented, looking down at Willow. His eyes were warm and a smile teased his lips. God, he was so likeable this way, now that he'd dropped some of his barriers.

"You'd be better with the first aid than me," she replied. "Being a fireman and all."

"Yes, but you have a better bedside manner."

Her cheeks heated again. She really wished she'd stop doing that.

Connor stood nearby, spooning in ice cream as fast as he could. "Dad, can I go see Jimmy or something? I mean, after the ice cream?"

"I should take Ronan home. You can see Jimmy another time."

"But Dad, I'm bored. And Ronan won't be able to play now, and I'm bored."

Willow looked at Ethan. "Two 'boreds' in there. It's serious."

He rolled his eyes. "Connor . . ."

"Please, Dad? Jimmy's mom did say to come over anytime. We've been working on a fort and stuff."

Ethan sighed. "Let me call her first and make sure it's okay."

"I wanna go," Ronan said, flopping his bowl down on the futon.

"Dad, I have to take him everywhere. Can't I just go alone?"

Ethan held up his hands. "Stop, everyone." Willow watched him take a deep breath. "Ronan, not this time. Connor, let me check with Jimmy's mom. Willow?"

"Yes, Dad?" she teased.

He blushed. She watched embarrassment creep up his cheeks and was delighted. Even Connor, in all poutiness, started to giggle. Ethan was so handsome when he didn't look so stressed. Not just handsome . . . sexy. He was too rough and rugged to be strictly handsome. There was a physicality about him that was alluring. A strength and confidence she admired. It suited him far more than the chip he usually carried around on his shoulder.

"Sorry." He looked a little sheepish. "I got a bit carried away."

"Why don't you make your phone call, and if it's okay, you can take Connor wherever he needs to go and Ronan can stay here with me."

Ronan protested, but Willow leaned over and whispered into his ear, and he quieted instantly. Within a few minutes it was settled. Connor was going to Jimmy's for the remainder of the afternoon, and Ethan would be back to pick up Ronan.

Ethan hesitated right before he left. "You're sure it's okay if he stays here? You always seem to have something to do, and I don't want to interfere.

She smiled. "Ronan and I will be just fine, won't we?"

Ronan nodded. "We has a secret."

Once Ethan and Connor were gone, Willow and Ronan darted over to the hanging chair, Ronan limping a bit because of his toe but fast just the same. Willow sat inside first, and then gathered Ronan onto her lap. She kept one foot on the floor so that she could use her toe to move the swing back and forth in a slightly rocking motion. Ronan grinned up at her. "I like your chair, Wil-low."

He was utterly enchanting. He smelled like laundry soap from his clothes, and like a little boy—a little bit dusty and a little bit baby-ish. Her heart turned over when he snuggled into the crook of her arm and looked up at her. He was so trusting. It made her feel . . . whole. Worthy. In a way she hadn't in a very long time, if ever.

"Tell me a story," he said.

Oh, dear. Little-boy stories were not something she was familiar with. "What sort of story do you like?"

"Any kind of story. I like books."

"So do I." She thought for a minute, before she came up with the story of the Three Billy Goats Gruff. It was an old standard, but it would work, particularly if she could do a troll voice.

She was only on the second goat crossing the bridge when she felt Ronan's little body relax further in her arms, and his lashes started lingering on the tops of his cheeks as he blinked. She softened her voice and kept her toe moving the chair in that ever-so-slow rocking motion. By the time she'd ended the story to the best of her recollection, he was out.

She leaned back and closed her eyes. Ronan was so sweet, so trusting. And for the first time in a long time, she allowed her mind to drift, allowed the memories to wash over her, the questions and what ifs, and she thought about her own child. Her little boy or girl would have been . . . well, nearly ten by now. She didn't think of it often. The pregnancy and the end of that pregnancy were a part of her distant past. But with Ronan in her arms, sleeping soundly, it was impossible to forget.

The day she'd found out she was pregnant was the first day of a hell that had lasted over five years. She'd had so many emotions to contend with, and no emotional support. No one she'd confided in. She'd been an achiever. Type A, controlling, driven. And scared, so scared. Desperate for her mother's attention; eventually accepting attention from the wrong place. Then the abortion . . . and the horrible, secret way she'd dealt with all the stress and heartbreak. And she'd done it all alone.

Her lip trembled as she thought of how she'd healed since then. She was happy with her life and who she'd become, but she still got emotional about it from time to time. Being with Ethan and his boys brought a lot of those feelings back, and she knew the best thing to do was to sit with them, acknowledge them, deal with them, and let them go.

Ronan snuffled and burrowed closer, and she tightened her arms around him. Maybe it was time she admitted to herself that she still wanted children. She didn't want to be alone forever. Admitting it threatened the peaceful life she'd built for herself, and trying to picture herself as a wife and mother seemed impossible. How on earth would she manage everything?

And yet a very real part of her felt the yearning, burrowing a hole into her heart that longed to be filled. It frightened her. It frightened her more than anything had in a very, very long time.

She only had to deal with one day at a time, she reminded herself. Besides, it was only acknowledging the desire. Despite the vibes running between her and Ethan lately, he wasn't in the market for a wife. And she certainly wasn't looking to step into a ready-made family.

She looked down at Ronan's peaceful face and sighed. No matter how adorable they were.

CHAPTER 9

Ethan hadn't tried to be quiet as he'd climbed the stairs, but when he re-entered Willow's apartment, the sight that greeted him stole his breath.

Willow and Ronan were in her swinging chair, and they were sound asleep.

He took the moment to study her. The pink streak was nearly invisible in her hair, tucked back into a ponytail somewhere on the back of her head. The simple style kept the hair off her face and highlighted her delicate cheekbones and the sandy color of her lashes. Her lips were full, too, not too much, but soft-looking; the kind of lips a man wouldn't mind kissing now and again. He'd nearly done that earlier this afternoon. There was no sense in pretending otherwise. They'd been alone in that stock room and she'd looked up at him and *boom*. There was no other way to describe the feeling than attraction. Normal red-blooded attraction, the type any sane man would feel when faced with someone as pretty and vibrant as Willow, right?

Now she was cuddled up with his youngest son, and the sight did something to his heart. There was no denying the vision of the two of them sleeping was precious and made him sentimental. But it also highlighted the fact that Ronan didn't have a mother to hold him close after a boo-boo and reassure him he was all right. He had aunts and grandparents, but it wasn't the same. Nothing and no one could take the place of a mother.

It would probably be better if he didn't let his sons get too attached. As nice as Willow was, and a good person, he wasn't in the market for a replacement. He couldn't even imagine what it would be like to fall in love again. He'd done that once and had his heart shattered into a million pieces. How could he willingly go there again?

Not that what he felt for Willow was anything like his feelings for Lisa. Lately he'd just found himself thinking about it. Willow was the first woman he'd even come close to feeling any sort of attraction to, and he supposed it was just another stage of his grief coming to a close. Besides, attraction aside, they were too different.

Except that she wasn't quite as "different" as he'd thought. He'd misjudged her in a lot of ways.

In the quiet of her apartment, he heard a sigh escape Ronan's lips, and watched as his son shifted and snuggled more firmly into her embrace. Willow slept on, but her hand moved in response and settled on Ronan's back, keeping him close and safe.

He couldn't watch any longer. Instead he backed out of the apartment, shut the door quietly, and went back downstairs to the food bank. Perhaps he could still be of some good there while his son slept.

* * *

While there'd been a fair amount of hoopla surrounding the setup of the temporary food bank, the actual first day of operation was anti-climactic. Willow knew that was deliberate. Clients deserved privacy, and it was even more difficult to come by with the facility being housed right on Main Street rather than its former location.

As a result, they'd made a slight restructure on Friday afternoon. Those in need would enter through the front door, but now they could make their way through, select groceries according to their needs, and exit through the back. It helped with congestion to keep everything going one way, and Willow had very little to do. The administration was all left up to the volunteer coordinator and the food supervisor. She'd take a volunteer shift a couple of times a week, but other than that, she could now be hands-off.

She did set up a few things that she thought helped welcome the clients. For one, she put a plate of homemade cookies under a domed lid, so that the children who came with their parents could have a treat as they "shopped." She also arranged to have a basket of fruit available for the same reason. By talking to her suppliers, about seventy-five percent of the food bank's produce was organic. Stocking the fresh stuff would be her responsibility, on an "as available" basis.

Once she was sure everything was well in hand, she made her way back to The Purple Pig. It almost felt like a relief to be back in familiar territory, baking scones and brownies and wrapping up sandwiches.

There was no sign of Ethan all day, and she couldn't help but be disappointed. Not that she particularly wanted to be; things with him were complicated at best. There was so much about her he didn't know, and with his history, her additional baggage would have him running for the hills. Then there was her own troublesome reaction to their almost-kiss the other day. She'd wanted him. Wanted him in a way that she had no right to. She couldn't stop thinking about it, and it made her both afraid and nervous. She longed to know what it was like to feel his lips against hers, but also wanted to avoid feeling too much.

"Damn therapy," she muttered, slamming together a roasted peppers and gouda sandwich. Therapy had taught her that she needed to sit with her feelings and deal with them. But what if they were too over-whelming? Why on earth did she have to overthink *everything*?

Laurel came in at five, still dressed in her Ladybug Garden Center golf shirt and a pair of jeans. "Hey, good lookin'," she called behind the counter.

"Hey yourself." Willow perked up and smiled at the welcome distraction. "What's shakin'?"

"Well, I came to ask a favor. I know you're crazy busy, but I wondered if you'd come out to the Galla-ghers' with us tonight. They're having one of their cookouts and I'd like you to come."

Willow's eyes narrowed. "You wouldn't be trying to set me up or something, would you?" She certainly didn't need any help in that department. If it wasn't Ethan she was thinking about, it was the kids. She'd fallen asleep with Ronan in her arms on Thursday, and it had been too sweet for words.

"Set you up? No." Laurel's cheeks flushed a bit. "Um . . . I just want you there, that's all."

There was something in Laurel's expression that threw up a red flag. After their discussion the other morning, perhaps Aiden and Laurel were going to make some sort of an announcement. Willow swallowed against the lump in her throat, and wanted to ask the question. She refrained, though. If Laurel was expecting, she probably wanted to tell everyone all at once. And if that were the case, Willow wouldn't spoil the surprise.

"I can't possibly leave here until six thirty. I'll have to ask Emily if she'll close."

"That would be perfect, Wil. Thank you." She beamed again. "Hannah will be there. We can make it an unofficial girls' night."

It had been a long time since they'd done that. Summer was the busiest season for both Laurel and Willow. "Anything I can bring?"

Laurel shook her head. "Just yourself." Then she nodded at Willow's apron. "Maybe wear something cute."

Willow smiled. "You don't like my apron?"

"About as much as you like my golf shirt." Laurel grinned. "You're really going to come, right?"

There was a hopefulness in Laurel's eyes that fueled Willow's suspicion. Of course she'd be there. Laurel deserved all sorts of happiness after her troubles of the past few years. Marrying Aiden had just been the start of her wonderful new life.

"I promise."

"Great. Now I've got to run. I need to go home and shower off the dirt before we head over."

Willow rushed through the next few hours, doing as much prep as she could after bribing Em to stay by guaranteeing her an extra afternoon off the following week. By five-thirty she was in the shower, and by six she'd decided on a maxi dress of pink lotus flowers on an aqua blue background. She grabbed a sweater out of her closet for when the air cooled later in the evening, and headed for her car.

Most of the time she walked anywhere she needed to go in Darling, unless she was picking up supplies for the café, so her car was strictly a "point A to point B" vehicle. The Gallaghers lived too far to walk, so she put her purse on the seat and headed to the sprawling house with the wide lawns and boisterous family.

She wasn't as intimidated this time. Because of Laurel, she now knew Aiden quite well, and Hannah was quickly becoming the older, pushier sister she'd never had, not to mention her new "truce" with Ethan and her fondness for the boys. That just left John and Moira, then Rory and the twin girls, Cait and Claire. All were friendly, and if what she suspected was true, everyone was going to be in a very good mood.

The yard was full of cars, and despite the order to not bring anything, Willow had a bottle of wine for the hosts. She went through to the backyard and found the most wonderful kind of bedlam. Food, laughter, running children, music . . . all indicators of a big happy family.

She kept behind the gate for a few moments, just watching. She'd never had this growing up. Never had it . . . ever. She'd never known her father and had been brought up by her mother, who'd worried far more about work than about her daughter. No brothers or sisters . . . and the moment she'd graduated, her mom had taken a transfer and she'd finally been totally abandoned, rather than just neglected. It didn't matter to Josie Dunaway that her daughter had been close to breaking down, that she'd needed her mother. Once high school was over, Josie was gone. Like her duty had been fulfilled. It had always been that way; her mother's career had come first.

It hadn't mattered how hard Willow had tried. She knew that now. She'd stopped feeling like the failure in that relationship long ago. But she'd always longed for a family like this. Loud and loving and fun.

"Afraid to go in? We can be a little intimidating."

A shiver ran down her spine at the sound of Ethan's voice just behind her ear. "I didn't hear you come up behind me."

"Not much wonder. Rory's got the music blasting and there are enough Gallaghers in there to deafen the pope."

She laughed despite herself, and turned halfway around. "Oh my God. Did you just crack a joke?"

He shrugged, looking more relaxed than she ever remembered seeing him. "It's been known to happen."

She narrowed her eyes. "I think having some time off has been good for you. You look rested."

He lifted an eyebrow. "I can't imagine why. Those two boys in there run me ragged, and I'm ten times slower because of this." He lifted his arm. There was a new drawing on the cast. It looked like a roughly drawn soccer ball.

She peered back inside the gate. "Actually, I was just watching your family. I was an only child. This sort of thing is way out of my depth. But you . . . you're probably used to it."

He came up beside her. "Yeah. It can be a pain, but I wouldn't trade it for anything." She felt his gaze on her profile. "Don't you get together with your mom?"

She laughed. "Not really. I get happy birthday calls and a Christmas present and the odd update."

"I'm sorry."

"It is what it is. It's why I value my friends so highly."

He was quiet for a moment. "Do I count among those friends?"

She turned and met his gaze, and that slow, melty feeling started to come over her again. "Do you want to?"

"Hey, you made it!" Laurel bounced over, looking adorable in capris, a cute top, and a perky ponytail. Ethan didn't have time to answer her question, and Willow let herself be pulled along into the backyard where all the action was happening. She was welcomed by Moira and John, who were sitting on patio swing, and she gave them the bottle of wine. Then she was greeted by Hannah, who disappeared to get another drink, and was set upon by Connor and Ronan, who nearly tripped over themselves to say hello.

"Boys! Slow down. Don't knock Willow over."

"Willow! I got a new soccer shirt! But Dad wouldn't let me wear it. It's green!"

"Green is my favorite color," she stated, ruffling Connor's hair. She knelt down in front of Ronan. "Hey, kiddo. How's the toe?"

Solemn brown eyes looked into hers. "It turned black, Wil-low. *Black.*"

She raised her eyebrows, met his gaze with an equally serious expression, and said, "*Cool.*" She drew the word out impressively.

He stuck out his foot. "You wanna see it?"

"By all means."

She tried not to laugh as he plopped down on the ground, pulled off his shoe and sock and stuck out his cute little foot. "Ooooh. Awesome." It did, in fact, look a bit disgusting, but she figured the less fuss made, the better.

"Ronan, put your sock and shoe back on. Gross."
Ethan gave the order but half laughed as he said it. "All
boy, that one," he murmured, close to her ear. She shiv-
ered again.

"Both of them," Willow observed. "Can't imagine
where they get that from."

Laurel came over again. "Did you get a drink, Wil?
I know you're driving, but there's lemonade." Willow's
suspicions were further reinforced by seeing that Laurel
was partaking of that particular choice.

"Lemonade sounds perfect."

"I don't think it's made from organic lemons," Ethan
said.

A few weeks ago she would have been offended at
that, but now she just rolled her eyes and made opening and closing motions with her fingers, as if to say,
Blah, blah, blah.

He laughed. An honest-to-goodness, unable to stop
himself choke of a laugh and she grinned like a fool.
She hadn't heard him laugh before. It was an amazing
sound, rich and deep and . . . rusty, like the color of his
hair.

Oh dear.

She went with Laurel for the drink. "What's going
on with you and Ethan?" Laurel asked. "And the boys,
too. They came right to you. All this after one soccer
practice and ice cream date?"

"Oh, that." Willow dismissed the comment with a
wave of her hand, though there was a knot of anxiety
balled up in her stomach. "They all came and helped
with the food bank on . . . Thursday, I guess. Even the
boys helped stock the shelves. Ronan's black toenail is
courtesy of a can of tomatoes."

Laurel poured a glass of lemonade, topped hers up,

and faced Willow. "Sweetie, I haven't seen you laugh with a man since I moved back here. And the way Aiden tells it, the last time you were here, you and Ethan didn't exactly hit it off."

"I'm freaky, remember?" She laughed lightly. "I'll admit we got off to a rough start, but he's nice enough now."

"Is that all?" Laurel sounded disappointed. "You blushed when I mentioned ice cream the other day."

"Yes, that's all." One hesitant moment in a dimly-lit room didn't count for much on the romance scale. "He's nowhere near over his wife, anyway."

"I know." Laurel's face fell. "It's just . . . I'm so happy. I want everyone in the world to be this happy." A soft smile formed on her lips. "That sounds so sappy, I know . . ."

"It sounds lovely, and you deserve every bit." Willow put her hand on Laurel's arm. At that moment, Hannah came up to the two of them and started relaying a story about something that had happened during their week, and in typical Hannah fashion, she had them laughing in moments.

Willow ate way too much food to feel comfortable, laughed more than she could remember laughing in years, and with a red face, obligingly did her troll voice when Ronan demanded it. "Okay, that's it," she said, turning him around and sending him on his way. "Go ask your Aunt Hannah for more ice cream."

Moira sat down beside her and handed her a cup of tea. "You're good with them. You like children?"

The question sent a pang through her heart. "Yes," she answered. "I do. When they're that age, they have no bias, you know? The world is just an endless adventure. And hopefully, when they go to bed at night, someone they love is there to tuck them in and kiss them good night."

She'd got carried away just then, and when she bashfully looked over at Moira, she saw understanding in the other woman's eyes. "I know you didn't have a great home life," Moira said softly. "I remember. But you turned out to be a really good person, Willow. Hannah talks about you all the time and you were so good to Laurel and Aiden. And now Ethan . . . well, he's been more relaxed and easy tonight than I remember him being in months."

"Oh, that has nothing to do with me," she replied quickly, hoping she wasn't blushing.

"Doesn't it? He keeps looking at you."

She couldn't help it. She lifted her gaze and caught Ethan watching them. They both looked away, but not before Moira smiled.

"I don't think either of you is in a hurry," Moira said gently, taking a sip of her tea. "But I've been so worried about Ethan. He's kept everything so bottled up inside. Even if you're just friends . . . well, I'm grateful for that."

Willow was touched. "I don't know what to say."

"Don't say anything." Moira smiled. "Just enjoy your tea."

She did. She sipped at it and leaned back in her chair and soaked up what was left of the summer evening sun. Before long, everyone had mellowed and Willow watched as Aiden pulled Laurel onto his lap as he sat on the bench of the picnic table.

"So, uh . . . since everyone's here, Laurel and I have an announcement."

Claire and Cait had shown up partway through the

food, and they squealed together, while Rory paused, his beer bottle halfway to his mouth.

Laurel's eyes shone as she admitted, "We're pregnant."

A delighted cacophony of congratulations went up from the family.

"Well, now! That didn't take long!" John Gallagher clapped his hands together. "More grandsons, Ma!"

Moira laughed. "This one might be a girl, you know." She looked at Laurel. "How're you feeling?"

Laurel's cheeks were bright pink. "Well, tired. But it's too early to feel much of anything else. I'm hoping I don't get sick."

Hannah winked at Laurel. "Hey, Willow, we get a sober driver for the next what, seven months?"

Willow grinned, playing along. "Longer, if she breastfeeds."

Cait and Claire gave Laurel a hug. Willow was starting to really notice the differences between the twins, though they were faint. Their hair was just a little bit different, and they dressed a bit differently. Claire was more conservative, but not much. A slightly more professional appearance, in keeping with her summer job at the town office.

"This means we can go shopping for baby stuff!" Claire exclaimed. "Oh, I hope it's a girl this time."

"If it's a boy, there's lots of baby stuff at the house. I won't need it anymore. You're welcome to the gender neutral stuff anyway." Ethan had been standing behind, but he stepped forward now, with a handshake for Aiden and a hug for Laurel.

Willow looked up at him, her heart softening. It had to be hard for him to say that. But she hoped that it wasn't true. He was still young. He could remarry, have more children. She imagined Connor and Ronan with a little sister. They'd spoil her rotten, and defend her against any bullies who dared hurt her.

"Thanks, bro," Aiden said quietly.

"Yes, Ethan. Thank you."

The moment got a bit awkward, so Moira jumped in with questions about pregnancy and due dates. The chatter continued, but then Willow noticed Ethan backing away from the gathering, his face somber.

So the offer had cost him. She wasn't surprised.

She snuck off, too, following him around the corner of the house to the side bordered with Moira's rosebushes.

"Ethan, wait."

He spun around, a look of surprise momentarily blanking his face. His lips dropped open and she glimpsed a bit of embarrassment in his features.

"I'm fine, Willow. Go back to the party." He started walking away again.

"You're not fine. I saw your face." She hurried to catch up to him, the hem of her dress brushing against her ankles. "Ethan."

She put his hand on his cast, but it was enough to stop him. They were at the corner of the front porch now, with the rosebushes on their left and the lattice-work at Ethan's back.

"Willow . . ."

"I'm sorry. It must have brought a lot of memories up for you."

"They deserve to be happy. I don't begrudge them that."

"Of course you don't. But it doesn't mean it doesn't hurt."

His jaw ticked as the muscle there tightened. "I just . . . we'd talked about having more kids. And the boys need a mother, and . . . Goddammit."

She didn't think, she just acted. She stepped forward, and put her ear against his chest and her arms around his waist. He was broad and strong and smelled like fabric softener and masculine-scented soap, a heady combination.

"What are you doing?"

"Giving you a hug. I don't think anyone's given you a hug in a very long time."

He chuckled just a bit, one soft, hitching movement of his chest, but it warmed her heart. "Did you know that a twenty-second hug releases oxytocin, which relieves stress and anxiety?" she asked.

His un-casted arm came around her, resting along her lower back. "Exactly twenty seconds?" he asked softly.

"Give or take," she murmured against his shirt. "How're you feeling now?"

"Willow . . ."

Oh my. He'd never said her name in quite that way before. She bit down on her lip and closed her eyes. "Maybe just a few more seconds," she suggested. "Cheapest therapy in town."

"I don't need therapy," he replied, his voice strong again.

She backed away just a little, but her arms were still partway around him, resting on his hips. His eyes were so intense she started to lose herself in them. "What do you need?" she asked, her pulse beating so fast she could hear it in her ears.

"This."

He tightened the arm at her waist, drawing her flush

against his body, then dropped his mouth to hers. He kissed just as she'd imagined, only better. Commanding, but not forceful. Deliberate, but with a seductiveness that was as fragile as a question. She closed her eyes and held on, gripping the fabric of his shirt as she met him equally. Oh Lord . . . she wasn't sure she could feel her legs anymore. It was all his lips, the soft, full feel of them on her mouth, the rasp of his whiskers as they grazed her chin, the feel of his hard body pressed against hers. The body of a man who ran into burning buildings, who wrestled with his children, who strode into her café with a singular purpose and made her heart sing.

She was in so much trouble.

The kiss tempered, slowed, until he pulled away, a little regretfully, she thought. Her breath came in short bursts, the cool evening air doing nothing to chill the desire rushing through her. The very sensation scared the hell out of her; made her feel incredibly vulnerable and needy. Two things she never really wanted to feel again.

"Hell." Ethan stepped back, stopping when his back hit the edge of the porch. "Willow, I . . . I . . . damn it."

Willow just stared at him. She didn't know what to say. On one hand, she wanted to see where this led; she was that turned on and caught up in the passion of the moment. He was an extraordinary kisser. Her head still swam with the taste of him. On the other hand, neither of them was the sort to jump into bed without any thought to the consequences. They were both too broken and neither of them wanted to be broken further. They didn't need to bare their souls to understand that much.

"Ethan," she finally whispered, and touched her fingers to her lips.

"Don't do that," he ordered, his brow wrinkling. "Just don't."

"I'm sorry."

"Don't apologize." His gaze locked on hers. "I should apologize. I shouldn't have done that. I don't know what I was thinking."

"I started it. I hugged you."

And it had felt so good. It all had.

"Ethan . . ." She stepped forward, tilting her head up to look at him. "It was just a kiss. And I liked it. I like you, Ethan. Can't we just leave it as simple as that?"

"Maybe. Except I'm not simple. And the boys . . ."

"You're more than a father, Ethan. You're a man, too. But you've been dealing with so much on your own, and focusing so much on the kids, that you've probably forgotten. And I'm . . ." She swallowed against the lump in her throat. "I'm a woman. We're two consenting adults and it was just a kiss."

Just a kiss. Understatement of the century.

He stared at her for a long moment. "Well," he said quietly, "I have to admit, I've had a hard time figuring you out. But I never took you for a liar."

Her insides trembled. "I don't think either of us is ready for the truth. So let's call it a kiss and let it go. It would probably be for the best."

"Right."

"You're really not my type anyway," she insisted. "I'm a little too weird for you, and you're too conventional for me." For someone who wasn't a liar, she felt as if she were doing a fantastic job at it. Right now the pulse hammering at her wrist and neck said that Ethan was exactly her type.

"Right. Conventional." His jaw ticked again.

She backed away, suddenly very afraid of what this all meant. Her sandal caught on her hem and she stumbled, then righted herself as heat rushed into her face.

All the lessons she'd learned had been for nothing. Here she was again, scared, vulnerable, not in charge. Ethan didn't even know the power he possessed. No one, not in all the years since she'd started therapy, had gotten past her barriers. Not until now. It left her feeling naked and afraid.

"I've got to go. Tell the boys . . . tell Laurel . . . I said goodbye. I have to open the café in the morning and it's already been a long day."

"Sure. Whatever you want." His voice was utterly polite, and it was both a relief and a source of regret.

Then she remembered her bag, tucked in beneath the picnic table. Great. She'd have to make another appearance anyway. She turned her back on Ethan and inhaled deeply, setting off for the backyard again, pasting on what she hoped was a calm smile.

She grabbed her bag and went immediately to Laurel. "Hey, thanks for inviting me, but I have to go. I'm opening tomorrow and it's already been a very long day."

"Of course. Thanks for coming, Wil. It means a lot to us."

Willow's eyes stung a bit. "I'm very, very happy for you. You guys are going to be great parents." She cleared her throat. "Now let me get out of here. I'll call you soon."

She probably should have stayed and thanked Moira and John, but Ethan was coming back around the corner of the house and she needed to escape. She headed for the gate, reaching into her bag for her keys as she went.

When she backed out of the driveway, she chanced a look up at the house. No one was watching her leave, and a part of her was disappointed. Another part was relieved. She had to go home, back to her sanctuary. Back to the place she knew she belonged. The home she'd made for herself, filled with all the things that made her whole again and none of the things that unraveled her threads.

CHAPTER 10

Ethan was starting to go crazy staying at home.

He loved his boys; of course he did. He loved doing stuff with them. It was admittedly nice to look after laundry and the house without the added pressure of working shifts. But he was starting to understand why Lisa had liked having a car at home and had joined a mom-and-baby group when both boys had been small. At least with Lisa, he'd come home at night, or in the morning, and they'd managed some time together. Some adult conversation. Lately all that he'd been conversing about was soccer, the Tonka trucks out in the sandbox, and what was to eat at the next meal.

He took the boys to their soccer practice and sat on the rickety bleachers to watch. He'd been there for maybe ten minutes when the seats shifted as a newcomer climbed up his row. Ethan looked up and saw his dad coming over, dressed in his ever-present Levis and the Red Sox hat that had seen better days.

"Dad. How'd you know the boys had practice?"

John settled on the bench next to Ethan. "Took a

chance. You didn't answer the phone, and it's a Tuesday night. Chances were good you'd be here."

They watched for a few minutes. Again, the full soccer field was split into two to accommodate the young age groups. Ronan's group was nothing but chaos, about ten balls going at once in a configuration reminiscent of some sort of drill. Connor's side was slightly more organized, with a scrimmage in progress. They watched as Connor passed the ball up the field and then ran ahead toward the goal.

"They're going to be thrilled you came," Ethan said. "Grampa hung the moon and the stars, if you ask them."

"They're good boys. Like you three were. And nearly as busy." John grinned and rested his elbows on his knees. "How're you doing with that cast and being off work? Stir-crazy yet?"

Ethan chuckled. "Something like that. I can't wait to get this stupid thing off. It's great being with the boys, but . . ."

"But you miss work. Of course you do. We're all just glad you're okay."

"I didn't mean to scare anyone. Mom had a bird about it."

John chuckled. "You're her golden boy. Of course she did. But we're both dead proud of what you do, Ethan. And since Lisa . . ."

His father let the sentence hang unfinished. They both knew what he meant.

"You're starting to move on," John remarked quietly. They kept their eyes on the soccer field, but the words settled into Ethan. If he was, it scared him to death. He didn't know how to move on.

"I don't know, Pop. I just don't. She's gone. At first I didn't know who I was without her. And now I don't know who I am without . . ." He wasn't sure what word came next. It was a vast, scary world now. When a person stepped out of the dark and into the sun, it took a while for the eyes to adjust.

"Without grief," John supplied. "I haven't lost a wife, Ethan, but I've lost people I cared about. Deeply. Grief becomes your companion until it, too, leaves you alone. And then you either have to move forward or stay in place." John looked over at Ethan. "E, I have to tell you. Happiness does not come from staying in place."

Ethan let out a sigh and watched the boys for a few more moments. His dad didn't usually say much, but when he did, all the kids knew to shut up and listen. In the past months, John had been strangely silent. Maybe he'd been waiting for the time to be right.

"How do I know when it's right?"

John chuckled. "Well, damn, E. I don't have all the answers. But it did seem to me that you were making eyes at Willow Dunaway the other night. I never pegged her as your type, but she could be just what you need. She's pretty and . . . light. I don't know. Free, I guess. And she was making eyes right back."

"We're too different."

"The boys sure seem to think a lot of her. Connor filled us in on her homemade ice cream and some sort of chair she's got at her place? And she did step in to get the new food bank up and running. She's good people."

Ethan didn't need reminding of her good points. He still couldn't get the picture of her and Ronan sleeping in her chair out of his mind.

"She's completely different from Lisa."

"Maybe that's just what you need."

Ethan looked over at his father's shrewd face. "Did Mom send you over here?"

John laughed, his blue eyes twinkling. "Maybe we agree about something. It doesn't happen that often, you know."

"Hmph." Ethan huffed and looked away. "She's never held back before, or sent someone else to do her dirty work."

His dad laughed again, and Ethan couldn't stop the smile that spread across his face. Dad-laughter had always had that effect on him. It seemed that when John Gallagher laughed, the world smiled along.

"Well, I'll tell you," John said, with a sigh. "Your mom means well. But she's not a man, and sometimes it takes another man to understand. I've loved your mother for nearly forty years. It's a partnership, there's no doubt about it, but I always felt the responsibility of providing for the family. For being there. For . . . leading. And I've relied on your mother to keep me steady, to smooth out the bumps along the way. I don't know how I would have managed to bring you all up if something had happened to her. We balance each other out. Without her, a piece would be missing. I know that Lisa was that piece for you, but God, Ethan. I don't want you to be alone forever. If you're interested in this woman, ask her out. Give yourself a break. Let her smooth out some of your rough spots. Maybe it'll turn into something, maybe it won't. But don't be afraid to try."

Ethan was touched and also floored. His dad rarely spoke of matters of the heart. Usually they didn't say much at all. Just twisted the top off a beer, put on the game, and let the silence work it all out. For him to say so much meant he'd been thinking about it a long while.

"I'm scared," Ethan admitted. "And it's not fair to

her for me to use her as a guinea pig to see if I'm ready to get back on the horse."

"You are a decent man," John declared, shaking his head. "But sometimes that moral compass of yours needs shaking up. If you tell your mother I said that, I'll deny it." He leveled a finger at his son. "Not for one minute do I think you'd be thoughtless. I just don't want you to be afraid to give it a chance, if there's really something there."

Oh, there was something there. The kiss the other night had proved it. He hadn't been able to get it out of his head. She'd been sweet, but darkly passionate, too, something he hadn't expected. Maybe it was that his dry spell had been long, or that the kiss had been unexpected. Either way, she'd walked off not knowing how shaken she'd left him.

"On my own time," he finally answered, as the coach blew his whistle and the boys went running to the center line. It was good advice, but he wasn't about to be pushed into something he wasn't ready for. Besides, Willow had been the one to run away. It didn't matter if he wanted to pursue something or not. She had a say and her last words—and actions—had been loud and clear. She'd been scared to death.

Both father and son now left the topic alone, and instead talked about Aiden's pending fatherhood and the new roof that John hoped to put on the storage shed out back. Good, safe topics that had nothing to do with Ethan and his personal life.

But as the practice ended and Ethan stood to stretch, he caught a glimpse of the Kissing Bridge. He and Lisa had kissed there when they'd been young and full of dreams. When their love had been indestructible. They'd believed in the legend; believed that their love would last forever and their future would be bright and shiny. A year later he'd taken her to the golf course overlooking the town and had proposed.

That bridge was nothing more than stone and mortar. It didn't hold any special qualities or powers.

Ethan finally realized what he'd lost when his wife had died.

He'd lost his innocence. And he'd lost his hope, too.

Was it possible to get them back? Did he even want to?

In the week following Laurel's announcement, Willow threw herself into work at the café, and when she wasn't there, she was getting back on track with her chosen lifestyle. She added a nightly yoga routine after the café closed, then finished her day with chamomile tea and a meditation. At work, she organized her day with precision, blocking off time for administration and bookwork, and also creating new menu items with in-season local ingredients.

She should have been completely blissful. Instead she found her thoughts drifting to Ethan Gallagher whenever she let her guard down the slightest bit.

Long ago she'd made a vow to never let her heart be at the mercy of someone else's. And it wasn't that she'd lost her heart . . . it was more that she suddenly felt as if she weren't in the driver's seat. She wasn't in absolute control. While her life philosophy was largely based on acceptance rather than control, it was on the principle of that acceptance coming from within herself.

She wasn't quite sure what to do now that her thoughts were shifting all too frequently to someone else.

Right now, on a very sunny Thursday morning, she was outside the café, watering the hot pink impatiens and purple lobelia in the window boxes and planters. She'd given Laurel free rein with the flower choices and she loved how the colors complemented the building exterior.

"Good morning."

A familiar, deep voice came from behind her, and her stomach did that swirly-catchy thing that was part excitement and part nerves. She turned around and saw Ethan standing there in cargo shorts and a golf shirt, his hair still wet from his shower. She hadn't seen him for nearly two weeks, not since the kiss in his parents' backyard, and she was pretty sure he'd been avoiding her.

She was sure because she'd been avoiding him.

"Hi," she answered, then realized she was pouring water from the can onto her toes.

His grin widened. "Hoping to grow a few inches?"

She righted the can and looked up. She wasn't exactly short, but Ethan had several inches on her, particularly when she was wearing little flat sandals. Ethan's eyebrow lifted as he stared at her feet. "Turquoise nail polish. And nice toe rings."

Heat rushed into her cheeks. "What can I say? I like pretty toes."

His brows came together now. She wondered if he realized how expressive they were.

"But not your hands. No nail polish, no rings."

She shook her head, wondering why on earth he was noticing such little things. "It's a food-service thing."

"Right."

"Something I can do for you, Ethan? Did you want

a coffee or something, or did you just come by to pester me while I water my flowers?"

A sneaky grin slid up his cheek. "Do I pester you?"

"Yes. Especially when you tease me. I'm not used to it."

"Should I growl instead?"

Oh my word. He was flirting. Her stomach took another little lift as she realized it. Bad enough she couldn't get him out of her thoughts; now he was right in front of her and it was like she couldn't see anything else. She took a deep breath, but it felt as if her chest wasn't big enough to hold all the oxygen. "It's more what I'm used to."

"I'm trying to do less of that. I discovered I like smiling more. I'm just rusty at it."

"How's the arm?" She tried to change the subject. They were outside the café, the sidewalk traffic was brisk, and the last thing she needed was to be openly flirting. Neighborly conversation would be much better. And then perhaps she could calm down. He shouldn't be able to fluster her so.

"It's getting there. Only another week and I might be able to get the cast off. Then it'll just be a matter of getting my strength and range of motion back."

"Another week?" She gripped the watering can with both hands. "But that's only . . . well, four weeks."

"They'll do an X-ray first. I'll be glad if I don't have to do the full six weeks in this thing." He held up his arm. "The sooner I'm back in shape, the sooner I can go back to work."

"Oh."

An awkward pause sat between them for a few moments, and Willow's stomach did that crawly thing again. Hell, she was going to need to do a meditation to calm down after he left. If he ever left . . .

"What are you doing after you water the flowers?" he asked, putting his left hand into his pocket.

She swallowed tightly. His khaki cargo shorts emphasized his long legs, and the golf shirt was the same blue color as his cast and stretched across his broad chest. He had on some sort of sporty flip-flops, and she noticed a sprinkling of dark hair on the knuckles of his big toes. Did he have to be so very . . . masculine?

"Meditating," she replied quickly, hoping she wasn't still blushing.

"Of course you are."

Right. He didn't go in for all that "mindfulness" stuff. Though perhaps he should. There was a restless energy about him that put her on edge.

"Seriously, is there something I can do for you, Ethan? I have things to do."

"Go to a movie with me."

She stared. "What?"

"Go to a movie. You know, you walk in, buy your ticket, get some popcorn . . ." He shrugged his shoulders, but his gaze was fixed on hers.

"You're asking me out on a date?"

"Is that so hard to believe?"

"Yes." Once more, she answered without really thinking, and his lips thinned a bit at her sharp response.

"I see. Well, never mind, then." The humor in his eyes cooled into something distant and closed off, and she immediately felt badly for refusing so bluntly.

"Ethan . . ." She looked around, wondering if anyone was eavesdropping on their exchange. A couple of joggers went by, their puffs of breath punctuating the rhythm of their steps. "It's just . . . even though we kissed the other night, and we've been friendlier . . . I just . . ." Wow. She couldn't even put a sentence together. "I've had the impression that we don't have a lot in common. We're very different, you know."

"Because you're . . ."

"A nature freak. And you're . . ."

"A grumpy ass."

She laughed. Dammit, how did he manage to do that?

She didn't really like movies, if she were being honest. At least not in a theater. Everything was overpriced, and people talked or played on their phones or kicked the back of the seat in front of them. Still, she got the impression that it had taken a lot for him to even ask. If she put two and two together, she'd bet that he hadn't been on a date since his wife had died.

And he'd asked her.

She was flattered and terrified.

"What movie?" Was she actually considering going? She hadn't been to a theater in years. This would be a "pick you up and bring you home" kind of thing, wouldn't it? And there was no theater in Darling, so they'd probably go into Burlington.

"You pick," he said. "I haven't been to a movie in ages. Anything works for me."

"Are you okay with the later showing? I probably can't get away from here until eight or eight-thirty."

"Let me ask my babysitter. What night's good for you?"

She bit down on her lip. "I don't know. A week night? Weekends are really busy for me."

"How about Thursday?"

She swallowed again, so bungled up in nerves she was relatively sure she was vibrating. "Um, okay."

"I'll pick you up here."

"Okay."

"Eight fifteen?"

"Okay."

Wow. She was now down to one word in her vocabulary.

"See you Thursday, then," he said, and backed away toward the sidewalk.

"Yah," she answered, and smiled. The least she could do was smile. Pretend she wasn't just freaking out on the inside. Considering her last four sentences had been monosyllables, she wasn't sure she was doing so well on the pretending.

CHAPTER 11

After Ethan was gone, she took the watering can back inside and headed straight for the kitchen. She washed her hands and then went to work slicing breads for the noon sandwiches and made sure the sandwich station was stocked. She refilled the muffin and cookie display, put new coffee to brew, stocked the fridge, and still felt as if her chest were too small for her lungs. Keeping busy tricked her mind into not thinking about Ethan, but her body's response didn't lie. Up until now they had had chance encounters, or they'd met at family or community events.

But a date . . . there was a level of intent with a date. There was a statement that said *I'm interested*. And for all her self-confidence and cool advice for her friends, when it came to dealing with a relationship herself, she was an utter mess.

A few months ago Laurel had turned to her when she'd been so confused about Aiden. Now Willow wondered if her best friend could return the favor. Perhaps Laurel would be her voice of reason right now, since her own powers of serenity had deserted her.

When the lunch rush was over, she announced she was taking an hour's break and hotfooted it to the Ladybug Garden Center. Laurel was in the greenhouse area, helping a customer pick out flats of colorful annuals. When she was done, and the purchase had been rung through, she approached Willow with a furrowed brow and concern darkening her eyes.

"What is it? You look discombobulated."

"That's it! I am. I'm just . . . oh Laurel. I think I'm in trouble."

Laurel reached out for her hand. "Is it the café? You got cash flow issues?" They were both small business owners. Cash flow was always a concern.

"Café's fine. It's me."

"What happened?"

"Ethan Gallagher asked me out on a date."

Laurel let out a whoop, but then schooled her face when Willow didn't return her enthusiasm. "You don't look happy. Did you turn him down?"

"No, we're going to a movie on Thursday."

"Then what's the problem?"

Willow sighed, met her best friend's gaze, and admitted something she hadn't admitted to a single soul.

"I haven't been on a date in three years, and it's been four since I had sex."

"You're thinking about having sex with him?"

"No!" Willow blurted out her response, but now that it was in her head, she couldn't get the image out. Oh God, she was in more trouble than she'd thought.

Laurel was grinning from ear to ear as she tugged Willow over to the bench by the wildflower garden. "Sit down here and tell Auntie Laurel everything," she instructed. Then she leaned in closer. "Every. Little. Detail."

"You're enjoying this way too much," Willow grumbled.

"Are you kidding? You always have your shit together. It's kind of fun seeing you all freaked out about something."

"Glad you're enjoying yourself."

Laurel smiled. "I'm sorry. I know I'm having fun at your expense. It's just a date, Wil. It'll be fine. You don't have to have sex on the first date."

"Oh shit. You did not just say that." She rolled her eyes.

Laurel laughed. "Okay, so seriously. Why does this have you so upset? Is it because you guys don't get along? Because I thought you were doing better with that. At John and Moira's the other night—"

"I kissed him."

Laurel's mouth hung open, then she shut it with a clack of her teeth.

Willow dropped her forehead onto her hand. "He offered you the baby stuff and then he disappeared and I just knew he was upset. So I followed him around the side of the house and we talked. Offering you the boys' things . . . it was a reminder, you know? That he and Lisa won't have more kids, because she's not here."

"We hoped the announcement wouldn't upset him." Laurel pursed her lips. "Both of us are aware that he's still grieving, you know?"

"He's happy for you, really. He just needed a few minutes."

"And then?"

"And then I kissed him."

"How was it?"

Willow made a strangled sound in her throat, and Laurel laughed. "Oooh. That good, huh? Did it make your toes curl? Give you goose bumps?" She nudged Willow with her elbow. "Or something else?"

"Don't make fun of me."

"I can't help it."

Willow smiled, feeling a little less panicky thanks to Laurel's teasing. "He is a grumpy shit, you know," she admitted. "But he has such a good reason. And he's got a good heart underneath. We stopped being at each other's throats a while ago."

"So you like him, and he likes you. What's the big deal?"

Willow hesitated. This was what she'd avoided since coming back to Darling. She prided herself on being "together." It was the life she built for herself and she clung to it fiercely. She never wanted anyone to see the scared, uncertain woman she'd once been.

And yet the thought of dating, of putting herself out there, told her that she was still that woman, deep down. It was a complicated mess of feelings. She was thrilled on one hand with the excitement of attraction and possibility, and scared on the other hand, wondering if allowing herself to be vulnerable would mean falling back into old thought patterns and habits. She never, ever, wanted to be that fragile and fractured again.

"Honey?" Laurel's voice was quieter now, and concerned.

"Sorry," Willow said softly. "I guess it comes down to me being scared."

"Scared of what?"

She looked up at Laurel. This was her best friend. Laurel had been through her own share of troubles, but coming back to Darling had been absolutely the right move. Willow was glad. She'd been a bit lonely until Laurel had shown up.

"There's a lot you don't know about what I went through. Everything I do is a conscious decision. So if I decide to go on this date, if I decide to just 'see what happens,' that's a conscious decision, too."

"But you always go with the flow and say that what's meant to be will be."

Willow laughed, but it was a short, harsh sound. "I thought so, you know? That I was like a river, just burbling over any rocks in my way. But the last relationship I had didn't go well. We were both fixer-uppers and found ourselves reverting to old and bad habits. I don't want to go back there again, Laurel. I can't." Her chest cramped at the mere idea of it.

"What happened that was so bad?" Laurel put her fingers on Willow's hand. "You've never said, but I know it was something big. And that it's taken you a long time to love yourself again."

Laurel's face blurred as tears filled Willow's eyes. She was so torn. Laurel was her best friend, but she still couldn't find the words to tell her the truth. That in their junior year she'd gotten pregnant, and that her mother had made her have an abortion. There'd been no counseling, no help. No choice. Her mom took one day off work to go with her for the procedure, and then she was right back to work again. She was rarely home. Willow had already felt like an inconvenience, even before the baby. Then she'd felt like a screwup. Everything had been out of control and she'd turned to bingeing and purging. She'd felt she could control at least that one part of her life.

The father of the baby had only been interested in

one night. Her mother wasn't interested in her at all. Willow had tried everything to get their attention. She'd nearly destroyed herself, and it had taken years and all her strength to overcome those challenges.

She liked her life, but it was lonely. And caring about Ethan Gallagher made her weak. The last thing she ever wanted was to go back to that needy, scared little girl who desperately just wanted someone to love her.

She'd been quiet a long time, but Laurel waited. Even though her business was booming and there was clearly lots to do, her best friend sat by her side. That meant more to Willow than any words.

"I don't know where to start."

Laurel smiled. "When you do, you know where I am. Day or night, okay? All on your own time." She touched Willow's wrist. "You know, maybe you could begin with this. What's troubling you has something to do with your tattoo, doesn't it?"

Her tattoo.

She'd already shared it with Ethan; at least the main points. She figured it said something important when she could share something so personal with him.

"When, Wil? And how?" Laurel's voice was soft with compassion.

Willow swallowed. "My first year of college. I took pills. And then I puked them up. I was very good at vomiting. My eating disorder came in handy."

Laurel said nothing. She simply put her arms around Willow and hugged—a firm "I got you" hug that absorbed some of the tension and strain from Willow's body.

She reached over, put her hand on Laurel's arm and squeezed. "Thank you."

"You are the strongest woman I know." Laurel sat

back a bit. "You are so grounded and smart and intuitive. I know you're scared, but you won't go back there again."

"How can you be so sure?"

Laurel smiled. "Because you learned. You learned why you felt the way you felt and you learned ways of dealing with it. Life isn't always going to be smooth, you know. You were bound to be tested—challenged—at some point. And honey, if Ethan Gallagher is your test, you're a lucky girl."

"You have to say that. You're married to his brother."

"I still have eyes in my head." Laurel chuckled. "It's one date. If he doesn't ring your bell, you move on."

"And if he does?"

"You're always telling me to live in the moment. Why don't you try that? Just take it one day at a time. No reward comes without a little risk. You know this."

"I didn't want to have to face my demons again."

Laurel grinned, but there was a softness of understanding around the edges. "Demons are funny that way. They never really seem to be banished. But know what? I had real trust issues when I came back to Darling, and Aiden helped me move past them. So did you. Don't you deserve a little romance, Wil? A little excitement?" She looked over at the ceramic bird bath, where a robin was making a huge splash and commotion. "All this inner peace and harmony stuff is great, but where's the joy? You should spread your wings, not have them clipped."

Willow watched the robin roll and flutter in the water. Joy, yes. And flying free . . . what good was serenity if it came camouflaged as a prison? Maybe all she'd managed was to cage herself away. Damn.

Didn't take away the fear, though.

"I'm so stupid. All this fuss over a single date."

"Exactly." Laurel tapped her knee. "Listen, Ethan's still raw from losing Lisa. He's not going to be a fast mover. He's probably just as scared about this as you are, so give yourself a break, go to a movie, and just have fun." She met Willow's gaze. "If you feel as if you're getting in over your head, you hit the stop button."

It sounded so logical that Willow immediately let out her breath and dropped her shoulders. "You're a good friend, Laurel."

"So are you. And I want to see you happy. We can hang out later if you want. I can't indulge in any wine, but I can make a wicked Virgin Daiquiri and we can sit in the garden and chill."

"That sounds good."

"Okay. Now, you get back to work and so will I, and I'll see you later."

Willow leaned over and gave Laurel a quick hug. "Thank you, sweetie. You were just what I needed today."

"Hey, I'm happy to finally return the favor."

Willow's steps were lighter as she made her way back to The Purple Pig. Laurel was right. She wasn't the same lost girl she'd been back then. Why shouldn't she go on a simple date and have a good time? This was only a big deal because she was making it out to be one.

It all sounded perfect, except she could still remember the feel of his lips on hers, and the way he tasted, and the touch of his hand on her hip.

Thursday was rainy and cool, so Willow dressed in jeans and a cute top, gathered with elastic at the hem and

neckline but with flowy sleeves. Pink and purple butterflies danced on the white background. She gathered
her hair in a semi-messy top knot and added a simple
necklace, then the barest of makeup essentials—a
little powder, a flick of mascara and a swipe of tinted
gloss.

Normally, this time of day would be dusk, but
because of the overcast skies, it was darker and felt
later. Willow looked out her window at the street below, watching for Ethan's SUV. Her shirt wasn't the
only thing with butterflies. Her stomach was fluttering
so badly she nearly felt ill.

"It's just a single date," she reminded herself, and
took three deep breaths. Then his SUV pulled up to
the curb and the delicate fluttering became a stampede.

Should she rush down to meet him? Or let him come
up and get her at the door? She bit on her lip, trying to
decide, and in the end, waited too long. He tapped on
the door and she grabbed her purse and went to answer.

"Hi!" She opened the door with a cheerful greeting
and damned near swallowed her tongue.

He wore faded jeans with some dark leather shoes,
and a black waterproof jacket that made his shoulders
look massive. The very end of his cast stuck out of the
sleeve, reminding her that he was still injured. And his
hair . . . the rain had darkened it to nearly mahogany.
It made his blue eyes stand out like bluebells in a field.

"Nice weather for ducks, isn't it?" he commented,
giving her a smile.

She could do this. She could make small talk. Be
flippant. "They'll all be swimming in the creek and
heading for the Kissing Bridge. Do you know I saw a
mama duck taking her ducklings across in the spring?
It was so cute."

There was small talk and there was babbling and she feared she'd just crossed the line.

"The boys would have loved that. They love watching the ducks. When they slow down long enough, that is."

Connor and Ronan. Safe topic. "They have a sitter tonight?"

He nodded. "Yes. A teenager from down the street." His cheeks colored a bit. "I didn't want to get the third degree from my family about tonight. I figured a babysitter was a better idea than asking my mom or one of my sisters."

So maybe they were both a little chicken. She wasn't sure if that was reassuring or if it made her even more nervous.

He smiled a little bigger. "Um . . . maybe we can get going. It's wet out here."

"Oh my gosh, of course!" She shut the door behind her and locked it, her knees wobbling as he stepped aside on the small landing, letting her pass by and go down the stairs first.

She held the railing and called herself an idiot.

Ethan opened the car door for her and she hopped inside, then fastened her seatbelt while he got in the driver's side. His jacket was speckled with raindrops, and he looked over at her and smiled again. "You look scared to death. Are you?"

Her cheeks heated and she nodded. "A bit. Which is ridiculous. It's a movie."

He sat back against the seat and rested his hands on the wheel, even though he had yet to start the engine. "Would you rather not go, Willow?"

She hesitated, then saw the tiniest flicker as the muscle in his jaw tightened. She thought about what

Laurel had said. Thought about how hard it must have been for him to even ask. The last thing she wanted to do was hurt his feelings. "I just haven't done this in a long time," she murmured, looking down at her lap. "I mean . . . go on a date. I think I've forgotten how."

Her last relationship hadn't even really started as dates. They'd met in yoga class. Got coffee a few times. He'd walked her home, kissed her, they'd fallen into a relationship in a series of steps that hadn't really involved dating as such. It had started as sharing their secrets and vulnerabilities, and ended with the very things that had brought them together pushing them apart.

"I know how you feel, if it helps. It took me half an hour to figure out what to wear. And then I figured the theater's going to be dark anyway." He chuckled tightly. "Maybe it was a mistake. If my dad hadn't . . ."

"Your dad hadn't what?" She looked up quickly, found him looking a bit chagrined at the slip.

"He told me I needed to get off my ass and start living again." Ethan shrugged. "I think I like you because you didn't know Lisa before. So you don't give me the 'poor Ethan' routine."

Context. She didn't have context and that was a relief to him. She had to admit, she felt a bit the same way. When she looked at him she didn't see just a widower. And when he looked at her, she hoped he didn't see someone who'd been utterly broken and whose pieces were precariously held back together with the glue of time and a lot of hard work.

They were just Ethan and Willow.

They could be whoever they wanted to be with each other.

"Let's go," she whispered. "Let's get out of Darling and go to a movie or get a glass of wine or take a walk.

I don't care where. Let's forget about being nervous and what we might expect from each other and just *be* for a few hours."

"No expectations?"

"God, no. None." Just saying it made her feel tons better.

He smiled again, this time free from the edge of stress that always seemed to line his lips. "Then I have a great idea. Something I haven't done in years."

"Are you going to tell me?"

He turned the key in the ignition. "Nope. I'm going to surprise you. Though you grew up here, so I'll bet you'll guess before we get there."

He looked so excited she couldn't say no.

They left Darling behind and hit the highway toward Burlington. As they put mile after mile behind them, the sky lightened and the rain stopped. It was still overcast, but not the gloomy, heavy clouds of before. When Ethan passed the exit to go to the movie theater, Willow looked over at his profile. Where were they going? And why was she so excited about it?

It all came together when he headed to Colchester and a small smile played on his lips. "We're going to the drive-in, aren't we?" she asked. She folded her hands in her lap but the little shiver of excitement was back. She hadn't been to the drive-in since she was sixteen, and a bunch of them had piled into a car—six of them, maybe—and had snuck in their own snack food rather than go to the concessions stand. They'd snuck some other stuff in, too, though they'd been responsible enough to make sure whoever was driving wasn't drinking.

Back when she was carefree. Just before she'd gotten pregnant and the world had changed.

"Hey, you okay?" Ethan's voice interrupted as he slowed and reached into his back pocket for his wallet.

"I'm fine. Just remembering the last time I was here. Good memories, and some not so good ones, too."

"High school's like that." He gave a half-shrug.

"Ain't that the truth," she muttered, determined to enjoy herself.

He looked over at her and grinned. "Hey, last time I was here was after college and the guys I was with hot-boxed the truck. I was twenty years old and I seriously thought my mom was going to spank my bottom with a wooden spoon when she smelled pot on my clothes."

Willow burst out laughing, both at the story and at the image of the small but fiery Moira putting a big, strapping Ethan over her knee.

He paid for their entrance and crawled along, looking for a good spot to park. Because of the showers, it wasn't busy, and he picked a prime space smack-dab in the middle. The screen was still gray and dark, as they'd arrived even before previews.

"Hey," he said gently. "The thing about mistakes when we were young is that they shaped us into who we are today. So there's no sense in regrets, you know?"

"I do know," she answered, surprised when he reached over and took her hand. "Thank you, Ethan."

"You're welcome." He looked uncomfortable for a minute, then puckered his brows as he met her gaze. "Willow, I'm going to ask you something and if you don't want to answer, it's okay. It's just . . ."

A cold jolt of anxiety flashed through her.

He tightened his grip on her hand. "Willow, what happened that made you . . . I mean, that led to . . ." He nodded at her arm.

Panic tightened her throat. She wasn't ready to

talk about it, and even if she were, this was so not the moment.

When she didn't answer, he pressed on, gentle but persistent. "It's just . . . I know you don't really *talk* about it, but any time you've mentioned your home life, sometimes I get the impression . . . I mean I know it wasn't the happiest place to grow up, but was it worse? Did your mom ever . . ." He trailed off, a lost look on his face, before Willow saw determination flit through his eyes. "Did your mom ever hurt you? Not that I'm assuming anything here, but if I need to be particularly gentle, I want to know."

"No," she said quickly, and let out her breath. "No, Ethan, not what you're thinking. I'm sorry if I gave you that impression." And she was particularly touched by the gentle way he'd asked.

"I'm glad. The thought of anyone hurting you . . ."

Her heart melted just a bit. The consideration was just overwhelming. And to think she'd thought him a grouchy old curmudgeon the first few times they'd met. Unhappy, maybe. Though lately he'd seemed easier. More relaxed.

"Oh Ethan, it's very sweet of you to ask, but I promise, the worst I suffered was, well, maybe neglect is the best way to put it. I was on my own a lot. And anytime I couldn't be avoided, it was made very clear that I was being more trouble than I was worth."

That was it, really. She hadn't been worth it, and she'd felt it every day.

"That's abuse in its own way, Willow. I'm sorry."

"It's okay. Look, I'll be honest. It's not physical intimacy that frightens me. It's emotional. I'm not afraid of *you*."

"Then who are you afraid of?"

She met his gaze and admitted, "Me."

He swallowed. "Oh."

"I've kept myself distanced from people, but I'm starting to realize that it's not the way to move forward. I've done a great job of dealing with my feelings and building myself this wonderful, serene life, but truthfully, I've avoided personal relationships for the most part, and then I don't have to deal with my real weaknesses. You . . . you've made me start facing them and it's difficult."

"I'm sorry."

Of course he would be.

"No, it's probably about time. And Laurel says that I should try to have fun once in a while . . . and she's right. Other than a few girls' nights here and there, I've buried myself in work and causes."

"Like I buried myself in work and bringing up the boys."

"We do what we have to do to get by, right?"

He nodded. "You know what happened to me. It's no secret, especially not in this town. Maybe someday you'll feel like sharing more about what happened to you."

"Maybe."

"It's okay if it's not today. This is already the strangest first date I've ever been on."

Did that mean he was thinking there'd be another? She knew she shouldn't feel so pleased. Just accepting this invitation had put her in a twist, and not in the spinal-twist-to-work-out-the-kinks kind of way. And yet . . . she felt safe. Like Ethan wouldn't do anything she didn't want, or press for something she wasn't ready for. Laurel had been right. This was his first date after losing his wife. Baby steps.

"Maybe someday," she said, but her voice was non-committal.

In front of them, the screen flickered to life, and Ethan adjusted the frequency on the radio. "You want something from concessions?"

She grinned. "I wouldn't say no."

"I'm not sure they have organic popcorn or naturally sweetened soda."

"I'll live." She flopped back against the seat with a satisfied huff, enjoying the novelty of the night off, the drive-in, the prospect of a taste of junk food that rarely passed her lips. "I think there are a lot of things about tonight that I haven't done for too long."

His gaze touched hers and awareness sizzled between them, but then the movie sound came blaring through the speakers as the previews started. She reached to turn it down and he hopped out and jogged to concessions.

Each showing was a double feature, but by ten-thirty, after sharing a bag of popcorn, a box of Milk Duds, and a soda, fatigue was starting to set in. She'd been up at five, had worked all day, and had fretted about the date as well. The movie was a drama, and it was full dark outside. The SUV was dim, and she let out a little sigh as she sank a little lower in the seat.

"Here," Ethan said quietly, his voice a low rumble. He shifted in the seat and lifted one arm along the back of the bench seat. "Tired? Do you want to go?"

She shook her head, but slid over a bit and leaned her head against his shoulder. The very top of his cast nudged her arm as he pulled her in a little closer. She rested on her left hip and put her feet up on the seat, letting her weight lean against his ribs. Lordy, he smelled good. She'd caught his scent all night, being enclosed in the car with him, but now she was close to his jacket and the shirt beneath it and she breathed in some sort of fresh-smelling laundry detergent and a manly, musky cologne or deodorant that reminded her of walking in the woods.

Oh, for Pete's sake.

"We might as well watch the end," she said quietly, keeping her eyes on the screen. "There's only another twenty minutes."

"Are we getting too old for the double feature?"

She laughed a little. "And finish at one a.m.? On a workday?"

He chuckled and his chest rose and fell beneath her.

When the credits started to roll at the movie's end, Ethan sat up a little and slid his arm away from her shoulder. He started the engine, and they followed the thin line of cars that were leaving after the first show.

CHAPTER 12

The drive back to Darling was quiet and held an awkwardness that hadn't been there earlier. The pre-date nerves were eclipsed by end-of-the-date anxiety, with the additional charge of attraction complicating everything.

Willow worried her bottom lip with her teeth. Would he drop her off outside? Walk her to the door? Kiss her good night? Maybe they'd stick to a handshake . . . ugh, how lame. Or a hug . . . would that mean she'd been friend zoned? What did she want for him to do? Could she step up and take the lead?

Were all these thoughts going through his mind, too?

She was more than grateful when he started up a conversation about the construction happening at the old food bank site, the upcoming date to get his cast off, and what their plans were for the Labor Day weekend. It was hard to believe that summer was winding to a close already, and soon kids would be back to school.

But still, under all the niceties, there was the undercurrent of what would happen next.

Ethan pulled in behind the building, next to where Willow's little car was parked, and shut off the engine. The butterfly stampede was back, tromping all through her insides, and as Ethan got out to open her door, she took a deep breath. For God's sake, she was an adult, not a fifteen-year-old kid. He'd walk her to the door. There'd probably be a rather chaste kiss good night. And that would be that.

He opened her door and held out his hand.

When she took it, she knew she was in big trouble.

He shut the door behind her. The earlier rain had passed, leaving a fresh, verdant scent heavy on the air. Droplets of water pattered through the leaves of the nearby birches and maples, creating a mystical sound in the inky darkness. Everything was magnified; the warmth of his hand enclosed around hers, the sound of their footsteps on the wooden stairs leading to her apartment. She reached into her purse for her key and tried valiantly not to tremble as she slid it into the deadbolt and unlocked the door.

Willow turned to face him, and found herself a mere two inches away from the wall of his chest. *Oh my.*

"I had a good time," she said, sounding unusually breathy. "Thanks for the date."

"Willow."

Dammit, when he said her name that way everything in her went all soft and gooey, like warm caramel. She lifted her chin but then she was even more aware of how close he was right now. How if she shifted the slightest bit, their bodies would be brushing. Little muscles in her body tightened in anticipation, in desire, in need.

He leaned forward, his jacket brushing against her, moving the silky fabric of her shirt over her skin like a whisper. His lips were close . . . so close . . . close enough she could make out the flavors of chocolate and butter and something indefinable that she craved. Was he ever going to kiss her? And still he waited, prolonging the agony, until he finally caressed her lips with his.

The kiss began as a feather-soft brushing of lips, something beautiful and fragile and incredibly arousing. It clouded Willow's mind and she reached out and gripped the sleeves of his jacket as an anchor. Ethan deepened the kiss by degrees, increasing the pressure bit by bit, opening his lips a little more, touching his tongue to the inside of her bottom lip, until it blossomed into a full-on kiss that swept her up in a wave of delight.

His good arm came around her and pulled her flush against his body. Even fully clothed, she reveled in his strength and size. Perhaps he'd been off work with his arm, but there was no denying that his daily conditioning left him in splendid shape. Willow kissed him back, giving herself over to the sensation, committing to the moment with everything she had. Ethan tightened his arm and lifted her a few inches off the ground, and then walked forward through her door and kicked it shut behind him.

A dark thrill raced through her body.

The lights were still off, but gray shadows lit the room through the large front windows. Willow shrugged off her jacket and dropped it to the floor, then reached for his and unzipped it before sliding her hands inside and around his ribs. Then they were kissing again, this time with her pressed against the wall next to her front door. God, his hips were pressed against hers and a feeling of utter carnality swept through her. This was no quick kiss good night. This was foreplay. Was she ready for that? Was he?

"Wrap your legs around me," he said roughly, lifting her again. She didn't even think; she simply obeyed, and he carried her to the small kitchen and the countertop there and deposited her on it. Now the apex of her legs was pressed close to his navel, and he ran his mouth over the taut tendon in her neck.

Visions of making love right here in the kitchen filled her brain and she moaned, as the muscles between her legs clenched in anticipation. She was a physical person, in tune with her own body, and it had been a long, long time since she'd been so sexually stimulated. She tightened her legs around him and gasped as he slid his hand beneath her top, reached around and undid her bra, and cupped her small breast in his hand.

His thumb grazed the nipple and she swore she saw stars behind her eyelids.

"Ethan," she whispered, completely overwhelmed and yet clamoring for more. "Oh."

He replaced his thumb with his mouth. The fever burned just as hot, but not as fast. Instead he gentled his movements, tasting her skin in savory licks rather than ravenous bites. She looked down at his dark head, touched her fingers to the mahogany hair as his head moved slightly. Oh, sweet mother. She was in so much trouble. Because it wasn't just desire right now, at this moment. It was tenderness. And something big and scary and wonderful.

He lifted her shirt and pulled it over her head. "I want to see you," he said softly, dropping the pale pile of fabric to the floor. He covered her breast, his palm so large that the whole of her breast was encompassed in the warmth of his hand. "You're so beautiful," he murmured. "The curve of your neck . . . Willow, let your hair down. Please."

She lifted her arms and he stood back. Something like feminine pride swept through her as she worked the topknot loose, knowing that her raised arms lifted her breasts to his hungry gaze. She shook her hair and let it fall, haphazard, over her shoulders, the tips of the blond and pink strands kissing her collarbone.

"Like this?" she asked.

He came close again, ran the backs of his knuckles down over her shoulder, the hollow of her throat, along her sternum, and the faint hollow between her breasts. "So beautiful," he murmured, leaning forward and kissing the hair along her temple. "So perfect. So . . ."

He stopped. Willow paused and held her breath, simply in response to him freezing up over whatever he had been about to say.

"Ethan?"

He didn't move for a few seconds. "Willow. I'm sorry. I can't . . . shit."

She swallowed tightly, wishing she had her shirt back so she could at least cover herself. "Was it something I did?"

"God, no." He stepped back and met her gaze, but the naked heat of earlier was replaced with an expression she could only read as guilt tinged with embarrassment. In the shadows she couldn't tell if he was blushing or not, but the set of his jaw and his awkward posture spoke volumes.

"I got carried away," he explained, his voice strained. "But I'm not being fair to you. It's just . . . it's too fast."

Okay. That she could deal with. She was pretty sure

that when the fog of passion lifted, she'd be feeling like it was a bit speedy, too. Just not right now, when certain parts of her body were still throbbing with want.

She tried a smile. "Well. At least we know there's a spark."

He laughed, though it was a short, brief choke of a laugh; one of surprise and perhaps understatement.

"There was a spark the day we kissed. I knew it. I avoided it. I really was just going to kiss you good night at the door, and . . ."

"And here we are."

"Here we are."

"About ten steps away from my bedroom."

"Yeah."

"But we both agree it's too soon."

"You think so, too?"

There was such relief in his voice, she answered with a half-lie, because her brain and body were sending her two different messages. "We were both nervous about even going on a date tonight. Sex is quite a leap, don't you think?"

"It's not that I don't want to."

"Nor I."

The words settled through the kitchen. That was it, then. They wanted each other. Willow slid off the countertop, her breasts jiggling a little as her toes touched the floor. Was it crazy that she felt both exposed and sexy at this moment?

She reached for her shirt and pulled it on, leaving her bra in a tangle on the floor. "Whew." She tried to keep her voice light. "Not bad for a first date."

A ghost of a smile flickered on his lips before disappearing. "I thought I could do this. I thought I was ready. And then . . ."

Willow knew where this was going. She'd felt the same when that wave of emotion had overtaken her. The things holding them back didn't just magically disappear in the heat of the moment.

"You thought about her, didn't you?"

He nodded. "Just that . . . Wil, you're so different. You're . . . you're like a fairy, with your hair and your eyes and you're so graceful and . . . well, Lisa was different from you. And I caught myself comparing you in my head and that's not fair." He stepped forward and cupped his left hand around her jaw. "When I'm with someone, I don't want to be thinking about anybody else."

Willow covered his hand with hers, filled with both understanding and sympathy and, yes, a bit of hurt that he had, indeed, been thinking about his wife while feeling her up. "You're not ever going to forget her, you know," she advised. "And that's okay. It is what it is."

"But . . . I thought . . . Oh hell. I don't know what I'm thinking."

She smiled and squeezed his fingers. "You're right, you know. I don't want you to be thinking about someone else, either. And it's not jealousy. I just wish your heart didn't hurt so much, Ethan."

"And I you," he answered, dropping his hand.

"Okay. Then let me just say thank you for a lovely evening. Because it was. The drive-in, the movie, the popcorn . . . all of it. This part, too."

"You're too good a person for the likes of me, Willow Dunaway."

"Now you are talking crazy." She smiled up at him as the heat of desire waned. Left in its place was a restless affection that needed time to sort itself out.

She walked him to the door. He paused in the doorway and frowned. "You said 'first date' earlier," he said. "Does that mean you'd go on another?"

Was she afraid? Yes. Maybe the physical attraction was off the charts, but tonight had proved that neither of them were ready to leap into anything serious. But had it been good? God, yes. She needed to *live*. Take chances. If he asked her right now, she'd say yes.

"You'll just have to ask me and see," she replied.

"Willow? Will you come over next Sunday and have dinner with me and the boys?"

Ah. A safe date because the kids would be running interference. "That would be nice."

"Okay. See you then."

He leaned forward and dropped a kiss on her forehead, a kiss that was quick and impersonal. Willow almost laughed. If he'd tried kissing her lips again, who knew where they might end up? He was scared, and playing it safe. It gave her a small measure of comfort.

When he was gone, she slipped back inside, brushed her teeth, went into her room, stripped, and got into bed. She ran her fingers over the tips of her breasts, remembering the feel of his fingers and mouth, filled with a longing so intense she curled up in the sheets to hold it close.

It had been years since she'd felt so feminine. Years during which she'd denied her own sexuality, focusing instead on her spirit and body and pretending those needs and callings weren't important. That she was somehow "above" desire and passion, and she was better for it.

And she'd been wrong. She was human, and she was meant to love and be loved. To feel joy and ecstasy. It was not something to fear, but something to rejoice.

And while she knew that stopping was the right

thing, she rather wished she'd been able to rejoice a little longer tonight.

Dinner with "the boys" wasn't a dress-up occasion, so Willow left the café in Emily's capable hands and was at Ethan's door at six sharp. The moment she rang the bell, she heard the stomping of feet and excited voices.

"Willow!"

"Wil-low!"

Oh my, their sweet faces. "Hey, guys. I brought dessert. I also have a little something for you in my bag. Let's go in so you can have it."

Connor was off in a flash, shouting, "Dad, Dad! Willow brought dessert and presents!"

Ronan grinned up at her and held out his hand. Her heart did a solid thump as she took it and let him lead her into the house. Both boys were 100 percent energy, but there was a sweetness to Ronan that caught her right in the feels. It was like something had happened that day they rocked in her suspended chair. A strange but lovely bond had been formed.

Ethan was at the stove, stirring something in a big pot. The kitchen, to her surprise, was spotless. She tended to be a bit of a messy cook, but the only indication that there'd been a mess at all were a handful of dishes drying in a rack in the sink.

She looked at his hand as it stirred and her mouth dropped open. "Your cast is off!"

He lifted his hand and wiggled his fingers. "Yes, I've got two working arms again." His gaze touched hers and she felt heat rise up her chest. His comment might have been completely innocent, but now a crooked grin sat infuriatingly on his lips.

Then he placed one arm beside the other. "I have major tan lines."

She laughed. Sure enough, one arm was tanned and muscled from working in the sun over the summer, while the other was pale and slimmer. She considered making a joke about building up the muscles in his right arm, but there were little ears about.

"Dad made 'sgetti. It's our favorite."

"I love spaghetti." It wasn't something she made very often, but when she was a kid, the few times her mom had cooked a special dinner it was usually spaghetti and garlic bread.

Of course, by the time she was in her senior year, she'd spent more time in the bathroom purging than actually eating. Adjusting her perspective to thinking about food as fuel and a way to honor her health changed everything. That mindfulness was a constant part of her life now.

"I'll confess I make it mostly from a jar and add my own extras," he said, putting the lid on the pot. "But I did buy organic."

She smiled. "Am I converting you to my tree-hugger ways, Ethan Gallagher?"

"Maybe. More like I wanted to make a good impression."

The boys were dancing around her feet, and she realized she was still holding the container of brownies and their "presents" in her bag. She put the brownies on a nearby counter and knelt down before them. "Okay, guys. Don't get too excited. It's just a few things."

She'd been shopping for new kitchen towels for the café and she'd popped into a Dollar Store on impulse. She took out the bag now, and withdrew two small bottles.

"Bubbos," Ronan said. His slight mispronunciation only made him more adorable.

"For you, too, Connor," she said, handing over the other bottle. She reached inside the bag. "I got one for your daddy as well."

"Thanks," Connor said, not quite as enthusiastic about the surprise as she'd hoped. She supposed bubbles probably weren't so exciting for a five-year-old boy who was used to wreaking havoc.

"I got this, too. I thought it would be easier for Ronan to catch than using a glove." She took out a bigger package. Inside was a red tennis ball, and two paddles covered in Velcro.

"Oh, cool!" Connor took to this present better, opening the package and taking out one of the paddles. Willow helped him slide his hand into the strap on the back, and tightened it to fit more snugly. Then she took the tennis ball and stuck it to the Velcro.

"How about you, Ronan? You want to try?"

She took the second paddle and adjusted it to Ronan's little hand. "There. All set."

Connor ripped the ball from the Velcro and gave it a toss. Instead of hitting Ronan's "glove," it smacked him right in the forehead.

"Ow! Connor!" Ronan's little brow puckered, and he started to cry.

Great. She'd brought presents and the immediate result was a wailing child. Good job.

"Suck it up, big guy. It's a tennis ball." Ethan's voice was steady and calm, and he knelt down before Ronan. "It's not even going to leave a mark."

Ronan's lip wobbled, but the wailing ceased.

"You two take that outside. No balls in the house.

And Connor, toss it underhand. No split-finger fastballs aimed at your brother."

"Aw, Dad . . ."

Ethan lifted one eyebrow.

"All right." Connor let out a dramatic sigh. "Come on, Ronan."

Ronan sniffled and asked, "Can I bring the bubbos?"

"Sure."

The two went out the patio door into the backyard, leaving Willow and Ethan alone in the kitchen.

"Sorry," Willow offered, feeling out of her depth. "I thought it would be fun. I didn't mean for Ronan to cry."

Ethan laughed and slid noodles into the pot of boiling water. "That? Oh, that's mild. Ronan tries to keep up with Connor. Connor gets impatient. And they've got lots of energy. Tears and frustration are par for the course."

"I don't know much about raising kids."

He looked over at her and smiled. "No one does, until they become a parent. And then they learn as they go. Like I said, no big deal. They'll have fun with that until one of them gets frustrated, then they'll break out the bubbles or something."

He was so relaxed about it, and yet he'd been firm with the boys. "You're a good dad, Ethan."

"I try. But . . . it's hard. Doing it alone. I just kind of muddle through."

"Then you're very good at muddling." She smiled up at him. "Is there anything I can do to help with dinner?"

He looked out the patio doors briefly, then back to her. "Just this," he said softly, then took a step forward and with both gentleness and confidence, touched his lips to hers.

She melted against him. That was simply it. He touched, she melted. There was no thought, no pros and cons, no restraint . . . it was just as simple as a flower bending in the breeze.

When their lips parted, she had to find a way to breathe again. He was so good at that.

He spun to find a strainer for the pasta and she swallowed, trying to clear her fuzzy mind. While he worked around the kitchen, she realized that she was here, in the house that he and Lisa had shared together. They'd probably brought their babies home here. Made love here. Had plans for the future. It was lovely and welcoming, but she couldn't stop the feeling that she didn't belong.

"You're very quiet," he commented. He put a bowl of salad greens on the counter.

"It's nothing." Lisa had stood between them the other night. She didn't want the same thing to happen today.

"I don't think so. Are you still bothered about the boys? Trust me, it's already been forgotten."

She met his gaze. Goodness, he was so good-looking, even when his eyebrows pulled together and his lips pursed. He seemed to be taking this much more in his stride than she was.

"I just . . . oh, it's silly. Let's just eat." She moved to the counter and picked up a bag of croutons. This was her problem, not his. Clearly he wasn't that bothered that she was in his house. And it was just dinner, for heaven's sake. She took a deep breath and let it out slowly. If he wasn't bothered, she shouldn't be, either.

He called the boys back inside and sent them to

wash their hands, then drained the pasta and started filling little bowls with noodles, sauce, and cheese. They scrambled into their chairs and Willow laughed as they dug into their pasta with enthusiasm while she and Ethan were still filling their plates.

"They are not fussy eaters," Ethan commented. "Thankfully. I think they inherited the 'iron gut' gene from the Gallaghers."

They sat down at the table and Willow took a first bite of pasta. It was good. Not fabulous, but the three of them wouldn't starve with Ethan doing the cooking. She loved to cook, and thought about her own marinara with fresh tomatoes and herbs from the garden behind the café, but this wasn't bad. She sprinkled some fresh Parmesan on the top and reached for the salad.

It was all so familial. They chatted about the boys' soccer teams, swimming at their grandparents' pool, and Ethan's anticipated return-to-work date, which he was hoping could be after the September long weekend, as long as his physiotherapist said his arm was strong enough. She laughed at Connor's slurping of noodles, and knowing he had an audience, he made a big show of sucking in a particularly long piece of spaghetti. The end of it whipped up and left a trail of sauce along the side of his nose, which made Ronan laugh and try to keep up by sucking on a strand so hard his cheeks hollowed out.

Ethan issued a gentle reminder about table manners and handed them each a napkin.

When the meal was over, Ethan washed hands and faces and sent them back outside for a while, then he started clearing the table.

"Let me help you," she suggested, reaching for her plate and cutlery.

"You're our guest tonight. Sit back and relax."

She pondered a minute, wondering how to proceed. She was a guest and yet she was made to feel like part of the gang. It wasn't a bad thing, but it hadn't been a particularly romantic meal either. "Honestly, it's no biggie. We can clean it up together, and it'll take half the time."

"You're sure? Because this won't take long at all."

She nodded. "We're just . . . friends, having dinner. It's no big deal, right?"

His eyes met hers, and looked slightly troubled. "Friends," he replied carefully.

Willow's stomach twisted as nerves got the best of her. "Well, I thought after the other night, we agreed that this needed to be low-key."

"Low-key is not the same as friends."

Oh my.

"I just thought . . ."

"I kissed you. Did that feel friendly?"

She swallowed, her throat suddenly dry and tight. "Not . . . exactly."

"Maybe we just took things too fast, that's all. That's what I meant. I want to be fair to you. I want to be fair to me. That doesn't mean I don't want to see where this might lead."

Oh *my*.

"Unless you've changed your mind," he added.

She could say she had. She could do that and walk away and retreat into her safe little bubble. It was comfortable there. It was familiar. That bubble was built on self-acceptance and love and peace, and reinforced with principles she believed in. But it was still a bubble, with fragile walls that kept her protected from the scariest emotions.

Agreeing to take things slowly meant popping that bubble and stepping, ever so cautiously, into something new, without protection. It meant risk. The idea made her heart seize a bit, but there was longing, too. And a knowledge that perhaps her bubble had been holding her back.

Of course, she could be completely wrong.

"Slowly is probably the best way," she agreed, nodding slightly. "I'm just so out of practice—"

He laughed. "You think you are? The thing is, I don't want to hurt you, either, Willow. I think we've started something but I'm very unsure, and I don't want to drag you into something that might . . . oh, shit. I don't know what I'm trying to say."

"You're saying you want to move on with your life. You want to feel again. But you don't want me to be a casualty if it doesn't work out." She stepped forward, took the plate from his hand, and put it on the counter. Then she folded his hand into hers. "Which just proves that you are a good guy, Ethan. A lot of guys wouldn't take that into consideration. And I'm in the same predicament. I don't know if I'm ready, and I don't want to hurt you, either."

"So we could end it now, but—"

"But it still means that we're probably going to have to deal with putting ourselves out there at some point. We got off to a rocky start. We're very different in so many ways. But we're alike in a lot of ways, too. Maybe we can agree to just be honest about how we're feeling. Not expect too much of each other. Take it slow, like you said."

"I like you," he said, squeezing her hand. "A lot. I'm just not sure I'm ready to think about falling in love again."

There went her stomach again. "Hey, listen. I know I practice all this inner-peace stuff, but there are still things that scare me. Love is top of the list."

His thumb rubbed along the top of her hand. "Who hurt you, Willow?" He pulled her in close, into an easy hug that spoke of affection and comfort and caring. "Even if I'm not ready, it's not loving that scares me. Losing does. But love . . . it shouldn't hurt when you're in it."

A lump formed in her throat, lodged painfully there and she tried to swallow around it.

"Ethan, I . . ."

"Dad! Can we have Willow's brownies now?"

Connor came running into the kitchen, halting whatever Willow was going to say. Ethan sent her a telling look. "Saved by the kid," he said quietly. "But not off the hook. We'll continue this later."

Ethan moved to get the dish of brownies. Willow watched him with an unsettled feeling in the pit of her stomach. Her intuition said that things were about to get a whole lot more personal.

CHAPTER 13

Ethan was nowhere near as composed as he put on. Dinner had been easy . . . too easy. He'd wondered how it would feel to have a woman here, in the home he'd shared with his wife. He'd wondered if it would be awkward, or feel simply wrong.

Instead she'd come inside and fit in as if she belonged. He hadn't thought of Lisa once during dinner, but he'd found himself staring at Willow's lips, wondering when he could kiss her again. He couldn't deny the chemistry was off the charts, but it worried him, too. Was it his dry spell making him so crazy? Was that being fair to Willow? The last thing he wanted to do was string her along.

Or was it something more? And that was an even scarier proposition.

The boys were bathed and in pajamas when Ethan thought a fire in the backyard pit might be a good idea. Despite having brownies earlier, a good campfire meant some sort of treat cooked over an open flame. He gave the boys a cookie sheet as a tray and let them get out white bread and butter while he opened a can of apple pie filling and put in in a bowl. Willow was in charge of putting the chairs around the fire pit and he took a hatchet and shaved off some kindling to get things started. Within a few minutes the dry spruce started crackling and he looked up at Willow with a grin on his face. "Ah. My manhood is still intact."

She laughed, and the light sound rippled through the lavender twilight. Ronan opened the sliding door and Connor came out, carefully carrying the tray of pie fixings. "So, I've heard of a lot of campfire treats, but this whole pie thing has me puzzled."

"It's pretty sinful, particularly to someone like you." He went to Connor and took the tray, then set it on a small table. "Horrible, horrible white bread. Butter. And pie filling from a can. But I promise, it's delicious."

"I won't tell if you won't. But how do you do it?"

Connor and Ronan had zipped back inside to get milk. Ethan added wood to the fire and stood back, satisfied with the hum and snap of the flames. "This has to burn down a bit. Then we use these." He held up a strange apparatus—a long handle with a square metal box on the end. "It's a pie iron. Or sandwich. These aren't cast iron, because iron is too heavy for the boys. We've done grilled cheese, pizza pockets, pie . . ."

When he chanced a look over at her, she was grinning from ear to ear. "What?"

"I was just thinking I've never done this in my life. My high school campfires were more like chips and vodka coolers on the sly."

"You've never been camping?"

"No. It was just me and my mom, and . . ."

Her face changed when she stopped talking. Ethan

frowned. She said so little about her life before. Had she really been so unhappy, then? It hurt his heart a little to think of it. She was so full of life, so bubbly and smiling all the time. The thought of her being sad seemed so wrong.

He sat down in the camp chair beside her. "And what? I take it she wasn't the outdoor type?"

Willow laughed, but it was a humorless sound. "My mom was a workaholic. She did a great job providing for us, and as a single mom I know it had to be really difficult for her. But . . ." She sighed. "It wasn't a particularly loving environment, that's all. I felt in the way a lot of the time. Like an imposition."

Ethan thought back to his own childhood. He'd had his brothers and sisters to both play with and aggravate. His parents had always been loving and involved in their kids' lives. Sure, they'd done their share of "get out of the house and go play so we can have some peace and quiet," but their family had always been one of love and acceptance.

"You must have been really lonely."

"Friends got me through. Until . . ."

Once more she paused. Ethan was going to ask her "until what" except Connor and Ronan came back, carrying plastic cups with lids and straws filled with milk.

"Is it time, Daddy?" Ronan practically bounced on his toes, excited for his treat.

"Just about. Let's get them made, and by that time, the fire should be ready. You want to help, Willow?"

"Sure," she answered, her easy smile back on her face.

The four of them built the "pies" by buttering bread, sandwiching the slices together with pie filling, and closing the presses. Ethan arranged the boys' chairs so they were close to the fire but not too close, and they carefully held out the long handles so the pies were nestled in the flames.

"Once they have theirs, we can make ours," Ethan said. "We'll have to check them in a few minutes. Once they get a little brown, you flip them over and do the other side."

They watched the boys carefully, and checked the pies for doneness, flipped them over, and watched again. When they were golden brown on each side, Ethan carefully turned them out onto plates to cool. The boys were practically dancing with impatience, but Ethan made them wait. Burned tongues weren't fun.

In the meantime, he and Willow made their pies and put them in the irons. At that point the boys weren't going to wait any longer, so Ethan sat them down in their chairs with their milk and apple pies and he handed one of the irons to Willow.

She looked over at him as she held her iron in the flames. "This is fun. Do you do this a lot?"

He shrugged. "In the summer? Usually once a week or so. Either here or at Mom and Dad's. Though it's usually s'mores over there. He says they're for the boys, but Pop loves them."

"You have a great family, Ethan. I mean, I knew that from talking to Hannah and Laurel, but the more I know them, the more I realize how wonderful they are. And rare."

He hadn't really thought of it that way before. Sure, he appreciated them, but there was also the assumption that this was how families were. Boy, he'd been naïve. And had maybe taken them for granted.

He looked over at the boys. They were sitting in their

chairs, talking to each other, milk cups in the chair cup holders and half-eaten pies on their laps. For the first time in a long time, he felt lucky. Thankful. There was a lot to be thankful for, really, but he'd been too caught up in what he'd lost, and trying to be a single dad, that he'd stopped noticing.

Willow opened her pie iron and checked her pie, then latched it closed again and flipped it over to toast the other side. A lump formed in his throat as he watched her. He and Lisa had only managed to do this a few times with the kids. Ronan was too little to remember, and Connor had been the age Ronan was now. Even then, she'd been so sick that she'd sat in her chair and watched more than participated.

Those end days had been beautiful and awful. For a long time, Ethan had felt as if he'd died right along with her. But now Willow was here, and she was so vibrant. So alive. And she made him feel alive, too. No matter where this ended up going, he would always be thankful for that.

"What are you smiling at?" she asked. The firelight flickered over her smooth skin, and made orangey lights in her blond hair.

He turned away, embarrassed at being caught. "Oh, just enjoying myself, I suppose. Your pie's probably done. I'll put it on a plate for you."

She handed him her contraption and he busied himself with putting the pies on plates and then setting the irons aside to cool. When he took her the plate, their fingers brushed lightly, and she looked up and met his gaze. A jolt of something zipped through his fingertips, but then she licked her lips—had that been intentional? He didn't think so. Willow wasn't the kind to be deliberately provocative.

He cleared his throat and took his hand away, then went to put more wood on the fire.

"This is delicious," Willow said, and he turned to find her nibbling on the hot pocket. "It shouldn't be, but oh my."

Connor nodded. "Apple is my favorite. Aunt Hannah likes cherry."

"What about you, Ronan? What's your favorite?"

"Strawberry," he said. "But I like apple, too. Grammie Susan makes the best apple pie."

"I bet she does," Willow answered, and looked at Ethan. "Maternal grandmother?" she asked in a low voice.

He nodded. "Lisa's family lives in Montpelier. The boys are actually going to visit next week for a few days."

"Sounds like fun."

"It'll be quiet around here for sure."

A new awareness filled the air between them. Ethan would be home but without the boys to run interference . . . or get in the way. Did he want to see Willow again? Did he want to be uninterrupted? Would he back off once again if things got a bit intense? Man, he'd figured he wouldn't have to do this dating thing ever again, but here he was. Caught between a memory and a possibility, afraid to let go of one and afraid to embrace the other.

He was an idiot. Why the hell was he overthinking this so much?

And then he looked at Willow, with her very personal tattoo and the sad face when he talked about his big family and knew it was because she mattered. Knew that despite how cranky and broody he appeared on the outside, on the inside he would never deliberately want to hurt a living soul. And certainly wouldn't want to use someone for his own ends.

Maybe he should just back off. Until he was sure he was ready.

And then she looked up at him with her half-eaten pie and smiled at him and something warm expanded in his chest.

He was falling for her. Despite all the cautions, despite all the red flags, despite their different upbringings and views, he cared.

"Boys, it's time for bed. Finish up your milk, and then we'll go in and brush your teeth."

"Awww, Dad," Connor complained. "Do we have to?"

"Yes. It's already past your bedtime. Say good night to Willow."

With grumbling and much slumping, the boys crawled out of their camp chairs and heaved disappointed sighs. "When I grow up, I'm going to stay up as late as I want," Connor mumbled.

Ethan chuckled, and saw Willow hide a smile.

"G'night, Willow."

"Good night, Connor."

"Night, Wil-low," echoed Ronan. But he went over to her chair and went up on his toes to plant a kiss on her cheek.

"Flirt," Ethan accused, trying to ignore the ache inside at the gesture.

"Good night, sweetheart," she whispered, a telltale catch in her voice.

The boys ran off to the house, leaving Ethan and Willow alone. "Gosh, they're so sweet. Especially Ronan."

Ethan laughed. "He knows how to play you."

"I don't believe it," she said staunchly, defending Ronan. "There's not a manipulative bone in his body."

"See? You're completely fooled."

She smiled in return and sat back in her chair. "You know, when we first met, I felt sorry for your kids. You seemed so cranky. So . . ."

"Not fun?"

"Yeah. That."

"I'm not always fun. Sometimes I'm tired. Sometimes I'm frustrated." He took a chance and made a confession. "You've been good for me, Willow. I'd spent a lot of time with my family, but didn't make any time for friends. I think I was worried that they'd treat me like the fragile widower. Or that I'd just drag people down, so I stayed away."

"Not worried about dragging me down?" she asked, and he saw a twinkle in her eyes in the firelight.

"That's what I like about you. You can tease and hit me with honesty all at the same time. You don't treat me with kid gloves."

"Well, I'd been hiding away a bit myself, so I guess I'll return the favor and say that you've made me broaden my perspective."

"I'm not sure if that's a compliment or a criticism."

"The jury's still out."

Damn. She knew how to keep him on his toes, and he liked it. A lot.

"You go see to the boys," she suggested. "The fire's burning down a bit now, so I'll tidy up the food mess."

"Stay for a glass of wine? A beer? We could put another log on the fire and chill."

Wow, wasn't he the exciting host? Sitting around the backyard. He was sure she'd say she needed to head out, but instead she gathered plates and smiled. "That sounds nice."

He went inside and supervised the brushing of teeth and tucked the boys into bed. Well past their regular bedtime, both burrowed under the covers, their heads smelling a little like the smoke from the fire, their mouths like mint and apple mixed together.

"Good night, boys."

"'Night, Dad." Connor yawned and rolled to his side. Ronan didn't even answer, he simply closed his eyes and was out.

Ethan shut the door behind him, then hesitated for a minute. It had been a year and a half, maybe longer, since he'd tucked the boys into bed and looked forward to private moments with a woman. It was something he'd never actually thought he'd have again. For the longest time, it had felt as if he'd never move past his grief and loneliness. He hated to admit it, but perhaps everyone who'd said "It gets better" was right after all.

Willow was still sitting by the fire, staring into the flames that were softer now. He handed her a glass of wine, twisted the top off his own beer, and sank into the chair with a sigh.

"You got the monkeys off to bed?" she asked softly.

"It wasn't hard. They were pooped." He smiled a little. "Ronan was asleep before his head hit the pillow."

"They're great kids, Ethan. I know it's got to be hard, but they really are terrific."

"And busy, and dirty . . ."

"And little boys. They're just being kids."

"Have you ever thought of having your own?" he asked. "You're so good with them. Honestly, I find it hard to believe you're still single."

She didn't answer, so he took a swig of his beer and turned his head to look at her. Once more, the troubled look on her face gave him pause. "Willow? What's wrong?"

"Are we starting a thing, here, Ethan?" She met his gaze, her face utterly serious. "We had a great time at the movie, and after . . . but you stopped, and for a good reason. Tonight we took a step back to something more casual, but we're still . . . well, I'm here. I know I give you mixed signals. It's just hard for me to trust."

It had to be something pretty big for her to be so serious and so hesitant to share. "Does this have to do with why you've got that tattoo?"

She nodded. "It does. And I haven't told anyone. Not even Laurel, or Hannah. And I don't want to tell you, either, but I feel I should if we're moving into relationship territory."

He hesitated. Took another drink of beer. She had a sip of her wine. "I don't know what to say," he finally said, frowning at the flames. "I like being with you. I want to spend time with you. I think about kissing you . . . but I'm scared to put a label on what we have. I don't want to hurt you, but I'm not sure I'm ready for anything as heavy as an actual relationship."

"I understand."

"You need to know that. I don't want to stop seeing you, but I understand if it's not enough for you."

She laughed a little, but it was a sad sound. "I'm not exactly sure what a healthy relationship looks like. I have my own reservations. Not about you . . . about me."

"Me, too."

"But I like being with you. And the boys . . . maybe we just need to take time to sort things out."

He looked over again. She sipped her wine, and the

flames danced over her face and through the globe of her wineglass.

"Have you wondered if we're both just too damaged to do this?"

He was surprised he'd actually voiced that concern. He'd known from the beginning that there were shadows in her past. Even if she hadn't named them, they were there. Sure, she seemed happy and . . . serene. Yes, that was it. But his initial impression of her had certainly changed. There was a depth that wasn't noticeable at first glance.

She nodded. "You threaten everything I've worked for," she whispered. "My peace of mind. My confidence and security. You make me doubt. Sometimes I've wondered if you're meant to be a test for me. Or if you are meant to show me that I still have work to do. I thought I was whole. I think that might have been arrogant of me."

He didn't know how to answer that. Being with someone . . . it was supposed to make you more, not less. "You've made my life better," he replied. "But I think you're saying that I haven't done the same for you." It hurt to think he'd failed in that way.

"Oh, that's not it at all!" She turned in her chair and faced him head on. "Oh, Ethan. I don't mean for you to feel that way. You *have* made things better. If anything, it's made me take a good hard look at myself and realize what I've been missing."

"Missing?"

She nodded. "Love. Intimacy. The need to let myself be vulnerable. I've been looking inward to acceptance and happiness, and that's wonderful, but I've held myself back. I've avoided taking chances so that I wouldn't get hurt. That's not very realistic."

It was a heavy sort of conversation to have. He took another drink of his beer, and then held out his hand. "Take my hand," he said quietly. "Just for a little while. We can take this slow. We can avoid labels. We don't have to define anything."

A slow smile spread across her face as she put her fingers in his. "We can just be," she agreed. "In the moment. It's really the only way to live. We can't change the past, Ethan. And we can't predict the future. But sitting in front of a fire with you is a very nice *now* to be in."

Her hand was small and soft in his, and felt a bit foreign but also very right.

They sat there for a long time, until their drinks were gone and the fire was down to embers. Then, when the moon was high over the trees, they let go with a sigh.

CHAPTER 14

In the week leading up to the Labor Day weekend, Willow and Ethan snuck precious hours away to hang out. She went to Connor and Ronan's soccer game. He stopped in for coffee one morning on his way to his doctor appointment, to get the all-clear for his return to work the second week of September. There was a midweek supper at his family's place, where Rory told a story about Oaklee Collier hitting a stray dog and bringing it to the clinic, and then taking it home with her again a few days later, rather than sending it to the shelter. He had them all laughing when he told them about the dog peeing on her Kate Spade bag. Clearly the dog, affectionately named Buster, didn't care a bit about brand names.

But on Thursday, Ethan dropped the boys at their grandparents in Montpelier. They'd spend the long weekend there, and be back just before school started. Ronan would be in preschool and Connor would be starting first grade. In the meantime, Ethan had asked Willow on a bona fide date—no kids. Actual dinner, not at the café or diner but at the dining room of a local inn. Laurel had suggested it, since Aiden had taken her there when they'd been dating.

Right now Willow was going through her closet looking for something suitable to wear. She'd thought about asking Hannah to help, but it was a little awkward, asking for wardrobe help to go on a date with her brother. She'd left Emily in charge of the café—yet again—and was now scouring her closet for something a bit fancier than normal. Other than her usual maxi-dresses, the only thing she had was the bridesmaid dress from Laurel's wedding, and it was far too fancy.

When she heard the knock at the door her heart took a leap. The clock beside her bed said six-thirty, so it couldn't be Ethan. She tightened her robe and hustled to the door, hoping it wasn't something with the café. Nervous as she was, she was excited about the date. It felt grown up. Premeditated in a way the others hadn't been. Not casual like a movie, or "friendly" like spaghetti and a campfire.

She opened the door and saw Laurel standing there, grinning like a fool, holding a white garment bag in her hands.

"I figured that right about now, you'd be in your closet, despairing of something to wear," Laurel announced, and slid by Willow into the apartment. "Your hippy-dippy stuff isn't going to cut it at the inn. And you can't exactly show up in jeans and a pair of sandals."

Willow let out a breath. "This is so not like me! I don't get nervous before dates!"

"I know. You're the voice of reason. I haven't forgotten the bottle of wine we shared in my garden right around the time Aiden was sniffing around." She smiled. "I have to be honest. It's kind of gratifying to see the guru of sense be in a bit of a flap over a man. Even better that it's Ethan."

Willow wasn't sure whether to protest the guru bit, or that she was in a flap, or why Laurel was so happy it was Ethan. She wiggled her fingers. "Are you going to torture me all night, or show me what's in your bag?"

Laurel giggled. "Sure. But first . . . you need something to loosen up."

She pulled a small bottle out of her purse, one of those mini bottles of champagne that held maybe two glasses. "You want to pop it or shall I?"

"I'm not starting this date tipsy."

"Puhleeeze." Laurel drew out the word. "A thimbleful of champagne will just smooth your rough edges." Laurel dropped the bag on the futon and took the foil off the bottle. In seconds she'd popped the cork and was headed to the kitchen for a glass.

"Here," she ordered. "Drink this."

Willow did what she was told. Why was she so wound up? Maybe because she'd never eaten at the inn before. Maybe because she knew there would be no Connor and Ronan at home, or a babysitter that needed to be relieved. Nothing would stand in their way tonight, except whatever barriers they put up themselves. And she wasn't sure how sturdy hers were.

The champagne was dry and fizzy and she let the bubbles sit on her tongue. "Okay," she finally said, taking a deep breath. "Show me what you brought over."

"Well," Laurel said, reaching for the zipper, "you're smaller than me, particularly now since my buttons are all feeling tight. I picked out a few pretty things that I had left from when I was working in the office. No power suits—that's not you. But a few cocktail dresses I wore to events that you might like."

She pulled out a few hangers, and Willow perused the selections.

There was a red one that was cute, a shimmery fabric that would ride the hips snugly, had adorable cap sleeves, and a frilly peplum at the waist. It would suit Laurel, but not her. "Cute, but a little too . . ."

"Yeah, I thought you might say that. It's a bit stiff for you. How about this one?"

Next was a tank-style in a rose pink with a lace overdress. Feminine and a bit softer, but still not quite right.

"Your legs would look great in this one, Wil. And the color suits your complexion."

"Maybe. What else?"

The dress on the third hanger made Willow catch her breath. Ivory chiffon draped from tiny straps, creating airy folds around the neckline. The body was shaped to fit the figure but the skirt was a bit flowy, and the best part was the back. It was mostly backless, with a sparkly spiderweb of straps that she guessed would ride from just above her waist to the hollow of her spine.

It was feminine and sexy and had a wow factor Willow couldn't deny.

"I knew that would be the one," Laurel said softly. "Let's go try it on."

"But . . . I can't wear a bra with it."

Laurel laughed. "Sweetie, you are still young and firm and perky. Besides, the dress fits snugly, and the drape at the neck will help. Trust me."

Willow did. Laurel took another small bag out of her purse and handed it over. "You need seriously skimpy skivvies to pull this off."

"You bought me underwear?"

"I'm not sure you can call it underwear without feeling overdressed. But I knew you'd want to wear something . . ."

Willow opened the bag and drew out what she figured looked like a doily swatch with a shoestring attached. "You can't be serious."

"You don't want lines, and you can't have anything that goes up high on your waist with this dress."

"I've never worn anything like this in my life."

"It's bamboo. Sustainable and all that. Of course, not very sustainable if Ethan rips it off you later."

"Laurel!" Oh God. That was so not what she needed to hear right now. "It's not like that."

"Well, shit. That's disappointing."

Willow shook her head. "Why do I call you my best friend again?"

"Just put it on."

Willow shimmied into the tiny thong and then into the dress. She had to admit, the lack of undergarments felt just a little bit naughty. Laurel had been right—the bodice hugged her figure while the draped neckline made the dress look soft and classy. When she looked in the mirror, she did a half turn and gaped at the open back and the shimmering web of crystals that crossed her lower back. "Oh, wow."

"Right? And if you say that about yourself, imagine what's going to happen to Ethan's eyeballs."

Laurel disappeared into Willow's closet and came back out with the delicate sandals Willow had worn to Laurel's wedding. "Put these on. Oh, good. You painted your toenails. Pink is perfect." She got down on her knees and fastened the straps, then stood up again and stepped back. "Nearly ready."

"There's more, fairy godmother? What are you going to do, turn Ethan's SUV into a carriage? Or maybe one of my yoga mats into a flying carpet?"

Laurel grinned. "Drink your champagne while I dig through your jewelry box."

Who was she to argue? So far Laurel had been bang on with her choices. She sat on the edge of the bed and sipped from the glass, trying to remain calm. Moments later Laurel returned, holding a simple strand of pearls in her fingers.

"Oh," Willow said quietly. "Those were my grand-mother's. She left them to me."

"I didn't even know you had a grandmother. You've never said anything about her."

"I only remember seeing her twice. Mom didn't visit much, and she died when I was fifteen. Family never seemed very important to my mom, you know?"

"Well, maybe it can be important to you. You get to decide now."

"You're starting to sound like me."

"I try. You give good advice. Except to yourself. Here, let me hook these. And your hair. Your makeup is fine—understated suits you. But your hair needs to be up, and showcase that gorgeous long neck. French roll? Chignon? No braids today. You need less free spirit, more class."

In the end Ethan arrived as Willow was still putting the finishing touches on a loose roll, anchoring it in place with a few pins with little silk flowers on the ends. She heard Laurel's voice as she welcomed him at the door and then Ethan's answering one, deeper, and she pressed a hand to her belly as nerves began to quiver there.

For a fleeting moment, it felt as if all the years of

work—the body image acceptance, the self-worth, the peace and confidence—all led to this moment. She felt as beautiful as she ever had, and unbelievably sexy. Maybe that was the piece of the puzzle that had been missing. She'd never truly embraced her sexual self.

But rather than examine that whole issue right now, a very hunky firefighter was waiting for her to go to dinner.

She stepped out of her bedroom to the open part of the apartment and watched as Ethan's eyes widened and his lips dropped open.

"Well. I can see my work is done." Laurel reached over and touched Ethan's chin, closing his mouth. "You two have fun, now."

Willow's gaze flitted to her best friend. "Thanks, Laurel."

"Anytime, kitten."

She shut the door behind her.

"Wow," Ethan said, his gaze traveling over her. "You look . . . wow."

"Laurel loaned me the dress." She felt stupid as soon as she said it. Why couldn't she have just said thank you?

"It suits you. You're beautiful."

She felt her cheeks heat, but this time she just offered a bashful, "Thanks." She reached for her purse, which now looked old and frumpy next to such a pretty dress. "You're looking pretty spiffy yourself." She smiled, trying to lighten the atmosphere a little. He was looking at her as if she was dessert, and while she didn't know where things would lead tonight, she was pretty sure they should at least try to have dinner first.

"I clean up once in a while," he replied.

Indeed he did. He hadn't worn a suit—the weather was still quite hot—but he wore tan dress pants, a crisp white shirt that fit perfectly over his broad shoulders, and a precisely knotted tie in blue and beige stripes. When he turned to open her door, her gaze dropped to how the expensive trousers fit his backside and she pressed a hand to her belly again. They'd preened and primped for tonight, hadn't they? In hopes of what?

He opened her door and solicitously shut it again, then crawled in his side and adjusted the air-conditioning before ever pulling out onto the street again. To her immense relief, he started talking about the boys' trip to their grandparents during the drive, and Willow started to find her bearings again. She wondered, though, if she was glowing as much on the outside as she was on the inside—and it had very little to do with the glass of champagne she'd already had.

The inn was situated on rolling grounds with beautiful gardens. The restaurant was known as the finest of its kind in the county, and Willow looked all around her as they were ushered to a table for two that was set back in a corner, next to a window overlooking a marvelous bed of dahlias and asters in full bloom.

"This is really lovely," she commented. "Laurel must have gone crazy with all the gardens. She and Aiden came here earlier in the summer."

"Our family's been here a few times. And I came here one year on . . ."

He halted his sentence.

"You can say it, you know," Willow said softly, and reached out to touch his hand. "You and Lisa came here, didn't you?"

He nodded. "For her thirtieth birthday. It was just before her diagnosis."

"Then it was probably one of the happier memories, huh?" Willow smiled at him. There was no sense pretending that Lisa had never existed. Willow just didn't want to be compared to her.

A waitress came over and took their drink orders. Willow didn't usually indulge in anything other than wine, but there was something on the menu called a Gatsby's Girl that sounded delicious. Wasn't tonight an occasion for fancy drinks? If not, what was?

The drinks arrived and then they ordered appetizers: a berry and greens salad for Willow, while Ethan ordered calamari. Willow sipped at her drink and felt both indulgent and delighted. They chatted and laughed lightly, talking of inconsequential things, while the romance of the setting swirled around them. Her salad arrived, as did his calamari; they exchanged bites and pronounced both delicious. By the time they were finished, their entrees arrived. Willow looked down at the decadent crab cakes and wondered how she could possibly eat it all. Ethan's chicken was savory and rich with vegetables. Soft music played in the background.

Ethan ordered another iced tea for himself and another cocktail for Willow, and she wasn't sure she should. She was already feeling a little lightheaded . . . or was that because of the company she kept? The lobster béchamel on the crab did indeed make it too rich to finish, so she pushed the remainder aside as they lingered over last sips. Neither felt in the mood for dessert, so Ethan paid the bill and they decided to take a walk through the gardens instead.

She watched, fascinated, as Ethan rolled his sleeves

up to the elbow, then loosened his tie, slipped it off, and stuffed it in his pocket. Oh my. The pressed-and-dressed Ethan had been exciting and oh-so-handsome, but she much preferred this look—slightly undone and more relaxed. He reached down for her hand and she took it, looking at their linked fingers, noticing the fine bronze hairs on his arm, and the light freckles on his skin. It wasn't hard to see his Irish roots.

They meandered down dirt paths, through various gardens. There was one with bee balm, verbena, and other florals that attracted butterflies and bees. There was a shaded area with trees and shrubs and hostas, most of which were blooming, their light purple stalks standing firm against the summer breeze. There was a rose garden, a section that was a profusion of larkspur, lilies, phlox, Shasta daisies, and other flowers Willow recognized but couldn't name. "I swear they must have a full-time gardener," she said as they stepped through an arbor tangled with wisteria.

"You belong outdoors," Ethan said, squeezing her fingers. "You change when you're in the sun and fresh air. It energizes you."

"It does." She grinned up at him and then let go of his hand and bent down to slip off her sandals. "Take off your shoes, Ethan. And your socks. Stand with me on the grass."

Ethan's cheeks colored. "What are you doing?"

"I'm showing you what it's like to be grounded. Truly. It's a whole scientific thing."

He laughed. "By standing barefoot."

She nodded. "Yep. Not everyone believes in it, but I always feel better after being in contact with the earth. It has to do with positive and negative electrons and balancing them in the body."

He laughed again.

"Are you laughing at me, Gallagher?"

"Yes, ma'am."

She grinned. "At least you own it. Come on. Take off your shoes. No one will care."

She moved around on the square of lush grass, her toes sinking into the cool softness of it.

He stared at her for a long moment, then began to toe off his dress shoes and bent to take off his socks.

"I feel like an idiot."

"You look awesome." He stepped onto the grass beside her as she continued, "Have you ever thought about how good you feel after walking on the beach? Or if you lie on the ground, looking up at the stars?"

He looked over at her, his eyes intrigued. "I'm still not sure I believe you," he said. "But it does feel nice."

She smiled. "All our technology is supposed to make us feel more connected, but we've lost important connections along the way. With ourselves. With nature. And we're so connected that we're more lost than ever."

"I hate to admit that makes sense, but it kind of does. Like when you see people walking and texting, or sitting together but staring at their phones. They're missing out on so much."

"Right." She took his hand. "Come on. Let's walk. We can wash our feet later."

They stayed off the pathway and walked the edge of the property, their shoes hooked on their fingertips. The further west they got, the more the landscape opened up. The inn's property line bordered a nearby farm, and they stopped under a giant oak and watched a pair of horses graze in a pasture. Willow let out a deep breath. "If I weren't wearing such a pretty dress, I'd sit down right now and just breathe all this in."

"Maybe I can help."

To her surprise, Ethan folded himself into a cross-legged pose beneath the tree, then patted his knees. "Sit here. Your dress'll be safe."

"I'll hurt your legs."

"A little thing like you? Hardly."

"I'm almost five foot eight. I'm hardly a little thing."

"Try me. Sit on my lap, Willow."

Her heart stammered as she put her shoes beside his and then rested a hand on his shoulder, gently easing herself onto his lap. His back was against the tree, and his arms came around her, holding her in place. Because she was sitting higher than he was, his head fit the curve of her neck in a strangely nice way.

"There. One safe dress, and a few minutes to watch the horses and enjoy the evening."

"Sometimes you surprise me," she admitted. "I didn't expect you to be such a good sport."

"I like the outdoors. I like you. This is not a hardship." He tilted his head a bit and smiled at her. "And I like seeing you smile."

"I seem to be doing a lot of that when we're together."

"I'm glad."

"Me, too."

She leaned into his body, watched as the pair of horses plodded through the field, stopping now and again to snip at some grass, their tails flicking as the sun began to lower in the sky. His hand, warm and a little rough, slid along her upper arm, caressing gently, making goose bumps rise on her skin. She let out a breath, inhaled again, closed her eyes. Peace. That was what she felt right now. Peace, and gratitude for this moment, with this man.

His hair tickled along her neck as he turned his head, then she felt the soft press of his lips on the tendon next to her collarbone. Without thinking, she tilted her head a little, allowing him access, inviting him to keep going. He did, the butterfly touch of his lips stirring sensations that were completely new and yet achingly familiar. A sigh escaped her lips as his mouth slid up to the delicate hollow just below her ear.

"You taste good," he murmured. "Kiss me, Willow."

She opened her eyes briefly, found his gaze burning with the blue flame of desire. Her lashes slid closed again as she leaned down and pressed her lips against his.

For all the intensity in his voice and eyes, he didn't rush. The kiss was gentle, but full of erotic little nips and licks that made the muscles between her legs tighten with need. His hand slid over the soft fabric of her dress and pressed against the pebbled nipple, unfettered from any bra. He made a sound of surprise in his throat, and then slid his hand up over her ribs, letting his thumb ride inside the ivory fabric, over the soft side of her breast.

"Ethan," she breathed.

"I think you're right. I think there's something to this grounding thing." He nipped at her bottom lip, stroked the fullness of her breast with his thumb, up and down, up and down. "I am feeling very, very connected right now."

Willow felt more than connected. She felt . . . wanton. She had the terrible, wonderful urge to slide off his lap, unzip his trousers, and straddle him right here against the ancient oak. But she wouldn't. Not now. Even if there weren't Laurel's expensive dress to consider, she didn't want a quick coupling under a tree to be their first time. She wanted something more. They both deserved that.

"Will you take me home?" she asked, more than a little breathless.

"We haven't had dessert."

She moaned against him, wondering what would happen if he knew she wore approximately four square inches of fabric beneath the dress. It wasn't much of a barrier.

"You're killing me here," she whispered, and without thinking, pressed her breast more firmly into his palm.

"You're not wearing a bra."

"There's not room for much under this dress."

His hand paused, and he halted the progress of his lips and looked at her. "I think we should head back to Darling."

"I'll buy you a nightcap."

Willow disentangled her body from his and stood, then slipped on her sandals as her body hummed, both from his touch and from the inevitability of what was to come. Tonight had been all about deliberate seduction. The setting, the meal, the romantic walk in the garden . . . all just window dressing for a mating dance that had been coming for a while now.

Ethan put on his socks and shoes, handed Willow her purse, and took her hand. The walk back to the parking lot went much faster than the walk out, without any stopping at the gardens to see any flowers or plants.

It seemed no time at all and they were ensconced in his car and heading back to Darling and the new reality of their relationship. Though neither had explicitly voiced it, tonight things were going to change. Go to the next level. Willow know she should be nervous, and she was, but not in a scared way. She'd done a lot of thinking and meditating lately, and it didn't make sense for her to pretend like her sexual self no longer existed. And if she were going to choose a lover, she couldn't do better than Ethan. She'd never met a guy with more integrity or honor.

By tacit agreement they went to her place; it was probably still too soon to go to his. They climbed the stairs to her apartment; the café was still open downstairs, but wouldn't be for long. Emily would close up and Hannah's office was already vacated. The temporary food bank was also empty this time of night. Within the next ten minutes, there wouldn't be another soul in the building. The whole, big, quiet building.

She put the key in the lock, marveling that her hand wasn't shaking. Ethan stood close behind her, the warmth of his body radiating against the naked skin of her back. Once they were inside, she shut the door, slipped off her shoes, and offered him a drink. "Wine? I don't have much else."

"Wine is fine."

Normally she would have cracked a joke about rhyming, but not tonight. Instead she went through to the kitchen and got a bottle of merlot, uncorked it, and got down two glasses. When she moved to pour, he was standing by the counter.

She handed him the glass. "Cheers," she said weakly, touching her rim to his.

"Cheers," he echoed.

They drank, deeply. It seemed nothing would be done in moderation tonight, and it was a heady thought. She had no need of liquid courage, but couldn't deny the alcohol was fueling her hunger for him substantially.

While he drank again, she went to the bathroom, retrieved a small basin, and filled it with warm water.

"What's that for?" he asked. He finished the wine in his glass and reached for the bottle, pouring himself another few ounces.

"Didn't I tell you I'd wash your feet?" She smiled at him. "Come. Sit on the futon."

"You don't have to . . ."

"Trust me, Ethan. Sit on the futon."

His gaze burned into hers, then he topped off her glass, too, and moved to the living area where he sat on the futon. She put down the basin and knelt before him, spreading a towel over her knees to protect her dress. Before she started, she reached over to the side table and picked up her glass of wine, taking a long drink, savoring the rich flavor. Then she reached for Ethan's socks, rolling them slowly over his ankles and off his feet. She dropped the washcloth into the water, squeezed out the warm water, and cupped his heel in her hand.

At the last moment she looked up and saw his eyes darken with what she knew was arousal and awareness. Then she ran the washcloth over his foot, along his arch, over the ridge just below his toes.

He sighed and leaned his head back, eyes closed. "God, that feels good," he murmured.

She slid the cloth over his heel again, then along his toes. He jerked his foot a bit, laughing lightly. So he had ticklish feet. She smiled to herself, filing the information away for later. Right now she put the washcloth back in the basin and ran her fingers over his foot, rubbing her thumb into the center of his foot, right where the arch and ball met.

"Mmmm," he moaned, and the sound vibrated

through Willow, heightening her own arousal. She moved to the other foot, washing it, massaging the pressure points she knew would bring him pleasure and relaxation, until he was relaxed and putty in her hands.

"My turn," he said. "Switch places with me."

She did as he asked because she was dying for him to touch her again. He knelt before her, but put the towel on the floor beside him as he cradled her foot in his big hands. The cloth slid over her skin, warm and wet, and she bit down on her lip. The urge to close her eyes was strong, but she made herself watch him, the way he focused on her feet, the way his fingers moved over the sensitive skin of her arch. He cupped her heel in his palm, but dropped the cloth into the basin and, with his free hand, used his thumb to stroke the side of her ankle, right between the bone and her heel.

Did he actually know about that pressure point, or was he just lucky? Willow caught her breath, then held it as his hand trailed past her ankle bone up her calf.

Oh God. Oh God Oh God Oh God.

"Your skin is so soft," he murmured, tracing his fingertips along the inside of her knee. The scrap of underwear Laurel had given her was soaked now, and Willow gave up all pretense of composure and leaned her head back against the futon cushion. There was a scraping sound—Ethan moved the basin and towel aside—and then his fingers crept up the inside of her thigh.

"Wil," he said roughly, and she instinctively parted her knees a little more.

Heat rushed to each spot his fingers touched, and when he encountered her tiny thong, he made a sound of approval deep in his throat. He cupped her and her whole world was centered in the palm of his hand as she pressed into his touch.

"This is all you're wearing under that dress?" he asked.

She nodded, unable to speak.

"Good thing I didn't know that under the oak tree. We might never have made it back here. Damn, Willow. I want you so much."

Her heart sang with the admission. "Me, too," she whispered, opening her eyes. "I've been dying all night, waiting."

"Waiting for what?"

"Waiting for you to touch me. To kiss me. To be inside me."

His nostrils flared at that last part, and she knew she'd just tossed gasoline on an already burning fire. It had been so long since she'd had sex . . . longer still since she'd had great sex. She was a physical woman who'd denied herself that particular pleasure for too long. And for what? She suspected she knew the answer, but there would be time for that later. Not now. Now was about Ethan and her and slaking this crazy need that was consuming them both.

She got up from the futon and went to the wall of windows, drawing the bamboo blinds on each large pane. Light from the spectacular sunset filtered through the meshy fabric, giving them privacy but not darkness. No, not darkness. Tonight she would see him, and he would see her.

She went back to him and slipped her shoulders out of the dress, then let it fall to the floor. Nerves bubbled around in her stomach; she was practically naked before him, but they both knew where this was headed. Her bashfulness was balanced by a new sort of pride.

She knew she was strong, limber, slightly curved in the right places. Her breasts were smallish but perky, and right now her nipples were so hard they were nearly painful. Mere strings decorated her hips, leaving her bottom essentially bare. She couldn't hide a thing from him like this.

Ethan stood, pulled his shirttails out of his pants, and undid the buttons. She got a glimpse of his firm chest and the smattering of dark hair, then watched as he undid his belt and the button of his trousers. "You want it off?" he asked, a bit of grit in his voice that she now understood to be desire, need, arousal.

"I want it off. I want to touch you," she admitted.

"Then touch me, Willow."

Oh *God*.

She went to him and parted the sides of his shirt, then pushed it off his shoulders, letting it drop in a heap on the floor. Before she could put a thought together, she pressed her lips to his chest, sliding her tongue over to his tiny nipple while her hand slid over his still-clad bottom. His hand, meanwhile, cupped her breast fully, his thumb riding over the tip, and then slipped down over her hip to her center, where he deftly moved the strip of fabric aside and slid his finger inside her.

"Oh," she moaned, her knees weakening.

"Before we go any further, I need to know you're okay with what's going to happen."

His words brought her back to earth briefly. "What's going to happen?"

"I'm going to take you into your bedroom. I'm going to kiss every square inch of your body. And when you can hardly take anymore, I'm going to be inside you. Fair warning."

Holy Buddha. This new, take-charge side of Ethan was intoxicating. The way his fingers were moving right now would have her agreeing to just about anything. Never in her life had she wanted someone this badly. He was blowing up every one of her senses, and they'd hardly even begun. "I'm okay. More than okay. My warning is, I give as good as I get."

"Then we're in for a hell of a night."

As much as she hated to pull away, she did, but only so she could take his hand and lead him to the bedroom. He was holding her hand, trailing a step behind her, when he gave her fingers a tug. "Willow?"

"Hmm?" She half turned, but didn't expect the serious tenderness that was written on his face. It tugged at her heart, gave her pause for a moment. "What is it, Ethan?"

"You are so damned beautiful. I thought you should know that."

Something inside her wept and sang at the same time. She smiled at him in return, then led him onward to her bedroom and the soft mattress that would cradle them for the next hour. . . . or more.

And as he took her in his arms and made her his, the very last chain holding her back fell away as if it had never existed.

CHAPTER 15

One long, languorous stretch and Willow felt the welcome soreness that had been absent from her body for so long.

She was naked beneath the cotton sheet, and so was Ethan. She relaxed her muscles and shifted gently to her side, looking over at his still-sleeping form. The sun was barely up, and the pale light touched his face, now rusty with a night's stubble. She studied the freckles beneath his tan, examined how his eyelashes were a shade darker than his hair, noticed, for the first time, a tiny scar on his forehead.

Ethan had done what he promised. He'd loved her thoroughly, and more than once. The first time had been fragile and tender and overwhelming; an exploration of each other and their wants and likes. She scissored her legs beneath the sheet, remembering how it had felt when he'd slid inside her. It had been unbelievably sexy, but something more, too. It had been frighteningly right. There'd been a moment when he'd looked into her eyes and she'd felt this crazy connection that was exponentially greater than any she'd ever felt before.

Sexually, they were utterly compatible. If there'd been any doubt, the second and third time would have sealed that deal.

As he slept on, she realized what she was feeling was awe. At him. At them. At the kind of man he was—hard worker, good father, amazing lover. Perhaps a little broody at times, but Willow understood a lot of that now.

She rested her head on her elbow. Last night she'd realized something unbelievable. In that moment, just before they'd hit the bedroom, she'd finally understood why she'd never felt free to explore her sexuality. Tears stung her eyes and she blinked them away, wondering how, in all her years of self-examination and acceptance, she hadn't really got to the truth. It all went back to that junior year of high school, when she'd missed her period and had found out she was pregnant. She'd been so scared to tell her mother, but had thought maybe this time they'd work through something together. Instead she'd been forced to get rid of it. There had been no question of keeping the baby. And Willow had equated that guilt with her sexuality and had never quite felt worthy of sex being an enjoyable part of her life. She didn't deserve it.

Until last night. Last night it hadn't mattered anymore.

She shifted her weight, but the slight movement disturbed Ethan. His eyes opened and he lifted a hand, wiping away the grit in the corners.

"I didn't mean to wake you."

He smiled a little. "I'm not used to sleeping with

someone else in the bed. I don't mind the early wake-up."

"I think it's after five. Probably closer to six. I have to be downstairs at six-thirty. I'm sorry about that."

"Well, I won't say I'm not disappointed," he said, reaching under the sheet to curl his hand over her hip. He pulled her closer to him, and she felt just how awake he was. "But I'm a big boy. I can handle it."

"You certainly are," she teased, and did a little reaching of her own.

"Be careful. You might not make it to work on time."

"I have an understanding boss." She stretched again, then lifted her arm over her head, inviting him to partake of her breasts. He took the hint and she sighed with pleasure; and then sighs filled the room for another ten minutes.

"Now that's a good morning." Ethan flopped over onto his back and put his arm over his head on the pillow.

"You are a horrible distraction."

"Thank you."

She looked over at him, her heart dangerously entangled. "So, no regrets?"

He turned his head to look at her. "About last night? Are you kidding?"

"I don't usually . . ."

"Hell, I know that. Me, either."

"And you didn't like me at first . . ."

"You didn't like me, either. You told me I was in need of serenity."

"I'm sorry about that."

"Don't be. You were right. More than that, I had to

start living again. I got so caught up with resenting what I'd lost, I forgot to look at what was right in front of me."

"Yeah, you're human." She kept the sheet tucked beneath her armpits and smiled at him. "So we're good?"

"Of course."

They were quiet for a moment and then Ethan spoke again. "I don't want you to feel like there's any pressure, Willow. Despite what happened last night, we can still take it slow. You know, emotionally."

Message received: physical intimacy okay, falling in love on the back burner. It was precisely what she wanted. One complication at a time. Living in the present. So why did his statement leave her feeling strangely empty?

"It would be foolish to rush into anything serious," she agreed, but her smile was a little more forced. "You've got the boys to consider. We both have baggage to work through."

"Right. But damn . . ." he reached out and ran his fingers up her arm. "I want to see you again. Soon."

She laughed. "Well, there's always yoga tonight. Since I missed this morning's session."

He winked. "I did notice you are rather bendy."

She raised an eyebrow. "This is a new side of you. You're a tease."

"Only when I'm happy."

They lay there another few minutes, until Willow knew she couldn't put it off any longer. "I've got to get moving or Emily will quit. She's already been putting in extra hours."

"You should make her your manager."

For the first year and a half, the café had been Willow's entire life. Sure, she'd made time for Laurel and

Hannah now and then, but she'd been putting in mad hours and had yet to take any sort of holiday. Emily was more than capable. The way she'd stepped in during the organizing of the food bank was proof enough of that.

"I've considered changing her role, to be honest, but she's not managing now, so I've got to hop in the shower and get going." She slid out of the bed, slightly self-conscious that she was naked. "Take your time, though. Go back to sleep, use the shower, help yourself to breakfast. Whatever you want."

He laughed. "I think our roles are usually reversed."

She looked over her shoulder and grinned. "Yeah, but I'm not your usual girl."

"You got that right," he said, and she disappeared into the bathroom.

Ethan helped himself to the shower, enjoying the fresh scent of Willow's soap and shampoo that clung to the damp walls. He dressed in his clothes from last night, assessing the wrinkles in his pants and shirt. His tie was still crammed into his pants pocket. He needed to go home and change and then he was going to head to his mom and dad's to give his father a hand taking down a tree in the backyard. Aiden had the day off as well, and they'd planned it so they could both be there to cut it down safely and then clean up the mess. Better to do it now, than have it fall in the winter during an ice storm or something.

He was whistling a tuneless ditty when he descended the back stairs and headed for his SUV. At least he hadn't parked on the street. It was early enough no one else was around. The food bank wouldn't open for another few hours. The scent of fresh baking filled the air, presumably from the café, and his stomach growled. Still, he wouldn't embarrass Willow by going in for breakfast, doing the walk of shame.

"Oh my shit. You guys finally did it."

He looked up sharply to find Hannah staring at him from the corner of the building.

"Christ, Hannah." He ran his hand over his still-wet hair.

"It's about time you both got laid."

He scowled. "You do not want to go there. It's been a hell of a long time for you, too."

She shrugged, though two dots of color rose on her cheeks. "You don't know everything."

He raised an eyebrow. "What are you even doing here so early?"

She pointed at a garbage can at her feet. "My cleaning service of one is on summer holidays this week. I'm on janitor duty."

"Just my luck," he muttered.

"So, you and Willow. You're a thing?"

"Leave it alone, Han. It's nobody's business but ours."

"Sure. Just because you're my big brother and she's my friend, means I shouldn't care about either of you at all."

He stepped forward and looked his sister dead in the eye. "If you really mean that, you'll leave this alone and let us handle it ourselves. Willow's not the kind to want her personal life to be grist for the gossip mill, got it?"

Hannah tsked. "My, my. So protective."

"I'm not in the mood for your teasing, Hannah." Truthfully, now that Willow was gone, he was worried about what he'd said to her about taking it slow emotionally. He didn't want her to think he was only hanging around for sex, but he also didn't want to rush into anything where hearts were involved. "You don't need to take it upon yourself to inform the family."

Hannah's face softened. "Big brother," she said quietly, coming forward. "Willow is one in a million. I know she's had it rough, though she'd never really said why. But she's beautiful, inside and out. Maybe a little freaky with all her zen stuff, but I love her."

He laughed a little. Hannah liked her ironman training, but he couldn't imagine her sitting still through any sort of meditation or have the time for a yoga practice.

"I think you need someone like her," Hannah continued. "You've looked happier lately, like you're not carrying the weight of the world on your shoulders. If she's the cause of that, I'm glad."

He didn't know what to say. He was so used to the family either giving him crap or tiptoeing around him that her honesty was refreshing.

"I've surprised you."

"I shouldn't be, I suppose." He put his hand in his pocket, felt his tie. "Pop talked to me a while back, too. I haven't been ready to move on, Han. I still need to take it in steps."

Sympathy filled her eyes. "Of course you do. I'm just saying I'm glad that you've started taking those steps."

"I'm going home to change and eat and then I'm heading to Mom and Dad's with Aiden."

"The boys are still in Montpelier?"

"Until the holiday Monday. I have to go pick them up that morning."

She nodded, then turned with her trash can and took

it to the dumpster. "You're a good dad, Ethan. You deserve some happiness for yourself. And the boys love her. At least you don't have to worry about that."

She sent him a wink and headed back to her office, but Ethan stood there for a minute, thinking about what she'd just said. It was true; the boys loved Willow. She was good to them, and good for them, with her smiles and gentleness. She'd be a fabulous mother . . .

But what if the boys got too attached and things didn't work out? How could they deal with losing another person they cared about? And what about him? He was doing a good job of living in the now, but behind the bubble of happiness was a heavy weight, reminding him of what it felt like to lose the person you loved. Did he want to risk going through that again? Could they just keep it casual for now?

As he started his car, he frowned. "Casual" wasn't how he'd describe last night. Being with Willow, making love to her . . . it had blown his mind. Not just physically, but the way they'd been in tune with each other. The moment when their eyes had met, her hair spread out on the pillow and her delicate fingers digging into his shoulders, something had clicked, like a puzzle piece you didn't expect to fit but did.

It might already be too late for emotional caution.

CHAPTER 16

Willow sat in The Purple Pig office, doing up the week's order for baking supplies. She really should have done it last night, but with her date and all . . . She paused, her pencil hovering over the order form. She loved the café. She doubted she would ever put in less than a forty-hour week. But she'd been sneaking far more hours here and there for personal time, and she had two choices. She either had to stop doing that, or she had to reassess the café's manpower requirements.

The idea of making Emily a managing partner made a lot of sense. It would mean training someone new as regular staff; maybe two people. Steven would be starting school again in September, and even though he commuted, his availability would take a serious hit.

And to hire new staff, she needed to look at profitability and what she could possibly sustain. The landlord had given her three free months for the additional square footage for the food bank, but she had nine more months of the contract that she was on the hook for. She had to decide what she was going to do with that space.

Maybe she should seriously look at expansion. Fall was busy, too, and then there was a brief slowdown before ski season picked up again.

But first, she had to talk to Emily. The most important thing was to make sure the current arrangement was as strong as possible.

After the lunch rush, she grabbed a cup of tea and then asked Em to join her in the office. She didn't beat around the bush. "Emily, you've been carrying extra weight around here all summer, and I think it's time you had a proper title. Would you be interested in becoming the café manager, with the possibility of leading into partnership? I'd still be here, but I'd delegate more of the responsibilities to you. Things like weekly scheduling, deposits, that kind of stuff. I can't afford to give you a huge raise, but there'll be something. I trust you to look after The Pig."

Emily's eyes lit. "I'd love that! I haven't minded the extra hours, or the responsibility, but having something a little more formalized would be great."

"I've noticed you're very organized, so of course you'd like to have things official and laid out in writing. I probably should have done it before now. So that's a yes?"

"Yes. It does mean we're going to need some new staff, though. Steven's cutting his hours soon and while we've still got Mary and Tina, I think we need another solid day person. At least one. We might be able to make do with a few part-time high school students."

"I agree." They took a few minutes to go over staffing issues and then Willow sat back with a satisfied sigh.

Emily grinned at her. "You can tell I've been thinking about this a lot."

Willow nodded. "I'll draft up a want ad and post it in the weekly paper, plus the Chamber website. Oaklee is in charge of that, I think. And Em—I want you to sit in on the interviews."

"If that's what you want, of course." Emily smiled. "Thanks, Willow.

"Thank you, Em."

Emily sipped at the coffee she'd brought in with her. "So does this mean you're going to have a more active social life? Rumor has it you've been out with Ethan Gallagher."

Willow knew she was blushing; she could feel the heat in her face. "We've gone out a few times, but that's all. I just think it's time I paced myself a little better. Plus, if we decide to grow or do something with the space next door, I need to delegate more."

"Nice dodge, but that's okay. I know you're a private person." Emily grinned at her. "Just so you know, though, Ethan Gallagher is one hot DILF."

"Oh my—" Willow choked on a laugh, "DILF?"

"Dad I'd like to . . . you know."

"I know! I know! Just . . . God. I can't even right now." And she burst out laughing. What else could she do? It wasn't as if she disagreed.

They ended the meeting and Willow spent an hour in the kitchen, doing prep for lunchtime sandwiches and snacks. Traffic was busy, particularly as the weather was gorgeous and people were out enjoying the last of the summer vacation days with their families.

Once the rush was over, she organized the kitchen, baked enough muffins and cookies to replenish the front display, did supper prep, and then grabbed a sandwich for herself and disappeared into the office to draft a want ad and finish the weekly order. When it was sent, she checked her watch. Seven. Where had the day gone? She'd hardly had time to think about Ethan and try to make sense of what had happened last night. Or where they went from here.

At eight she turned over the CLOSED sign and locked the door, then everyone chipped in to make sure the floors were mopped, tables wiped, napkins and sugar dispensers filled, and the café readied for the next day. Willow rang off the cash and ran the reports, then locked everything in the safe for the next deposit.

Eight thirty. She sighed, said good night to the staff and headed upstairs. Her stomach felt uneasy and a strange sort of tension settled between her shoulder blades. She hadn't thought of Ethan much today, but now that the café was closed and she was all alone, she couldn't help but wonder what he'd been thinking since this morning.

She needed some tea and deep breathing and a slow, calming practice to quiet her mind.

She brewed a cup of jasmine tea, letting the flowery scent envelop her. She changed into her favorite yoga leggings—pale pink ones—and a top in light blue. The airy colors made her feel lighter, and once her tea was gone she sat on her mat, folded her legs, closed her eyes, and began to center herself with a So Hum meditation.

Sooooo . . . Deep inhale, filling her stomach, diaphragm, lungs.

Hummmm . . . A long, slow exhale, emptying fully, relaxing her shoulders, envisioning the tension leaving through her toes and fingers. Over and over, with nothing but the sound of her breath, the connection with her body and spirit. *So hum . . . I am . . .* and the quiet peace and strength that came from the simple mantra.

She opened her eyes slowly. Then she stood, anchored her feet in the center of her mat, took a long inhale, and stretched upward into a simple Standing Mountain pose.

A knock sounded at the door.

She exhaled and lowered her arms, while her heart abandoned its early calm and peace and started up a rapid tattoo of anticipation. Was it Ethan? She had said that tonight was yoga night . . . but she'd never really thought he'd show up so soon.

She padded over to the door, her bare feet soundless on the hardwood. When she opened it, there he stood, dressed in khaki cargo shorts and a white T-shirt with some sort of logo on the front in green. His clean, slightly spicy scent enveloped her—he'd just showered. In one hand he held a small bouquet of flowers.

"Ethan," she said breathlessly. So much for playing it cool, she realized. That breathy sound communicated exactly how she was feeling right now, seeing him again.

"For you. I didn't think you were the hothouse type. Laurel let me raid the garden."

"They're lovely. Thank you, Ethan. Come on in."

He stepped inside while she took the flowers to the kitchen and found a pretty blue bottle to put them in. There was one stalk of purple-blue delphinium, then several daisies, black-eyed Susans, colorful asters, and a few deep pink coneflowers. Nothing exotic, but she loved them because Ethan understood she preferred a simple, colorful bouquet over something more extravagant and showy.

She took them to the living area and set them on the

end table by the futon. "These are so pretty, Ethan, thank you."

He'd taken off his sandals and left them by the door. When she turned to speak to him, she couldn't help but look down at his feet. There was something personal about bare feet. She wasn't sure if it was humbling, or if it was a lack of artifice, but it was hard for a person to be something they weren't when they were barefoot.

And she was sure if she tried to articulate that, Ethan would look at her like she had nine heads.

"You're welcome."

She faced him, her throat tight with nerves. "You came back."

"You didn't think I would?"

"I didn't know." Heat crept into her cheeks. "I didn't want to take anything for granted. I wondered if you'd freak out, once what happened sank in."

His eyes searched hers. "Did you freak out, Willow? Should I not have come?"

The lump got bigger, and she shook her head. "I'm glad you did. I . . . oh, damn." She took three big steps and wrapped her arms around his broad shoulders, lifted her face to his and kissed him.

He kissed her back, openly, fully. His arms wrapped around her and pulled her closer to his body. "Oh, thank God," he muttered harshly, as they took much-needed breaths. "I was afraid you'd want to back off. And all I could think about all day was coming back here. Seeing you again."

Things were happening so fast. Willow's body was clamoring for one thing while her head—and her heart—cautioned her against moving too quickly. She gasped as he dragged his teeth along the tendon of her neck, but then pushed out of his arms just a bit. She needed space to think.

"We need to slow down," she said, her breath coming quickly. "You just got in the door, for heaven's sake."

His chest rose and fell with labored breaths. "It's a bit scary, isn't it? How . . . explosive this is?"

She nodded. "I feel like a damned horny teenager." And that was exactly who she couldn't afford to be. She stepped away and tried to clear her head. "Can I get you something to drink? Lemonade? Tea?"

"Lemonade would be great. It's a bit hot for tea."

She went to the kitchen and took out the bottle of lemon juice, then the organic sugar and a small pitcher to mix it in. He came into the kitchen; she could sense him behind her even though he wasn't crowding her space.

"You don't have to make it from scratch," he said. "I would have been fine with water."

She turned to face him and smiled, thankful to have something to do because her hands were itching to touch him again. "I make it all the time. Seriously, it only takes a minute. Besides, it's not like I'm squeezing the lemons or anything."

And if her hand shook as she stirred, she pretended not to notice. He didn't need to know how nervous she was.

The drink was slightly sweet, with a bit of tart that stung the tastebuds at the back of her tongue. The only place to really sit was on the futon or in the hanging chair. The chair wasn't built for two adults, so that left either the futon or the floor. Willow chose the floor, sitting on her bottom with her elbows resting lightly on her knees.

"You don't want to sit up here?" Ethan leaned back on the futon.

She smiled up at him. "Is it weird to say I'm more comfortable here? Besides, now I get to look at you."

"Good point." He took a drink of lemonade. "I interrupted your yoga, didn't I?"

"Not really."

"You've got the gear on. You look cute, by the way. I like the leggings. They make your ass look good."

Heat rushed to her face.

"Your hair, too. I like the braid. It's weird."

Willow wasn't used to all the compliments. "It's a Dutch braid. You do it from under rather than over."

"I don't understand any of that, but okay."

She laughed. Drank. Licked her lips.

He crossed his legs, balancing his right ankle on his left knee. "So how was your day?" he asked.

It should have been a bit awkward. There was subtext, after all. *How was your day* was also *how was your day after last night* and *did anyone say anything to you* or even *did you tell anyone what happened*. But now that the initial welcome was over, it wasn't awkward at all. That was the thing with Ethan. It felt so comfortable, even when they didn't see eye to eye. She realized that since they'd "met" at Hannah's birthday dinner, they had always been honest. Tactful, maybe, but honest just the same. Good and bad.

And honesty was only a step away from trust. It frightened her but also excited her that she might actually be ready to trust someone.

"I took your advice," she admitted, finishing her glass of lemonade. Ethan leaned over with the pitcher and topped her glass. "I asked Emily about managing the café and she said yes. We talked about staffing and

I did up a want ad that I'm going to post in the paper and through the town website. I'm going to need more staff, especially now that school's going in soon and I'm losing one of my full-timers."

"Good for you."

"I like having me time, I discovered. And you know, someday I might want to take a vacation. If I do, I need to leave the café in someone's hands."

"I know what you mean. As much as I've hated being off work, in some ways it's been nice. I've been able to spend more time with the boys over the summer. Connor's starting school after Labor Day and Ronan'll be back in pre-school. It changes."

"You go back soon?" A little bit of worry slid through her veins. Sure, he'd only broken his arm this time, but he did have a potentially dangerous job.

"Once the boys are back in, I'm back on the roster. Right now I'm working on strengthening my arm and getting some muscle and flexibility back."

Willow lifted an eyebrow. "Yoga can help with that. Just sayin'."

He grinned. "So show me," he said easily. "Show me some yoga."

She laughed. "That's not exactly how it works, you know. It's not just a 'do this' and then 'bend like this' thing. It's a philosophy. A way of life. There are physical and spiritual parts that complement each other." She met his gaze. "Honestly, one of the things I miss most about where I used to live is that there's no real studio in Darling. The rec center has someone teach a couple of classes each week, but it's not the same."

"Spiritual, huh?"

She smiled softly. "I know. You think it's hippy and weird. All I can say is, yoga taught me to accept myself and to stop beating myself up over not being perfect. I started to look for happiness within me instead of being desperate for someone else's approval. It saved me, Ethan."

"And I'm glad. Not sure it's my kind of thing, but I'm glad."

She laughed. "I could make you a believer."

"Oh, I don't think so."

"Is that a challenge?" she said lightly with a smile. Lord, she loved bantering with him. It lit her up like very little had in a long, long time.

"I'll let you try, but on one condition."

"Which is?"

"You show me how bendy you really are. What's the hardest move you've got?"

There were several, some that looked harder than they were, others that looked simple but were deceptively difficult. But she knew what he was getting at. Still, she frowned a bit.

"You know this isn't what yoga's about, right? It's not about being bendy or better than anyone else. That's the exact opposite of the heart of it."

"So you won't show me?"

She pondered. "I'll show you, if you agree to let me lead you through a mini practice."

"Deal. But I might need more lemonade to loosen me up. I'm used to pumping weights and going for a run. I'm not sure I'm the meditative type."

She couldn't help it; she laughed again. It was the mischievous look in his eyes and the slight quirk to his lips like he was trying not to smile but not quite succeeding. "Okay. But I'm only going to show you a couple of poses. Then I'll take you through a few moves. Break you in gently."

He got up from the futon, grabbed the nearly-empty pitcher, and poured them each a smidgen more. "Okay. Bottoms up."

He held out the glass in a toast. She clinked her rim against his, smiled, and said, "To Downward Facing Dog."

"What?"

"You'll see," she answered, and they both drank.

CHAPTER 17

Ethan wasn't sure what he'd gotten himself into, but if it meant seeing Willow bend over in those skin-tight leggings, he'd pay the price.

She had a way of looking at him, sort of starry-eyed, that did flattering things to his ego. Plus, she looked adorable in her leggings and top. Like cotton candy that melted on the tongue.

"Okay," she said, putting down her glass. "I'll show you one. It's called Dragonfly, or Maksikanagasana."

"Maksi . . . what?"

She laughed. "It's Sanskrit. Just call it Dragonfly. First I need to warm up. I can't do it cold."

He watched as she went through deep breaths and motions, bending forward at the hips, placing her hands flat on the floor. His mouth went dry. Then she stepped back into something that made her into an inverted *V*, holding it for several breaths, and he imagined moving behind her and grasping her hips. Which, he knew, would be totally inappropriate. She took this stuff seriously. It wasn't her fault that he couldn't watch her without getting turned on.

A few more moves, one where she balanced her weight on her arms, her knees on her elbows, and he had to keep his mouth from dropping open. She did it all with such precision and grace, but he knew it took incredible focus and strength.

"Okay." She unfolded herself and stood tall, then placed her right foot along the side of her leg. "Dragonfly opens the hips, but also takes a lot of core and upper body strength. Ready?"

He watched, awed, as she bended and twisted like a pretzel, and balanced only on her hands as one foot rested on the side of her arm and the other was off the floor, perpendicular to her torso. Was it sensible that her strength and physicality turned him on? They did nothing to detract from her femininity; they enhanced it. What sort of muscles did she have to have to do something like that?

"Holy shit."

She tilted her head up slightly and smiled at him. "It took me a long time to be able to get to this pose."

She took another deep breath, then unfolded herself back onto the mat. "You want to try something? We'll start small."

"I guess."

"Come here." She got to her feet and held out her hand. He put down his glass and stood, feeling a bit apprehensive. He'd never been very flexible.

"Okay. So the first thing you need to do is breathe."

"I am breathing."

She chuckled. "No, full breaths. Nice and slow, in

and out through your nose. Actually, let's sit down first. I'll get you a mat."

She unrolled a pink mat and he raised an eyebrow at her. She only smiled. "Okay, so sit in a comfortable position." He dropped onto the mat and crossed his legs. "Keep your spine long and tall. Close your eyes."

"Really?"

"It's fine, I promise. I'll close mine, too. But I'll know if you're cheating."

He chuckled, but closed his eyes.

"Inhale through your nose. Go slowly. Fill your abdomen, then your diaphragm, and finally, fill your lungs." He did as she said, and heard her do the same. "Then exhale through your nose, slowly, with control, letting out all the air from your lungs, your diaphragm, right down to your stomach."

"Do that four more times. Clear your mind. Relax your body. Shut out all the noise from your day, and just be in the moment, listening to the sound of your breath. In, out, through your nose."

Once, he opened his eyes. Hers were closed as she sat across from him. "Close your eyes," she said in the same calm tone. "Focus on your breath."

How had she known he'd opened his eyes? He let the question settle, then worked on the breathing. Huh. His shoulders did feel more relaxed. He kept breathing, losing count of how many breaths, but kept going, his body melting a bit each time.

"Good," she said quietly. "Now open your eyes. How do you feel?"

"Relaxed," he admitted.

"We're usually so busy going from place to place that we forget to just stop and breathe and be in the moment. I'm going to show you a few basic postures first, but I'm also going to show you a few exercises to help with the range of motion in your wrist. Ready? Stand up for me."

Lord, but she was graceful. He stood and listened while she dictated his breaths and he stretched tall into Standing Mountain. She demonstrated something called Half Moon, where she stood flat on her feet, jutted out one hip, and arced to the side. When he arched into the pose, which was harder than it looked, she stepped forward and placed a gentle hand on his hip, shifting his alignment slightly. He felt the shift in the stretch immediately.

"Good," she said, leading him through to the same stretch on the other side. "Now bring your hands down to your heart, like this."

He felt like a fool, but not as much as he thought he would. Not with her doing the same motion.

"We'll do one more before I get you to stretch out your wrists. Spread your legs on the mat, wide but not too wide. Your weight should be balanced across your whole foot."

He did as she commanded.

"Now take a big inhale, and open your arms out to your side. This is called the Five-Pointed Star. Let out your breath and relax into the pose."

Her voice kept on, soft and sure. "This is one of my favorite poses. I feel rooted and strong through my feet, but my chest and arms are open. My heart is open, too." She met his gaze, her eyes soft and a slight smile on her lips. "I knew I was on my way to recovery when I did this in class one day, and I shifted my palms so that they faced neither up nor down, but out. I felt like I wanted to hug the whole world. And I started to heal."

His throat tightened. She said it so calmly, so easily, but it was a very personal admission.

"I want to hug you right now," he admitted.

"Then do it."

He broke the pose and took two steps, off his own mat and onto hers. He folded her into his arms and she placed her palms on his shoulder blades. But best of all was the way she inhaled and then melted into his embrace. Like two trees twisting together.

Man, he was starting to get as philosophical as she was.

Maybe that wasn't such a bad thing.

"Thank you," she said against the soft cotton of his shirt. "For being you. For being you with me."

It shouldn't have made sense but it did. When he was with Willow, he didn't have to be someone's son or father or coworker or brother. He could just be Ethan. It was such a relief.

"I should be thanking you. Being with you the last month has let me start to heal. I was so worried about keeping up appearances for everyone else that I couldn't just be myself. You gave that back to me, Willow. For the first time in over two years, I feel happiness. Not just happy moments, but happiness."

As he said it, an unexpected warmth filled his chest.

She leaned back and looked into his face. "Me, too, Ethan. I thought I was happy, and I was, but I was still holding myself back from caring about someone. And now here you are. I know we're going to take it slow, but I want you to know that I appreciate you. I love being with you."

"I love kissing you," he whispered, and he dropped his gaze to her lips. But he didn't kiss her. The words were doing the wooing right now, and he wasn't in any rush.

"I love it when you kiss me," she acknowledged. "Both strong and gentle. Tender and tough. When you touched me last night, I felt like I was treasured, but I also felt desired." Her gaze burned into him. "You're a great lover, Ethan."

Christ. Her hands were sliding over his shoulders now, feather-light touches down his triceps, back up to his shoulders and along the hairline on his neck. The blinds were open tonight, and the muted glow of the fading sunset filtered into the room.

She didn't belong here, inside, with hard floors and walls and the confines of furniture. It was too manufactured an environment for a warrior woman. That's what she was, he realized. A warrior. A beautiful, big-hearted warrior that made his heart swell with pride that she was a part of his life.

He was falling for her, fast and hard. And he was unable to stop it. It wasn't just about sex . . . though he would be honest enough with himself to admit that he wanted her so much right now that he ached.

"If I could, I'd make love to you on a soft bed of grass, with the wind blanketing your skin and the moon above us. That's where you belong. Or by a river, where the water's cool and . . .

"Let's do it," she replied. Her cheeks were flushed and her breath came quicker than before. "I know where. Let's do it, Ethan. Let's go make love by the river. Let's be free."

He had to be out of his mind.

"I'll drive. You navigate."

* * *

Once upon a time, Willow's mother had said, "Sex changes everything." She'd meant it as a caution, when Willow had come home past curfew on the night she'd gotten pregnant. Not that her mom knew what had happened, but when a teenage girl starts breaking curfew and going out with high school jocks, cautions come with the territory.

Willow's fingers trembled as she folded them in her lap, not from anxiety or fear but pure, unadulterated anticipation. Her mom had been right. Sex did change everything. Sleeping with Ethan last night had changed their relationship. And it had made them both insatiable. Not just for the physical intimacy, either. The words they'd said tonight—and the ones they hadn't—were important.

Now they were on their way through a backroad, where Fisher's Creek met the river, the property of one of the farmers she knew. The drive through the small field would be blocked off by a gate, but it was a short walk to the river's edge and the natural beach. Fred had shown it to her when she'd taken the tour of his farm, looking for produce suppliers. At the time she'd commented that it was a stunning spot, and he'd revealed that it rarely got used, except during lunch hours when his workers would sometimes eat their lunch and then wade in the cool water before going back to work.

No one would bother them there.

She directed Ethan to a small pull-off spot in the shade of some birches, and he killed the engine and lights. "You're sure about this, Willow?" She could see his troubled eyes as he looked over at her. "I don't mean to be a killjoy, but Aiden and Laurel got caught in a compromising position on the golf course earlier this

summer. I don't want your friend coming after tres-
passers, you know?"

She smiled. "Fred's probably already asleep. His
morning starts at five. Besides, he's told me to stop by
for a swim anytime I want."

"And have you?"

"Not until tonight." She grinned at him, feeling a
little bit wicked. "Come on, Ethan. You, me, the moon,
some soft grass, the cool water on our skin . . ."

He opened the door and the dome light came on.
"Why the hell not," he replied.

They shut the doors quietly, and darted under the
gate and down the tractor path like guilty teenagers.
She hadn't felt this alive in ages. When was the last
time she'd taken a risk? Had fun? Since she was seventeen, those young moments of daring had passed her
by. She'd been too busy dealing with stuff to be silly or
impulsive. Oh, it felt good, particularly when he took
her hand and tugged her along with him, toward the
bottom of the hill and the secluded spot that was to be
their haven for a few hours.

The water lapped softly against the pebbled bank,
and the light breeze whispered with a hush through the
poplars, birches, and maples. They halted, and Willow
took a deep breath. Now that they were here, she wondered who would make the first move. Ethan, too,
paused, though he kept her hand in his.

Willow looked up, caught sight of the orangey harvest moon, and let the pull of her own sexuality guide
her actions. Slowly, she released her hand from his,
and took a step back. She was still in her yoga clothes,
and it took little effort to slide the loose tank over her
head. She slipped off her sandals and squeezed her toes

in the coarse sand, then shimmied out of her leggings. Her bra was the next to go, and she felt the slight weight of her breasts as the soft mesh fell away. She put it on top of her other clothes and then slipped out of her panties, so that she was naked before him. Naked and feeling gloriously free, like Eve in the Garden of Eden.

"You're beautiful," Ethan murmured, his eyes wide with what she thought was wonder. When had anyone ever looked at her in that way before? "Like a moon goddess. And I'm the crazy fool who thinks he might have a chance with you."

She smiled, so surprised and touched that she had to make a joke or else blurt out how she felt about him. "For a guy who seems so reticent, you've definitely been waxing poetic tonight."

"Maybe I'm inspired," he replied, too quickly for it to be a practiced comment. Her heart surged again.

And then once more as he pulled off his T-shirt, revealing his broad chest and the dusting of reddish-gold hair there. If she was a goddess, he was the Irish Faerie, seductive and sneaking past all her defenses. Tonight, in the moonlight, anything was possible.

His shorts followed his shirt, and his underwear, too. They were outdoors and utterly naked. No . . . not naked. Natural. There was a difference. And this felt so incredibly right. Last night had changed things. Tonight they would change again, and for once, Willow wasn't terrified.

He held out his hand and she took it. Stepped closer to him, and they spent precious seconds touching each other; arms, backs, stomachs, breasts. He ran rough fingers over the soft skin of her bottom, and she reached down between them and ran her knuckles over his silkiness. They weren't just touching, she realized. They were exploring each other, and it felt sublime.

When that wasn't enough, he lay her down in the soft grass and kissed her, worshiping her with his mouth, and she closed her eyes, letting the rest of her senses take over during the sweet torture—the touch of his hands, warm and rough; the soft, wet heat of his tongue. The sound of the wind in the leaves and the gentle lap, lap of the water on the gravelly bank. A lonely loon somewhere on the river, its call echoing through the clear night. She reached out again and wrapped her hand around him, and his hips surged forward, welcoming her touch. Cool night air kissed their heated skin as their hands and mouths grew more impatient.

"Come into the river with me," she said, just before licking his sternum. "I want to feel your hot body and the cool water on my skin."

They got up and ran to the river, gasping only a little as they entered the water in long, purposeful strides. When Willow was up to her waist she stopped and pulled him closer. He lifted her and she wrapped her legs around him, pushing against his hips, seeking relief. He took them deeper into the water, until the soft waves crested her nipples, the difference in hot and cold only heightening her sensations. They kissed and groped, with more urgency and less finesse than before. And then Ethan let go of her with one hand, reached down between them, let her slide a bit, and slipped inside her.

She nearly came at the first contact, but the water and the position together made for an awkward rhythm. Ethan walked them back to the shore until he got to where the water came to his knees, then he lay her down in the water and positioned himself above her. The water slid over her body and made her hair pool out around her, but it was shallow enough she could brace her feet and meet him stroke for stroke. His hot mouth met her water-cooled breasts; she cried out as he rolled a pebbled nipple between his teeth. The rhythm got faster and waves were breaking now from the movement of their bodies, ebbing and flowing.

"Willow," he said roughly, and she looked up to find him gazing at her with such intensity she felt it right in the heart of her soul.

"Ethan," she acknowledged. Just Ethan. Just his name. That was all they needed. *I see you. I know you. I love you.*

Their gazes clung, thrust after thrust, and when they came apart together, something shifted inside her. An inevitability, an acknowledgment, a benediction.

And when they caught their breath again, they smiled at each other and Willow pushed herself farther out in the water, away from shore. She swam a few strokes, then dove beneath the surface, the refreshing cold washing away the weight of the past, making way for a hope for the future.

She surfaced and found Ethan a few feet away, equally wet, smiling like a fool.

She smiled back.

CHAPTER 18

It wasn't until they'd dried off in the scratchy grass and were back in the SUV driving toward Darling that Willow's stomach clenched.

In all the heated rush, in all the unexpected intimacy, neither one of them had thought about a condom.

She fought for logic. The chances of one time creating a pregnancy were so slim. Still, she'd been rash, foolish, reckless. And so had he. It wasn't like either of them. And while she wanted to believe that being with Ethan was the best thing to happen to her in a long time, a little voice in her head nagged that if it was really and truly good, it would inspire good decision making and not poor.

Ethan Gallagher made her feel alive, and made her do rash things. The last time she'd been rash, it had nearly killed her.

Hold on, she reminded herself. *One tiny mistake doesn't negate years of work. Learn from it and move on.*

"You got quiet all of a sudden."

She looked over at him, his features illuminated by the dash lights. "Um . . . it just occurred to me that we didn't use protection."

His eyes widened as shock blanked his face. "Oh my God. Why didn't I . . . it was in my wallet."

"It's okay. I'm sure once won't . . . I mean, I'm not afraid of any STIs or anything."

"But pregnancy . . ."

The knot in her stomach tightened at the sound of panic in his voice. "The chances are slim, Ethan," she rationalized. "Let's not borrow trouble."

"But . . ."

He turned back and stared out the windshield, both his hands gripping the wheel. Her stomach flipped and flopped. Of course. Ethan had children. The last thing he'd want was a baby from a fling. He wasn't that kind of guy. And she was single, with a business to run. A baby would complicate everything. Still, her feelings were hurt that he was so completely freaked out. His jaw looked so tight she wondered if his teeth would hurt tomorrow.

"We're just getting started in our relationship. If you got pregnant . . . God, we were so stupid. I got so caught up in the whole sex outdoors thing. You dancing around like some wood fairy or something, and me too horny to think straight."

The words hit her like a slap. While she knew they came from a place of fear, it also took the intense, deep feelings she'd had when they were together and negated them utterly. She'd felt a soul-to-soul connection; he'd been horny.

She had been, too. But there was more. And maybe she was alone with that part. Maybe he wasn't so different after all.

"Sorry," he said quietly. "I didn't mean that the way it sounded. I'm sure it'll be fine. Like you said, the chance of getting pregnant from one time is pretty small."

And she thought of Laurel and Aiden who were already expecting, barely two months after their wedding. Thought of how it had only taken once when she was a teenager . . . was she still that fertile? Was he? The boys had been born close together.

They drove in silence for a few more minutes, the earlier spell utterly destroyed. He reached over and turned the radio on, down low, and the sound filled the heavy silence. Willow wanted to shrivel up and fly away, like a dry leaf on the wind. Earlier this evening they'd been face-to-face on the yoga mats, getting closer together by the minute. They'd connected in a way she hadn't expected, and now he was shutting her out.

She stared out the window at the darkness. The old words circled around in her brain, fighting to be heard. Not good enough. A screwup. Unlovable. In her heart she knew it was all lies, but right now her head was telling her differently.

So hum, she said in her head, breathing deeply. *I am*. She was not good, or bad, or lovable or unlovable. She just was. And that was enough.

She'd repeat it as often as she had to, to believe it.

They were nearing Darling town limits when Ethan broke the silence. "You could always go to the drugstore for a morning-after pill."

Her heart seized. It was the one thing she wouldn't do. She clenched her teeth and tried to stay calm, but inside she was in total turmoil. What if . . . what if by tomorrow morning, she'd already conceived? She'd messed with fate once before and it had been devastating. There'd been so much guilt, so much sadness to overcome. She didn't want a baby now, but if she and Ethan created one, she'd let nature take its course and not interfere. Not again.

"Willow?"

She looked over at him, unsure of what to say. He didn't know about her teenage pregnancy, or the abortion that followed, or the years she'd spent dealing with the fallout. Not only was she not going to take the morning-after pill; she wasn't going to ever allow anyone to dictate her choices ever again. The last time her mother had forced her to have the abortion, or at least, Willow hadn't been strong enough to fight against it. This time the choice would be hers.

"What?"

"I said, you can take the morning-after pill. I mean, that's what it's there for, right?"

"Right," she agreed, answering his question but technically not agreeing to any such action.

"I'm sorry I wasn't thinking straight. What I said before . . . I didn't mean it. It just freaked me out. Getting pregnant would blow the hell out of taking it slow. And the boys . . ."

"I get it, Ethan. Everything is just too soon. There's no sort of commitment between us, and an unplanned pregnancy would be a disaster." She wanted to mean the words. She did. And logically she knew the timing couldn't be worse. And yet a little part of her wondered if it might be a second chance.

For the love of Pete. She was thinking this way and it hadn't even been an hour. Talk about borrowing trouble!

"Well, that's good then." He visibly relaxed, his white-knuckle grip on the wheel loosening and his shoulders relaxed.

They got to her apartment and he pulled into the back parking space, next to her little car. When he moved to unbuckle his seatbelt, she put out her hand. "I'm tired, Ethan. And I've got to open in the morning."

He met her gaze, and she hated that he looked both confused and hurt. "Are you upset, Willow? Because it's going to be fine."

"I know."

"Are you angry with me? I'm sorry I forgot, truly. And I blurted out stuff I didn't mean . . ."

"I'm not angry, Ethan. The responsibility was as much mine as yours, so why would I be mad at you? It's just been a crazy night, and I need to sleep on it. Plus I really do have to open in the morning."

It was the first time in many years that's she'd lied to someone's face. She didn't like that about herself, either. But right now she could only deal with one thing at a time, and memories were crowding in her mind, clouding her judgment.

"Okay. As long as you're sure you're okay."

"I am." She fake-smiled at him. "Promise."

"You'll go to the pharmacy tomorrow morning?"

The question was like a dagger to the heart. "I'll look after it, Ethan."

"Good."

She leaned over and kissed his cheek. "I'll talk to you soon, okay?"

He nodded. "I pick up the boys on Monday. Maybe we can get together then." It wasn't just her, then. Tonight had scared him too, and he was taking a step back from getting too close.

"I'll let you know. I've been taking advantage of Emily. She might want a few extra hours off before the summer's over. Just call or stop in, okay?"

"We're okay?"

She nodded, on the verge of crying all of a sudden. Why couldn't he just let her get out of the car and go?

"Good night, Ethan."

She got out of the SUV and headed straight for the stairs, then turned at the top, pasted on a smile, and gave him a wave before putting the key in the lock and going inside.

She shut the door behind her and leaned against it, closing her eyes and fighting for breath. Her serenity was gone, broken. She'd fallen for him. The strong, tough, tender firefighter with two motherless boys. She'd done what she always ended up doing—nurturing, trying to fix things. Assuring herself she'd be okay, and then falling apart the moment she started to lose herself. All it had taken was one time forgetting a condom and she was rudderless, wondering what to do next.

She wanted. . . .

She wanted . . .

That was just it. She slid down the door, sitting on the floor with her back against the cool steel. She'd taught herself to be in the moment, to be happy with what was, and live in the now. She'd accepted herself, and her flaws, and her good qualities, but she'd forgotten one thing. She hadn't allowed herself to dream of the future. She'd satisfied herself with what she had because wanting more had always caused her grief.

And now she wanted more. And she needed to believe it was okay to want more for herself. What was wrong with wanting love, and a family? Did she even know how to not be alone? Had she worked so hard at being independent that she'd made it impossible to give herself to someone else?

Or was it worse than that? Was it that she didn't know how to accept love when it was offered?

And what if, by some miracle, there was a baby? What then? Ethan wasn't looking for another wife. He'd made that plain. And he certainly wasn't in the market for a baby mama.

Tears stung her lids and she dropped her head. Her hair fell over her shoulder and she smelled the river water. The woman on the riverbank seemed a lifetime away. She'd been wanton, reckless, beautiful, resplendent. Not small and slightly broken.

She crawled up from her sprawled position and went to the "studio" part of the apartment. Instinctively she went to the small stereo, and put on her favorite harmonium and chant recording, then gently lay down in Savasana. She let the drone and the ancient chant wash away the insecurities and fear. Whatever came her way, she could handle it. She'd been through worse, and she was older and wiser.

And she could do it with or without Ethan Gallagher.

The recording stopped and she slowly opened her eyes, looked down at her tattoo, and smiled. Her story wasn't over. Not by a long shot. Because even if she forgot all the other lessons she'd learned, one remained.

She was a survivor.

Willow threw herself back into her work. The holiday weekend was a huge time for tourists to get away for one last bit of summer, and the café had a steady stream of customers looking for light lunches or snacks to take on outings and picnics. At least once an hour she overheard customers talking about heading to the Kissing Bridge, the town's biggest tourist draw. Two by two they went to the stone structure and kissed, ensuring their love would last forever. All it did was remind Willow that things were unresolved between her and Ethan. Not from lack of trying on his part, though. He'd called three times already. Twice she'd let her voice mail answer, and the third time she'd picked up, hoping that talking to him would get him to cease and desist. Instead he'd asked her over for dinner.

She'd refused, even though it hurt. She might have considered it, except he was barely past the hellos when he asked her if she'd gone to the drugstore. She'd lied again and then felt horrible about it. And yet she couldn't tell him the truth, because then he'd ask why, and that would open a whole Pandora's box of issues she wasn't ready to share.

She told him she'd call when she was ready. That things had moved a little too fast, and that the contraception issue had highlighted how they needed to slow down for a bit.

His silence had sliced into her like a paper cut.

Labor Day moved into back-to-school days. She and Emily conducted interviews and hired one full-time person and two part-time students to work the counter after school. Emily took over scheduling duties, while Willow adjusted the menu to more fall-like offerings: apple tarts, curried squash soup, heartier breads. She went back to her daily yoga practices, meditated, and started to run numbers for expansion, though her heart wasn't really in it. She knew, deep down, that she was keeping busy to avoid dealing with her feelings for Ethan. And she knew it was the wrong approach. Her justification was that she'd wait for her period, and then once she knew for sure that they'd dodged a bullet, she'd figure out how she felt and then go to Ethan and talk it out.

It was a good plan.

Except for two things. First of all, her best friend was married to Ethan's brother, and her next-best-friend was Ethan's sister. Neither of them was good at minding her own business, and Willow wasn't comfortable sharing personal details.

Secondly, her period never came.

Willow rose the morning of September 10th and went to the bathroom as usual. Nothing. She checked her phone for her calendar, and she was four days late. That wasn't a big deal at any other time; she was usually a few days either side. But she didn't have any of the normal tweakiness in her back, or the burst of energy she normally got a few days before that had her cleaning and organizing. She sighed and fought the urge to go back to bed. The last few nights she hadn't been sleeping as well as she normally did. Maybe she'd do her yoga tonight and try to sneak in another half hour of sleep.

When she woke again, it was because her phone was ringing. She reached for it groggily, knocking it off her end table before groping for it on the floor and hitting the talk button. "Hello?"

"It's Em. Are you okay? It's nine thirty."

"Nine thirty? Oh God. I only meant to sleep an extra half hour."

"Don't worry about it. It's just not like you, and I wanted to be sure you're okay."

"I'm fine, just a little tired." But she knew that, too, was a fib. "Are you able to handle things until lunch? Since I'm already late, I might run a few errands if you've got it under control."

"Take your time. Like I said, I just wanted to make sure you're okay. Thought I could bring you some tea or soup if you were sick."

Sick. She swallowed against a lump of fear. Few days or not, the stress of the current situation was taking a toll and she needed to know one way or the other. The surest way to do that was to do a pregnancy test. And she'd be damned if she'd buy the test at the Darling pharmacy.

"I'm fine. Text me if you need anything while I'm out. I'll be back for the rush at noon. Promise."

"No worries. Glad you're okay. I'd better get back."

Willow hung up the phone and flopped back onto the covers. Pregnant. Was it possible? The slim chance wasn't feeling so slim anymore. She put her hand on her flat belly and wondered. Fear ran cold through her veins, but something else was there, too. Something that acknowledged that carrying a baby was a beautiful thing. And that if it was meant to be, she'd go through with it and the hell with the consequences.

She dressed and brushed her teeth and drove into Stowe, where not a soul would recognize her. She didn't even wait to go home to take the test. She peed on the stick in a bathroom stall in a coffee shop, then sat in her car and waited for the results. Early fall was all around her—an empty school bus went by, businesses opened their doors to the warm temperatures but put potted mums on their stoops instead of petunias and geraniums. The sun had lost its summer harshness and its rays were gilded and soft. It was Willow's favorite time of year, and she focused on it for a few minutes to give the stick time to form a definitive result.

She held her breath and checked it.

It was positive.

She was going to have a baby.

Her breath came out in a whoosh and she rested her head on the steering wheel. One time. Just once. She seriously had to have the most fertile eggs on the planet. How was she going to tell Ethan? He didn't want a baby. They'd only been together twice. Twice! He had a family and wasn't in the market for another.

And she'd lied to him. And now he'd know that she didn't take a morning-after pill like she'd said she would.

For the first time in two weeks, she felt sick.

She needed to eat. The nausea wasn't morning sickness, but instead emotional upheaval paired with an empty stomach. She took a few deep breaths and got out of the car again, and went inside the shop to buy a muffin and some milk. Once she'd eaten, she hit the road. She had to go back to Darling and The Purple Pig. Emily and the rest of the staff was relying on her. And she needed to speak to Ethan, but wanted to take a little time to get used to the idea first.

She was going to be a mother. Holy shit.

A mother.

She pulled over to the side of the road just before she burst into tears. Not panicked ones, not scared ones, but overwhelmed tears that welled out of her eyes and slid down her cheeks. The significance of what was about to happen hit her square in the chest. Her life was going to change forever.

She wasn't sure she'd ever have a chance to have another baby. She'd wondered if not having one would be some sort of a punishment. That she was . . . unworthy.

She'd always felt unworthy. She still did. Unworthy of her mother's love, unworthy of forgiveness, unworthy of Ethan, even. And still . . . there was a little human developing inside her. A cluster of cells that would divide and grow and soon have a heartbeat and little fingers and toes . . .

For some reason, she'd been given this chance. And she would be worthy of this child. She'd make sure of it.

When her tears were dried, she pulled back onto the road again and headed home. She'd figure this out step by step.

CHAPTER 19

Ethan didn't know what to do anymore.

He hadn't seen Willow since he'd dropped her at home that night. Sure, they'd forgotten to use protection, but it didn't make sense that she'd stop seeing him altogether. It wasn't like her. Willow faced things head-on. She was calm, rational, serene. She made sense, always. But nothing since that night was making sense.

She avoided his calls. She'd answered once and it had been so awkward he hadn't had the courage to try again. Maybe it was just too soon. Clearly, she'd freaked out.

Now Connor was in school and loving every minute, Ronan was in preschool and jealous of his brother going to the "big" school, and Ethan was back at work. Not a single person in the family brought up Willow. Hannah had tried to, once, but he'd shot her such a dark look that she'd stopped mid-sentence and hadn't asked again. She must have spread the word, because the rest

of the family was back to acting like they were on ten-
terhooks around him.

He was off shift and trimming the shrubs in the
backyard just to keep busy when she came around
the corner of the house.

His first reaction was pure, unadulterated pleasure.
His heart gave a solid thump. She wore dark jeans with
a loose, light sweater in pale blue, one of her favorite
colors, he now knew. She had a new stripe in her hair—
turquoise—and as she came closer he noticed the
diamond nose ring had been changed out to a sapphire.
His little bluebird, he realized. Just as delicate and
beautiful.

"Hi," she said quietly.

He put his trimmers down on the grass, stood, and
brushed his hands off on his jeans. Now that the moment of pleasure was over, other emotions snuck in.
Resentment. Hurt. Confusion.

"Hi. Something I can do for you?"

His sharp tone hit its mark. He saw it in her eyes
and the quick intake of breath.

"I'm sorry, Ethan. I've been avoiding you."

"No kidding."

"You're not going to make this easy."

"It hasn't been easy." He shoved his hands in his
jeans pockets. "I've gone over what went wrong about
a million times, and I still don't understand. And it's
not like you were willing to talk."

"I know. I . . . I was confused, too. And I needed to
tell you some things but I wasn't ready. So I kept away.
I'm not proud of it. It's not how I usually do things."

"Yeah. Tell me about it."

He picked up the trimmers again and headed to the
garage. It hurt to see her. That night at the river . . .

he'd been so close to falling in love with her. It had been amazing and terrifying all at once, but it had been profound. It had taken a lot for him to even come close to caring about someone that much, and for her to do such an about-face . . . it was going to take him some time to get over it, too.

"Ethan . . . we need to talk."

She'd followed him toward the garage, and he turned to face her. "On your schedule, right? Maybe *I'm* not ready to talk." He was being an idiot, and he knew it. It was childish to play this game, and yet he wanted her to know that what she'd done hadn't been okay. "Willow, you were the one who accused me of being closed off when we first met, but the truth is I wanted to work out whatever went wrong and you wouldn't even have a simple conversation."

"I know." Frustration bubbled in her voice. "I know. I didn't know what else to do."

"I'm sure you meditated on it."

Wow, and didn't he sound like a dick now?

"I did," she answered softly, not taking the bait. "A lot. I'm not perfect, Ethan."

"Nobody's perfect. I didn't expect you to be. But I didn't think you'd run, either."

Their eyes clung. Damn, he really had got himself in deep. For all his joking about her free-spirit ways, that night when she'd showed him how to breathe, how to move . . . he'd started to understand. And in that tiny bit of understanding, their connection had deepened. Deepened into the best sex of his life. He could finally admit it to himself. It took nothing away from his relationship with his wife, but it did speak to the depth of his feeling for Willow.

She smiled a little, a sad little curve of her lips.

"I think I fooled myself into believing I had it all together. Had all the answers. But I don't, and caring about you shone a light on a lot of my flaws. I didn't like what I saw."

Well. He hadn't expected that. So what now? Did he want to try to work things out with her? Or just have a decent ending? That silly word, *closure*. They couldn't stay this way, because caring about someone else was taking its toll.

"Can we please sit down and talk?"

"Come up on the deck. I'll get us something to drink. Want a beer?"

She gave him a funny look. "Just water for me, thanks."

"All right."

He went inside to get drinks and get a grip on his emotions. Something bigger was going on than just "talking." Something was off with her, but he couldn't put his finger on it. It was just a feeling he had. Usually she was so open, so transparent. But not today. Today her guard was up.

She waited for him, sitting beneath the umbrella at the patio table. Her skin had darkened over the summer, just a bit, and her freckles were more pronounced. It made her look very, very young. And he felt very, very old.

"Here you go." He put the glass down in front of her, and then took a chair at the table and leaned back, taking a swig of cold beer. The September weather was still hot enough that he'd worked up a slight sweat in the yard and the beer quenched his thirst.

She sipped and then put down the glass. "How are the boys?"

"In school. Having a blast. Wondering why you're not around anymore."

"God, Ethan." She rested her forehead on her hand. "Every time you speak to me, it's a verbal slap. I know I was wrong. I'm sorry, okay?"

"It was one of my worries, you know. If I got involved with someone and it didn't work out. I told myself that you wouldn't be the kind to just disappear from their lives. That you'd be too sensitive for that." It was one thing for him to hurt. It was a very different thing when it was his kids. They'd been through enough.

"Bring them by for an afterschool snack," she suggested softly. "Or if you really don't want to see me, maybe Hannah or Laurel could."

"They'd like that."

She sipped her water again, and silence surrounded them. Awkward, weighty silence, and Ethan made himself sit and wait her out. She'd come here. She wanted to talk, so she could say what she had to say. And then maybe he would, too. It would give him time to figure out exactly what that was.

"Ethan, that night at the river . . ." She looked up at him, but her fingers played with her glass, like she was nervous. "I felt a connection to you that was unlike anything I've ever felt before. It was scary but it was beautiful, too. I felt myself falling for you. For the first time ever, I wanted a future. And then I realized that we'd been careless. Both of us, not just you. None of this was your fault."

"It sure felt like it was."

"I know. I'm sorry. It's just . . . well, the thing is, I was careless once before. A long time ago." Her fingers twisted together. "And today I came over here to tell you about it, so maybe you'd understand."

"Understanding would be good, because I've played that drive home over and over in my head and I don't get anywhere. We were crazy that night, Wil. So into each other. And then it was like someone flipped a switch. Do you know how hard it was for me to put myself out there again?"

She looked away for a moment; he saw her bottom lip quiver for a mere second before she squared her shoulders and took a breath. "I'm sorry. I didn't mean to hurt you."

He swallowed, kept his voice low, even though he was frustrated as hell. "Then explain it to me."

It took her a minute to begin. In those moments, he saw her bite down on her lip, twist her fingers. Then she sat straight in her chair and took three long, deep breaths, just like the ones she'd shown him. When she was finished, she opened her eyes. They were clear and blue like the September sky above them.

"The night of our first date, you asked about this." She held out her wrist, then tucked it back against her belly. "I wasn't ready to go into details that night. But I need to tell you now."

He didn't say a word, just watched her steadily, resentment still burning in his gut.

"I was sixteen, nearly seventeen. I liked this guy a lot, but he wasn't that into me. I was so thrilled when he finally asked me out. I was devastated when I realized he'd only wanted to score. More devastated later when I hated myself for letting him."

"Teenage boys are assholes. I know. I was one." He sensed there was a story coming, and he eased off his snarky tone. He'd made his point, and that was enough.

Whatever she was going to tell him had caused her to run out on them, and it was clearly hurting her now. He didn't need to pile on.

"A month later I found out I was pregnant."

He hadn't seen that coming. He set the beer bottle down on the table and let out a breath. "Jesus."

"That's what I said, too. My mother had a few other things to say—about my behavior and my stupidity. I was so scared, Ethan. I already felt so alone. High school is brutal at the best of times. I was a straight A student. I was on Student Council and on a thousand committees because I was so . . . lonely. I had lots of 'friends' but few I could really turn to. No one knew about the baby. Can you imagine what people would have said if they'd known? And my mom . . ."

Her voice wobbled, but he waited it out. He couldn't stay angry. Not with her. He'd never really been angry, anyway. He'd been hurt and confused. Anger had been the easy way to deal with it.

"Your mom . . ." he nudged gently.

"She was always at work. She provided for both of us, and I always felt like a burden. Like she'd be doing so many other things if she didn't have to look after me."

"Your dad?"

"Left when I was a baby."

"I'm sorry."

"I tried so hard to be perfect for Mom. Like if I did everything right, all her sacrificing would be worth it. Once I grew up, I realized that she's a workaholic. She lives to work, and she never really wanted to be a parent. It hurts, but I've accepted it. But at the time, I couldn't understand why she didn't seem to love me like other moms loved their kids. We never did things together. Had girlie days. She'd tell me I should be happy to have so much independence, and isn't that what I wanted?"

"Of course it wasn't. You wanted a parent to care enough to set boundaries."

"I wouldn't have admitted it then, but yes. I needed a parent, and instead I had a landlord."

Christ, that was sad. He thought of Lisa and how she'd doted on the boys. There were always kisses and hugs and smiles, even when she'd been sick and it had cost her precious energy. And Ethan, too—he knew he was grumpy from time to time, but God, he hoped the boys knew how much he loved them.

And he'd always felt love from his parents, too. What would it have been like, growing up feeling that your only parent didn't care about you?

"So you can imagine what it was like when I told her I was pregnant." She gave a bitter laugh. "I actually thought for a moment that maybe this time she'd be there for me. That it would bring us closer together."

"It didn't?"

Willow shook her head. "Hell no. She was furious. I was already struggling with feeling isolated and, well, depressed. Add a perfectionist streak onto that and it was a dark, dark place in my head. I wanted her to hold my hand and tell me it would be okay. Instead she drove me to an abortion clinic."

Ethan had been about to take another sip of beer, but his hand paused halfway to his mouth. He'd figured this was leading to her losing the baby. But not this. Her voice was so cold as she said it. So flat.

"You went through with it?" He put the bottle back down.

"I didn't have a choice, don't you see?" Her troubled

gaze lifted to meet his. "I didn't know how to stand up to her, and she threatened to kick me out. I didn't know what else to do. I couldn't have a baby without her help, but I . . ."

Her voice had been strong throughout the whole thing, but now she turned her head and made a small sound. He gave her the space she needed, while he tried to wrap his head around what it would have been like to be in high school, pregnant by a stupid jock, and without the support of the one person who was supposed to be there for you.

She reached for her water with a trembling hand and he saw her tattoo again, just below the cuff of her sweater. Isolation, depression . . . and an abortion. It would have been enough to put her over the edge, wouldn't it?

His stomach clenched as he asked the question. "So that's what led to your . . . your tattoo? God, Willow. You have to know I wouldn't judge you because of that. I can't imagine how awful that was for you."

"I stopped eating. And then I'd eat and I'd . . . I'd purge. I honestly don't know how I fooled people, or how I managed to graduate like I did. But once the ceremony was over, I lost it. I couldn't pretend anymore. I ended up in Boston, at a clinic. I didn't want to live anymore."

Tears stung his eyes. "Honey," he said, and reached for her. But she pulled away, her eyes flashing a warning.

"I've never told anyone about this, Ethan. Not even Laurel. And I wasn't planning on telling you, either. Not . . . not yet. But I had to because . . . because of that night at the river."

He frowned. There was so much to take in, and he knew that somehow it was all going to link together, but he couldn't for the life of him see how. She'd run scared that night . . . had it been too intense? Was being with him making her depressed again? His heart hurt just thinking about it. She'd said only minutes ago that she was flawed, imperfect. That being with him had shone a light on those flaws. Maybe he wasn't good for her after all. It was tough to think about, because despite the last few weeks, she'd been very, very good for him.

"I'm sorry about the things I said that night. I know I got upset . . . you have to know I care about you, Willow. So much. I couldn't have been with you if I didn't."

Her voice was clogged with tears as she answered, "I know."

"But you're not okay, are you?"

She looked at him and shook her head, tears glimmering in her eyes. His stomach seemed to drop to his feet.

"I'm pregnant, Ethan."

If it was possible to feel the blood leach out of his body, he was sure it would feel like this. Pale, empty, like a shell of a person. Like one of those cartoons where the character gets the crap scared out of him and he turns white. *I'm pregnant, Ethan.* The words bounced around in his brain as he stared at her.

Pregnant. A baby. His baby.

But they'd talked about this. She'd promised she was going to go to the drugstore in the morning. The morning after . . .

He stared at her as the truth settled on him. "You didn't take a morning-after pill."

She shook her head. "I couldn't. Please understand."

He rested his elbows on the table and dropped his face into his hands. Jesus. A baby.

"You lied," he accused. "Shit, Willow, you lied right to my face."

Willow watched the emotions cross his face. Shock. Understanding of the situation.

Despair.

She'd known all along that he wouldn't want this baby. He'd had his family, with his wife. And sure, maybe someday he'd want to get married and have another child, but not with her, right? And definitely not outside of marriage. How would he explain it to the boys? To his family?

"I didn't exactly lie. You said, 'Isn't that what the morning-after pill is for?' And I said yes. It *is* what it's for. I never said I was going to take it."

His eyes were steely blue and he pinned her with them, like one of the dragonflies on Styrofoam she'd seen in a museum one time. "Don't argue semantics with me." He pointed a finger at her. "You knew what I meant at the time. It's not worthy of you, Willow Dunaway."

He was right. She'd known it at the time, and it was a flimsy justification. "I know," she acquiesced weakly. "I just couldn't tell you that night. And I couldn't take the pill. Not . . ."

She gasped for air. "Look, when I was seventeen, I wasn't given a choice. Do you know what it was like? Can you imagine?" Her voice rose and she strove to temper it. The neighbors weren't that far away, after all, and they were sitting outside. "My mom took me there. Filled out the paperwork. I had it done and came out and she drove me home, then left me and went to work for the rest of the day. She left me, Ethan. I had no counseling. No one to hold my hand. No one to make me tea or soup and tell me it was going to be okay. I was not given the basic right to choose. I was stripped of everything that day. I couldn't take a pill this time and pretend like nothing had happened. That's what she made me do, don't you see? I was supposed to act like nothing had happened. No one knew, so it didn't happen, right? But I knew. I knew, dammit."

She couldn't stop the words now, or the broken sobs that came with them. "So yes. Yes, I lied to you. Because this time I was going to make the choice and live with the consequences. Me, no one else. We didn't use protection and I'm pregnant. I'm going to have this baby, and I swear to God it will feel the love I never did. With or without you."

He got up from his chair and paced a few steps away. Ran his hand over his head. Turned toward her, then away again, breathing heavily. She knew he wanted to say something, and she was afraid of what it would be. She hadn't expected him to forgive in an instant and pull her into his arms, but she hadn't quite expected his cold reaction, either.

When he turned to her, his expression was bleak. "But don't you see, Willow? By lying to me, by not telling me the truth, you took away *my* choice."

"So you want me to get rid of it? Treat it like a mistake, sweep the whole issue under the rug so no one knows your dirty little secret? You banged Willow Dunaway and got her knocked up."

He frowned. "Of course not," he snapped. "Dammit, Willow. I'm a father. I'm not your fucking mother."

The words held in the air, while the two of them stilled. Of anything he'd said today, this was the most basic truth. He wasn't her mother. But she'd treated him as if he was, and she hadn't trusted him. And that was on her.

"You don't want another baby," she whispered.

"No, I don't. We just started seeing each other. We both wanted to take it slow because of our pasts. It's impossible to do that with a baby on the way. This just took a giant leap from exploration to . . . Christ."

She had never heard him swear so much. He was always careful around the boys, too. But he was upset and probably scared. She got it.

"The timing is all wrong," he said. "I just don't . . . I don't know anymore. I'm not . . ." He was stammering now, and there was a thread of panic in his voice. "I'm not ready for any of this. Seven years ago . . . seven this month, Willow, I stood on that stupid kissing bridge in town and kissed Lisa and said our love was forever. Until death do us part, and that's exactly how long it lasted. I didn't want to love somebody else. I didn't want to go through any of that again. And now you're telling me I'm going to have another son or a daughter and I just want to . . ."

"Run," she finished for him. "I know the instinct well, Ethan."

And yet another emotion joined the smorgasbord of feelings—resignation. What had she expected? That he'd jump up and hug her and say let's be one big happy family? Of course not. But maybe some sense of "don't worry, we'll figure it out". Some sense that he'd be there for her when she needed him. Maybe he wasn't her mother, but he wasn't prepared to step in, either. Not if he wanted to run.

And she did not want a reluctant father for her child.

She'd had a reluctant mother and she'd be damned if her baby would be brought up begging for a parent's attention.

She stood, her knees wobbling, and she gripped the edge of the table for a moment until she was sure on her feet. "I'd better go," she said quietly.

"Are you kidding? You're going to drop this bomb-shell on me and then beat it?"

The exhaustion that was so familiar weighed on her now. "We're not going to solve anything today. You're too upset. You need time, Ethan. And we've got time. A little over eight months to figure it all out. I'm tired. So I'm going to go and look after me." She met his gaze. "Look after us."

"You've already made up your mind about everything," he accused.

She sighed. "Not everything. This is not how I would have planned it, you know. But I forgot the most important thing that I learned so long ago. I forgot that I need to not only accept my flaws, accept my life—I also have to embrace it. It's the only way I'm going to be whole. And my child deserves that."

She belatedly realized she said "my" and not "our," but Ethan didn't seem to notice.

Ethan just stood there. He didn't agree or disagree. He just stared at her like a stranger might. It couldn't be more clear. He didn't want this baby. And he didn't want her.

"Tell Hannah to bring the boys by sometime. I think Connor will like the new apple turnovers I've started making."

Her voice caught when she said Connor's name. Oh, those boys. She'd fallen for them, too, but she would never, ever put them in the middle of a grown-up situ-

ation. And Ronan with his sweet kisses and hugs, cud-
dling in the hanging chair. It made her heart ache.

She turned and hurried down the three wooden steps
to the back yard, then half-walked, half-ran around
the corner of her house to her car. Once inside, she put
the key in the ignition and looked up, but Ethan hadn't
followed her. He wasn't coming after her. Part of her
wept inside, but she steeled her spine and buckled her
seatbelt.

She was stronger now, and in charge of her own life.
And she could do this. Perhaps that was the lesson she
needed to take away. She was not that helpless, scared
little girl any longer. She was a woman, a mother, with
the heart of a lioness.

CHAPTER 20

She wasn't feeling so lioness-y four days later when the first bout of morning sickness struck.

Her alarm went off at five as usual, but there was no way she could stomach her customary green tea. It smelled different, somehow. She settled for water, but it made her queasy and came right back up. By the time she'd finished her yoga practice, she was feeling weak and had a sick sort of headache.

She made some hot buttered toast and had a crazy urge for hot chocolate once her stomach settled. When she got downstairs to the café, she prepared a mug of it for herself and took it into the kitchen.

"Hey, are you okay? You're looking a little pale today."

Willow looked up at Em and tried a smile. "Just feeling a bit off. Must be a . . . oh, something I ate." Wow, this lying thing was becoming a little too easy. It sat with her about as well as the idea of food.

"We've got the new woman in today at eight for

training. I won't be able to spend as much time out back. Are you okay handling most of the kitchen?"

Willow preferred that to dealing with customers this morning, particularly if her stomach acted up again. "I'll be fine. What do you need first?"

"Eggs. The breakfast biscuits are starting to get really popular. We open in twenty, so if we could have some made up in advance I can put them in the warmer along with the Canadian bacon."

Eggs. Simple enough. While Em took biscuits and muffins out of the oven, Willow cracked two dozen eggs into a bowl and whipped them with a whisk while the griddle heated. The trouble started when she poured the beaten eggs into the Teflon rings. The smell made her stomach turn again, and she swallowed against the extra saliva in her mouth.

She soldiered through four different times, putting the finished circles in a warming tray and sliding it into the unit behind the counter. A knock came to the back door, and her bread supplier dropped off the day's supply of rolls, wraps, and loaves. Her hot chocolate was long gone, but she was feeling a bit better, so she took thirty seconds to grab a Greek yogurt from the fridge. Calcium and protein, she reminded herself. She couldn't let a little morning sickness put her off her normal eating habits.

She baked through the morning. Cookies, brownies, banana muffins, apple turnovers . . . she thought of Connor and Ronan as she sprinkled the tops with coarse sugar. More eggs—the smell wasn't so bad this time—and then sliced free-range chicken and grass-fed beef for the lunchtime sandwich crowd. For some reason the red meat appealed, and she put on a beef barley soup for lunch and then a Harvest Vegetable, thick with carrots and zucchini and a rich tomato broth. Bile rose in her throat as the beef browned in the stock-pot, but by the time she'd added the other ingredients and tasted it, she was ravenous. At ten-thirty in the morning she sat down for a brief break and inhaled a bowl of soup.

This was her new life, wasn't it? Work, caring for herself, thinking about being a mother. The foot traffic in the café was brisk, and she heard the happy greetings and chatter from the front. For the first time, the sound didn't bring her pleasure. Instead she realized that any plans for expansion would be on hold. She couldn't afford the money or the time to make it a reality right now.

She was disappointed, but not resentful. She wouldn't ever be resentful toward this baby.

By two-thirty she was exhausted. The lunch rush was over, and she dragged her butt through the kitchen, washing dishes and working on supper prep. Emily would only be working until three, and then a shift change would happen and one of the full-timers would take over. The staff would be balanced out by one of their high school students. Normally Willow took a break this time of day, in order to avoid working fourteen or more hours. But not today. Training new staff was time-consuming, and she couldn't possibly impose on Emily further.

Besides, it wasn't as if she had any social life.

By the time she started slicing vegetables, she knew she'd been on her feet too long. She sat on a stool at the counter instead, giving her feet a break, and sliced some extra carrots and cucumbers to munch on. The cucumbers especially were crisp and fresh.

"You look pooped. Boss working you extra hard?"

She looked up. Hannah stood in the doorway to the kitchen, her teasing words belied by her solemn expression. "Hey, Han. Come on in and pull up a seat. I'm cutting vegetables."

"I can see that." Hannah stepped into the kitchen, pulled up a stool, and perched at the edge of the stainless steel work table. "Sweetie, what's going on? I talked to Laurel. She said she hasn't seen you for practically weeks. Ethan's snapping at everyone . . . whatever went wrong, you have to know that we're your friends. You can talk to us."

Willow's eyes watered, and she couldn't blame it on the onions since they were still on the table, waiting to be chopped. "Oh Hannah. I've screwed everything up. Or rather . . . we have. It's such a mess."

"You fell in love with him, didn't you?"

She looked up at Hannah. "And are you going to go running back to Ethan and tell him what I say?"

Hannah frowned. "Admittedly, there's a conflict of interest here. And I do want to see both of you happy. But I will not run back to Ethan if you don't want me to. Truth is, I think you guys need to talk it out. I just want to make sure you're okay."

A lump formed in Willow's throat and she looked away, and gave her head a tiny shake.

"I did fall for him. I might even . . . love him. We were just getting closer when it all went wrong. And now . . ."

She halted. She didn't know if Ethan had told anyone in the family or not. They'd certainly never discussed when to tell people.

"Now what?" Hannah reached over and put her

hand on Willow's. The cucumbers sat forgotten on the cutting board. "Why did it go wrong?"

It wasn't as if it could remain a secret forever.

Hannah pressed on. "Is it about Lisa? Is that it? Because I know for a fact that he cares for you. He was so happy. Happier than we've seen him for a long while, that's for sure. And then a few weeks ago he started snapping at everyone."

Willow wasn't quite sure how to begin, so she eased into the topic. "You know how we talked about expanding the café? That you thought you'd like to go in on it with me? I can't do that now, Han. The timing is wrong." She realized that she'd just mimicked Ethan's words to her about the pregnancy. "The truth is, I'm pregnant."

Hannah stared at her. A full-on, open-mouthed, wide-eyed stare.

"Pregnant."

"You're the first person I've told. I found out about a week ago."

"Does Ethan know?"

"He knows."

"Crap on a cracker."

Willow choked out a laugh despite herself. Thank God for Hannah. "I was shocked, too."

"You and Ethan . . . having a baby. This is just . . . wow."

"Apparently we are very fertile people." She kept her voice low and glanced at the door every few seconds, not wanting staff to overhear. "It was a new aspect to our relationship. And this is really weird, talking to you about having sex with your brother."

It was Hannah's turn to laugh. "I grew up with those

boys. Hardly anything fazes me. Let me guess, it was the week the kids were away."

Willow's cheeks heated. "How did you know?"

"I ran into Ethan one morning, sneaking out of your apartment. I was taking out the trash from the office and there he was, doing the walk of shame." A sad smile lit her face. "I was worried for him, but happy, too. Happy he was moving on with someone as lovely as you."

Willow didn't feel so lovely, but it touched her that Hannah seemed to think so. "It was the next night," she admitted. "We were stupid. We got caught up and forgot . . . you know."

"Oops."

"That wasn't exactly what he said. He's not happy about it, Hannah. I can't go into what happened. I hope that's okay. It's between Ethan and me. But I told him and he's never called or stopped in or . . . or . . . asked how I am."

"Ethan's not the kind of man to not take this seriously."

"I know that." She did, deep down. "But he's hurt, and he's angry, and it's going to take some time for him to come to terms with it."

"You could try talking to him."

She could. But she wasn't ready for that, either. She bit down on her lip, picked up the knife, and started slicing the cucumbers again.

"It's complicated, Hannah. I'm sure we'll get around to it. But I have to be honest. It hurts to see him right now. I had to face a lot of things from my past that I didn't want to, just so I could be free to love him. To have it end like this . . . I'm hurting, too." The back of her nose stung, like it did when she plucked an eyebrow hair and hit a nerve. "I miss him. I miss the boys. I . . . I don't want to be alone."

"Oh, sweetie." Hannah got off her stool and went to Willow, putting her arms around her. "You're not alone. Maybe you both do just need some time to sort through some stuff. But trust me. When the chips are down, my big brother will be there for you. Promise. Because if he's not I'll give him an atomic wedgie."

Willow laughed, and Hannah reached into her bag for a tissue. "Here. Blow your nose. Sanitize your hands before you cut into any more of that produce. Don't worry about the expansion; we'll figure something out. This is my specialty, remember."

"I've signed a lease, remember?"

"Which you don't have to pay for until the first of November. That gives me time to think of something. You are not alone, honey. Ethan'll come around, and even if he doesn't, I'm here for you. Laurel and Aiden will be here for you, and so will a lot of other people in this town. Know what else? You're going to be an amazing mother. So chin up."

"I love you, Hannah."

"Love you too, kiddo. By the way, talk to Laurel. She's going to be thrilled that your babies are only going to be weeks apart." Hannah rolled her eyes. "Good God. Ethan was a busy boy, wasn't he? You could hardly stand each other the night Laurel made her announcement."

Willow smiled and dabbed at her eyes. "That's what you know. We kissed that night."

"Sneaky thing." Hannah dropped a sisterly kiss on Willow's cheek. "I'm going to check on you every day, you know. Make sure you're eating and feeling okay. Get used to it."

"I will."

"And don't overdo it."

"Yes, Boss."

Hannah winked. "Okay. I have to blast off. Hang in there, sweetie."

"Thank you, Hannah."

"Anytime."

Hannah's visit had cost Willow about twenty good minutes of prep time, but it had been exactly what she needed to get through the day. She wasn't alone. She had friends, and support, and a home where she belonged.

The only piece of the puzzle that was missing was Ethan. Unfortunately, Willow was starting to realize that the final piece was the one that made the rest of the puzzle make sense. Hannah hadn't called her on it, but Willow had used the word "love." She did love him. She thought maybe she had from the moment on the first night when he'd cradled a sleeping Ronan on his lap and managed to eat birthday cake with his free hand. Or maybe it was the night he'd offered Laurel his baby things . . .

She put her hand to her mouth. Oh God. Baby things . . . he'd never expected to need them again.

But he would. She just needed to give him time to get used to the news. Maybe he'd never love her the way she'd wanted him to, but he wasn't the kind of man to turn his back on his child. In all the confusion and hurt, she'd lost sight of that. Perhaps he had, too. But it wouldn't last forever.

And he would never need to know how much she cared about him. And maybe someday it wouldn't hurt quite so much.

CHAPTER 21

"You're a goddamn idiot."

Ethan frowned and pointed at the stairs. "I just put the boys down and they're probably not asleep yet. Watch your language."

Why on earth was Hannah barging into his house at eight o'clock at night? He'd bet twenty bucks it had to do with Willow. Just what he needed. He already thought about her every damned day. She was across town running her business and carrying his baby and he had no idea what the hell to do about it.

If the boys didn't have big ears, he'd do a little cursing himself.

Hannah lifted her brows and he could practically hear the sarcastic "really" in her head. "Don't look at me like that," he groused. "And if you're here to stick your nose in my business, you can turn right around and go back out the door."

"Ooooh. Look at you, being all tough."

He made a dismissive sound and turned his back on her. "Baby sisters are the bane of my existence."

"Oh, I doubt that. Right now I'm guessing there's a blonde across town that's causing you fits."

"Stay out of it, Han," he warned, his voice low. "It's complicated."

"Having a baby usually is."

He gaped at her. How did she know? He couldn't imagine Willow telling anyone yet, but he could be wrong. And Hannah was quick to pick up on a situation.

"She's tired and scared, Ethan. What are you going to do about that?"

He frowned and opened a cupboard, reaching for a bottle on the top shelf. "I think I need a drink for this conversation."

"This is nothing compared to what Mom will say when she finds out. Accidents happen, we all know that. But you guys need to work it out."

He loved his family, but they did have a terrible tendency to stick their noses in. He poured a few fingers of whiskey into a glass, mentally said screw the ice, and downed it in two gulps.

"It's not your business, Hannah. You might as well go home. We'll fix this on our own."

"Right. Both of you stubborn. Both of you hurting. She loves you, do you know that?"

"Did she tell you that?" Was that hope blossoming in his chest? No, impossible. He wasn't that gullible, was he?

"Not in so many words."

"Right." That sounded more like it.

"But she hinted at it. A lot. And if I weren't your sister I think she might have opened up more. But I don't have to be a rocket scientist to see what's right in front of my face."

"She lied to me, Hannah. Did she tell you that? She told me that . . ." He hesitated. How much detail did he want to get into? And yet . . . Hannah was here because she loved him. Her harsh greeting aside, he knew that ultimately she wanted him to be happy. He hadn't breathed a word about the baby to a soul. Maybe he could use another perspective.

"She told you what?" Hannah asked.

He met his sister's gaze. "Do you want a drink?"

"Stop avoiding the issue. And no, I don't want a drink."

Instead he took a seat at the kitchen table, taking the whiskey bottle with him. "When we realized we'd forgotten to use protection, I suggested a morning-after pill. Willow led me to believe she was going to get it. She didn't."

"Maybe she just changed her mind."

"She *never* intended to. I won't go into why—it's a long story, and it's hers to tell. God, Hannah. I've got the boys to consider. Willow and I . . . we were just getting started. It wasn't that long ago that we started acting on our attraction for each other. It's a huge leap from that to bringing a baby into the world. To parenting."

"So you're what? Sitting here pouting? Thinking that if you avoid the situation it'll go away? That's not like you, Ethan. You face things. You deal with them. And you care for her. You need to do right by them both."

"You mean marry her?" He laughed and poured another liberal helping of whiskey. "This isn't the fifties, Hannah. Maybe I'll want to get married again someday, but that day's a long way off." Ache surrounded his heart as he looked at his sister. "You know what it was like when I lost Lisa. I don't ever want to go through that again. What's the point in loving someone if you're just going to lose them?"

"Bullshit." She stared him down. "Do you know how lucky you are to have had two really great women love you? You didn't have a choice with Lisa. She got sick and maybe it shouldn't have happened but she died, Ethan. She didn't leave you. Now you've got a choice—a chance at happiness—and you're deliberately pushing her away. Willow's having your baby, Ethan. And she's sitting over there thinking that you don't care about her. Why? Because she didn't take a stupid pill? You're going to let something trivial like that stand in your way?"

"I don't want another baby!" He blurted it out, then let out a long breath. "Do you understand that, Hannah? I have the boys and I love them so much, but being a single dad is a crazy amount of work and worry. She knew it. It would have been so simple. It's not trivial. Not to me. Maybe you don't understand. You've never been in love this way. But that thing you call trivial broke my trust."

Hannah didn't even blink at his harsh words, but he instantly felt bad for speaking them. Hannah took enough grief for being unmarried from their parents. She didn't need it from him, too.

"Willow'd be a great mother to them, too, if you gave her a chance."

It scared him that she was right. Willow had taken to the boys right away, and them to her. She was gentle and kind and firm. "We dated maybe a month. Isn't it a little soon for that?"

"What does time have to do with anything? You can know a person for years and not really know them.

And someone else you can see across a room and know they're going to change your life." She raised one eyebrow. "Or so I'm told."

He deserved that. "She's going to have a baby. Do you really think she wants to be saddled with two rambunctious boys, too?"

"Why don't you ask her?"

He turned away. What if Willow said no? She was so independent, and no matter what Hannah said, he doubted she was in love with him. She hadn't said anything of the sort when she'd come to tell him. She hadn't even hinted at wanting them to try to be a family together. It wasn't just him. He was a package deal.

And yet she'd dated him, knowing his situation.

Hannah stood. "You think about it. You think about a good woman who cares for you, who is carrying your baby, who loves your boys, and how you're sitting here and she's sitting over there because you're scared and need to be right more than you need to be happy."

"That's not fair."

"Life isn't fair, Ethan. You of all people know that. That's why you need to grab at happiness while you can."

He stared at his sister for a few minutes. Hannah was particularly passionate about this, and he wondered why. She was interfering at the best of times, but tonight she was truly put out with him and he wasn't quite sure where she was coming from. He'd had the same feeling when Willow had shown up here over a week ago. Damn, he'd never understand women. It's like they said one thing and then really meant something else.

"You sit and stew if you like. I didn't think I'd be able to change your mind, but you should at least talk to her, Ethan. You can't go on this way. Avoiding reality isn't going to change it."

"I know," he admitted. "It's just such a mess I don't know where to start."

"You could try being honest with yourself about your feelings."

She went over to him then and put a hand on his shoulder. "You are one of the best men I know," she murmured. "But sometimes you do need a loving kick in the ass."

"Go on," he grumbled.

She left, and he sat in the kitchen still, nursing the last few swallows of alcohol. Being honest with himself wasn't the problem. He already knew what he felt, and that was what scared him the most. He knew what he wanted, and that terrified him, too.

No one that he knew had lost a spouse. They didn't know what it was like. And asking him to forget the hell he'd been through was like asking a songbird to forget how to sing. It was a part of him.

Willow was a part of him, too, whether she knew it or not. And now she carried his child. Someday soon he was going to have to figure out how he was going to deal with that.

But that day wasn't today.

Not yet.

He finished the drink, put the glass in the dishwasher, signed Connor's agenda, and went to bed.

Alone.

CHAPTER 22

It was Laurel and Aiden who finally brought the boys in for a treat.

"Willow!" Connor ran through the door and barreled toward her, a huge grin lighting his face. "Where've you been?"

She fought against the bittersweet welcome and smiled, crouching down to greet him with a hug. "Hey, tiger. I've been right here, working. Coming up with some new recipes and stuff. How's school?"

"My friend Jimmy is in my class. He brought a frog to school yesterday in his lunch bag. Our teacher got mad and made him take it outside, and then threw out his lunch because it was unsan . . . unsan . . ."

"Unsanitary?"

"Yeah, that's it. I thought it was cool."

Lord, but she'd missed these two.

Ronan was waiting his turn, a little more quietly than his brother. She opened her arm and drew him into a quick cuddle. "Hello, sweetie."

"Hi, Wil-low."

Her heart turned over.

"And how are you? I think I have an apple turnover with your name on it."

He looked at her with his big, soulful eyes, and asked, "Why haven't you come to see us?"

"Oh. Well, the café's been really busy."

"We ran out of bubbles. And Daddy doesn't laugh as much. You should come over. I got a new video game."

"I've missed you guys, too. You hungry?" It was hard work keeping the smile on her face, but she did it.

She stood and saw Aiden and Laurel waiting, both with hesitant smiles on their faces. "It's okay, isn't it?" Laurel asked. "We took the boys after school today and they were begging us to come see you. I know something happened with you and Ethan . . ." Laurel kept her voice low.

"It's more than okay. I've missed them a lot. Let's grab a table and I'll bring out some stuff. What do you want, Laurel? Tea? Milk?"

Laurel touched her belly. "Mint tea seems to be hitting the spot right now," she said.

"I'll be back in a minute."

She returned a few minutes later with a plate heaped with sweets, two glasses of milk, two mugs of mint tea, and a black coffee for Aiden, since she knew that was how he liked it. The boys dug in right away, both heading straight for the turnovers. Connor, she'd learned, liked fruit and pastry. And Ronan was partial to chocolate but didn't ever want to be outdone by his big brother.

Laurel sipped at her mint tea and picked at a piece of shortbread. "How're you feeling, Laurel?" Willow wondered if her friend was still having morning sickness. She wished, too, that she could share her news with her best friend. She wanted to, so badly. She wanted to compare notes on pregnancies. To ask questions, share worries. She wanted someone to be excited with. Instead she spent precious private moments resting her hand on her tummy, wondering about the baby inside, how it was developing.

"Mornings are rough. I treat Aiden to what I call 'shower music.' He gets in the shower, I throw up. Once I have breakfast I'm better. And then it's just the odd thing that throws me off. But otherwise I'm great." She smiled.

Aiden grinned. "I started keeping barf bags in the car just in case." He reached over and took her hand. "But hopefully it'll be better soon. And I still think she has a glow."

If Willow didn't like them so much it might be sickening. It did, however, highlight what she was missing. A partner. Someone who looked at her the way that Aiden looked at Laurel.

She handed napkins to the boys, then talked to them for a few minutes about school and soccer and whatever else was going on. Apparently Moira and John's dog, Waffle, got an abscess on his leg and had to wear a big cone on his head. Connor threw his arm wide describing it, and Willow barely kept his milk glass from spilling as they all laughed.

It was Laurel who finally asked in a low voice, "Is everything okay with you?"

Willow shrugged, trying to remain nonchalant. "It's busy here. Emily's managing things now, so we've been training some new staff. It's good, though. She's taken over some of the administrative duties, and once we smooth out the newbie wrinkles, it'll be good for me."

"I don't mean work." Laurel looked over at Aiden who was deliberately keeping the boys occupied. "I mean you. What happened with you two?"

"It's a long story." Willow looked over at the kids and then back to Laurel. "Too long to go into now."

"I wish we could find some time to really talk."

"We will. It's just complicated right now, that's all."

"Sweetie." Laurel put down her mug. "You're never complicated. You always put things in perspective. Do you see why I'm worried?"

She did. She even agreed. "Well, what can I say? Sometimes something or someone comes along to stir things up." She smiled. "We will talk, Laurel, I promise. I've missed you."

"You're not happy." Laurel persisted, and Willow found the continued probing a bit tiring. There was no way she'd talk about any of this with Ethan's children around. Laurel usually took the hint, but since she and Aiden had married, she'd tried to fix the lives of those around her. It was sweet most of the time, but not so much when Willow was the target in her sights.

"No one is happy all the time," Willow asserted firmly. "And I'm not unhappy, either." She wasn't, not totally. Each day she made a point of counting her blessings, being grateful for the good things in her life.

"All right. If you say so."

A few minutes later they finished up the last Hermit cookie and macaroon slice on the plate and Willow took the tray back to the kitchen. When she came out again, she walked outside with the foursome, hesitant to say goodbye. She didn't know when she was going to see the boys again. Part of her wanted to invite them up to her apartment. To ply them with ice cream and let them sit in her chair. But she had no claim to them. Never had. Instead they seemed to have claimed her.

"Willow, watch me! I can walk like a crab!" Connor dropped to his bottom, braced himself up on his hands and feet, and started a goofy crab walk on the grass by the sidewalk.

"Be careful, Connor. Don't get in the way. There are people walking."

Connor could see people coming and going, but Ronan decided he wanted to walk like a dog, up on his toes and hands. He was prancing around with his head down when Willow saw the cyclist turn the corner, heading straight toward them.

Connor scooted out of the way, but Ronan gave an awkward doggy-hop and lost his balance, tottering erratically on the sidewalk.

"Ronan, look out!" Aiden yelled, but it was Willow who jumped toward the pavement. She hooked her hands around his little waist and pulled him out of the way, tossing him in a heap onto the grass in front of the café. The cyclist tried to avoid them, but Willow leaned backward after letting go of Ronan, her body trying to counterbalance the abrupt action. Teenager and mountain bike careened into her, sending her sprawling. The cyclist fell one way, the bike another, the pedals and handlebars landing on Willow's arm and thigh.

Ronan was wailing, Connor didn't know what to do with himself, and Laurel was by her side in seconds. "Oh my God, Willow. Are you okay?"

The cyclist picked himself up from the pavement. "I'm so sorry," he said, taking off his helmet and kneeling beside her. "Oh my gosh. You've got a cut on your head. Are you hurt? I didn't mean to . . . I came around the corner and . . ."

Aiden put a hand on the lad's shoulder, and the kid turned around and paled.

"Oh God. Officer Gallagher."

"You should be on the road, not the sidewalk, if you're going that fast."

"I'll slow down, sir. Promise."

"Hey, it was an accident. Don't panic. I'm not going to arrest you or anything."

Willow waited for the kid to lift the bike off of her. The boys stood a few feet away, still crying, and Laurel helped her to her feet. A pain shot through her right hip and she cried out a bit. When she looked down, a scratch from the teeth of the pedal ran down the side of her leg, marked by a thin line of blood and a dusty smudge where her skin had been rubbed by the metal and plastic.

And she might have been able to wave everyone off and insist she was okay if Hannah hadn't come running out of her office.

"Oh my God, are you okay? I saw you fall from my window."

"I'm fine, really." Willow smiled through her teeth.

"You should get checked out. You're bleeding."

Willow looked down at her leg. "It's just a scratch, Hannah. Stop fussing."

"Not your leg, you ninny. Your head. I saw you get hit, Willow. You need to go to the hospital and be sure."

"I'm fine," she insisted, shifting her weight onto her left leg more, trying to smile so that Hannah didn't see the agony she was in. But as she tried to move, her hip pained her again and she gasped. When she touched her face, her fingers came away sticky with blood.

"Willow. For the baby's sake," Hannah said the words down low, but Laurel and Aiden both heard. Suddenly Willow felt like a bug beneath a magnifying glass in the sun. Trapped and on the hot seat.

"Willow?" Laurel's hesitant voice broke the silence.

Tears stung her eyes and her throat closed. Aiden sent the cyclist on his way, the boys sat on the grass and whimpered instead of crying, and Hannah had the grace to look guilty as hell.

"Fine," Willow said harshly, angry at Hannah for being such a big mouth, sore from the fall, tired of it all. "Thanks a lot, Hannah. Maybe you'd go grab my purse from the apartment so I've got my ID with me."

"I'll take you, Willow." Aiden was by her side and said it quietly.

"I'll watch the boys," Laurel said. She reached out and touched Willow's arm. "I wish you'd told me," she said, and looked like a kicked puppy.

Willow fought for serenity. For calm. For peace. None of it came to her. She was simply hurting, and nothing was going to fix that right now. The only way past it was through it. She'd told Ethan that once.

"I'll take you to the hospital," Aiden repeated gently, helping her into his truck. "You'll . . . you'll need an ultrasound won't you? You won't find that at the clinic here in town."

"Sure." She doubted she was far enough along for an ultrasound, but at this point she wasn't going to argue with anyone.

Hannah brought out her purse. "Sorry," she offered weakly.

Willow didn't trust herself to say anything; she took the bag and dropped it by her feet. She wanted to simply sit and cry, but she wouldn't do that in front of Aiden. For his part, he pulled away from the curb and didn't attempt to make conversation much on the drive. Once they hit the highway, he looked over. "The bleeding on your forehead is stopping. Are you feeling okay? Any cramping or anything?"

"Not really."

"Good. That's good."

He waited a minute.

"It's Ethan's?"

"Yeah. I'm not up to a lecture or anything, Aiden, so if that's what you're—"

"Not even close. It's got to be a complicated situation and it's none of my business. But he's my brother and you're Laurel's best friend and we'll do whatever you need us to do. That's all."

She looked over at Aiden. He resembled his brother so much, in coloring and mannerisms. His face had a softer look, probably due to his well-known sense of humor. But right now he was as serious as she'd ever seen him, and without warning she started to weep.

To his credit, he just kept driving. After a bit he told her there were napkins in the glove compartment if she needed them, and she took one out and blew her nose. She'd needed the cry so badly, and had been trying not to fall apart. The pain of the crash along with the spilling of the beans and then Aiden's consideration toppled her over the edge.

They arrived at the hospital and he parked in the emergency lot, then went around to her side and helped her out of the truck, putting an arm around her waist and helping her hobble to the doors. "I'm sorry I cried," she said quietly.

He only smiled softly. "I'm married to a pregnant woman. I'm getting used to hormonal tears. It's no biggie, honey."

Ethan checked the speedometer and wondered if he dared drive any faster.

Hannah had called him at work and he'd clocked out right away, citing a family emergency. Even though she'd assured him Willow was fine, she thought he'd want to know what happened. A tumble, some cuts and bruises. Sounded innocent enough, but any fall could have consequences when a woman was pregnant.

And he hadn't been there for her. It had been Aiden who'd taken her to the hospital to get checked out. Was she scared? Hell, he didn't even know how she was feeling. Hannah was right. He was a stubborn asshole who put himself in a bubble rather than deal with the issues right in front of him.

She was having his baby. His child. What if she lost it now? Getting pregnant had been a total accident, and one that was guaranteed to mess up their lives and put a strain on their relationship. To someone on the outside, a miscarriage might look like a blessing.

Instead, the idea pierced him right in the heart, stealing his breath. He didn't want her to lose the baby. He wanted to see him or her be born and grow and giggle and play and be a brother or sister to Connor and Ronan. How that would all play out, he didn't know. But for the second time in his life, he experienced that moment of clarity when everything that was important became crystal clear.

Did the drive usually take this long?

Eventually he pulled into the lot and parked, then jogged to the emergency doors. He scanned the wait-

ing room and didn't see her; his stomach dropped to
his feet. Then he saw Aiden, sitting solemnly in one
of the vinyl chairs, checking his phone.

"Aiden." His brother looked up and stood as Ethan
approached. "Where is she?"

"They took her right in, on account of the baby."

"You knew?"

"Hannah blurted it out when Willow was getting
up. I don't think Willow's too pleased with Han right
now." Aiden put a hand on his sleeve. "But I think she's
okay, E. It's just a precaution. We've both had first aid.
She's got some cuts and bruises but she said she wasn't
having any cramping or anything. Take a breath."

He did. He let out a deep one, then sat in the chair
next to Aiden. For a few seconds he closed his eyes and
breathed deeply, trying to quell the panic cramping his
chest.

"Oh man, she really has done a number on you. Are
you . . . meditating?"

Aiden's warm voice drew him out of his focus. "No.
Now shut up. The breathing helps. You should try it.
Besides, you'd be the same way if it was Laurel in
there."

Aiden nodded, his smile slipping. "I know. Except
I'd be in there with her because we're a team. Why
don't you tell me why you and Willow aren't?"

Ethan didn't have a good answer. Yes, he was still
scared. Yes, he was still wondering what the hell they
were going to do. But he'd pushed her away rather than
holding her close. He should have been assuring her it
would be okay, instead of stubbornly refusing to call.
He loved her. He did, and he'd known it for some time.
It had hit him like a truck the night of the drive-in
movie, when he'd nearly taken her to bed.

"I don't know," he answered honestly. "Probably because I'm a first-class jackass."

"That's a given. What else?"

Ethan laughed a little. Maybe he should have talked to Aiden earlier. Truth was, he'd been embarrassed. He was the responsible one. The boring one. "It's your fault, you know," Ethan said, trying to keep the mood light so he didn't worry so much about what was happening inside the exam room. "You probably don't even remember, but you told Mom that I needed to get laid."

"Well, brother, there's a difference between scratching your ass and tearing it all to hell. Getting laid is one thing. Being irresponsible is another. See, Laurel and me, we did it right. We got married first."

Ethan snorted. Aiden had a different way with him. He'd joke and commiserate, whereas Hannah lectured. "Don't be smug," he said. "I know I should have told you. I just didn't know how. I was trying to wrap my head around it, and Willow . . . she's not what she seems. She comes across as so sweet and . . . uncomplicated. But she's been hurt, a lot. And so have I. And we both let that get in the way. Me especially. She's the brave one, and I'm the coward."

"It's never too late."

"She might not want anything to do with me. I'd deserve it."

"Why don't you ask her?"

Ethan's brow furrowed, and then he turned toward the sliding doors that came out from the exam area. Willow stood there, in a skirt and a shirt that had streaks of dirt all over it. Her leg was red and scratched and she had a bandage on her forehead, the white square standing out against the tanned skin of her face.

Oh, God. He'd failed her in so many ways.

He got up from the chair and started toward her, and she took a few halting, limping steps, and before he knew it she was in his embrace, her arms around his shoulders and her face nestled against his neck.

The backs of his eye stung. "I'm sorry I wasn't here. Willow, are you okay?"

She nodded against his skin and he let out half a breath.

"And . . . the baby? Are you both okay?"

She pulled out of his arms a bit and met his gaze, her face streaked with tears. "Everything's fine. We're both fine."

"Oh, thank God," he said, and pulled her close again.

"You mean that?" she asked, her fingers digging into his shoulder blades.

"I do. We have so much to talk about. And I have so much to apologize for."

"Oh, Ethan." She sniffled against his neck, and he blinked rapidly, trying to clear the moisture in his eyes.

Aiden laid his hand flat on Ethan's back. "I think you've got it from here, brother. I'll be heading out. Willow, let us know if you need anything, okay? And take your time. We'll take the boys to Mom and Dad's. They were going to stay there anyway while you were on shift, right?"

Ethan nodded. "Thanks, Aiden."

"That's what family's for. Check in later, let us know how you're doing."

Aiden left them there, and Willow pulled back, wiping at her face and looking a bit chagrined. "So much for no public scenes," she joked, biting down on her lip.

"Maybe it's time we both stop hiding away," he suggested. "Come on. Let me take you home."

CHAPTER 23

Ethan handed her into his car with such care that she wanted to start crying all over again.

She couldn't believe he was here. That he'd left work—he was still in his uniform—and rushed to her side. More than that, he'd seemed so relieved that she hadn't lost the baby.

She was, too. The entire time she'd sat in the exam room, she'd prayed for her baby to be safe.

Maybe the timing was wrong. Maybe this was more complicated than she wished it was, but when the doctor had come in and said everything looked okay, she'd realized that none of that mattered. She wasn't going to be a mother; she was a mother already. And it was a blessing.

"Are you in a lot of pain? Hannah said something about your hip, and your head."

She shook her head slightly. "It's okay. The doctor said I could take some stuff for it, but I'd rather not. I'll put some ice on it when I get home and take it easy for a couple of days."

"I know what 'take it easy' means to you. Stay off your feet, listen to your body, and take rests, okay? When Lisa . . ."

He halted, but she reached over and touched his hand. "When Lisa what? You can talk about her, you know."

He looked over at her briefly before focusing on the road again. "When Lisa was expecting the boys, she said she got tired really easily, especially at the first and the last of the pregnancy."

She smiled softly. "I do get sleepy, right around two o'clock every day. Thanks for telling me, Ethan. For sharing."

"I haven't shared much of anything lately. Mainly myself. I want to change that, Willow."

"I'd like that. I've . . ." She swallowed against a thick lump of emotion. "I've missed you."

"Me, too."

They drove in silence after that, somehow tacitly agreeing that they'd hold off on the serious conversation until they were home. He took her to her apartment, and when she would have hobbled up the stairs to her door, he picked her up in his arms instead and carried her to the top.

She didn't want to be thrilled, but she was. He was so strong, so capable. When he wasn't around she'd felt a little lost. When he was nearby she felt safe, protected. It had nothing to do with not being able to do for herself, but everything to do with feeling cherished and valued, something she'd been missing for too many years.

Willow Dunaway was strong enough now to realize that caring and loving someone made her stronger, not weaker. It made her vulnerable, but brave. He put her down on the futon and then sat beside her, brushing a strand of hair away from her face and tucking it behind her ear. "Do you need anything?" he asked. "Ice? Something to drink? Do you want to lie down?"

She smiled at him. "All three, but later. Thank you for bringing me home."

He took her hand between his. "When Hannah called . . . you know how sometimes people say they have a moment of truth? Mine was when she said Aiden had taken you to the hospital."

"It wasn't that serious. It was just a bike, you know. Hannah overreacted and honestly, going to the hospital was just a precaution."

"Of course it was. You're pregnant, Willow. I know I've been a jerk. More than that. I've been a coward. You shouldn't have had to deal with this all alone. I should have been there with you. It took two of us that night. And yeah, I was upset when I found out you lied, but to shut you out? That was fear, pure and simple. Fear and denial."

He rubbed his thumb over the top of her hand as his gaze held hers. "I understand why you did what you did. And I'm so, so sorry that you ever had to go through that as a girl. But it's made you into the woman you've become, and . . ."

He inhaled sharply, searched her eyes, and said, "And I love her."

She hadn't expected such an admission, and she didn't have a response right away. Love? Had he really just said he loved her? The man who was so determined not to put himself out there again? Who wasn't ready for whatever love might mean for a relationship?

"You're not just saying that because of the baby, are you?"

"I get why you'd think that, and all I can say is that I'll spend as long as it takes trying to convince you. I love the stripe in your hair—I like the blue by the way—and the way that you laugh, and how pale blue is your favorite color. I like how you smile and that you take care of everyone without them really noticing." His voice broke a bit. "I love walking in here and finding my son curled up in your arms in that silly chair, both of you asleep. I love how you kiss me and make me feel about nineteen again, and like I can conquer the world. I love it all so much it scares the hell out of me, because I think I'd die if I lost you, too."

"Oh," she said, the word barely more than a squeak. As speeches went, it was rather magnificent, and she suspected that if she tried to say more, she'd burst out crying—something she was doing more often lately.

"I pushed you away rather than deal with those fears. And a funny thing happened."

"What's that?"

"I lost you anyway. And it still hurt, even though I tried to tell myself it didn't."

She put her free hand over his. "You love me? But I'm . . . oh, Ethan. I'm so flawed. I thought I had my shit together and clearly I don't. Maybe I never will, and maybe that's the point. We're both so damaged . . ."

"You told me once that your last relationship ended because you brought each other down rather than making each other stronger. Willow, you make me stronger. I was a grumpy hermit when we met. I tried to be happy for the boys but I know eventually they would have figured it out. Then suddenly I wasn't snapping at anyone anymore. I looked forward to seeing you. I thought about you when we were apart. You took a moment when I was hurting and you kissed me and made me feel like a man again. You made me more, just by being you."

Tears quivered on her lashes. Damn, he was doing a very good job, but she needed him to know how she felt, too. He wasn't in this alone.

She swiped away at the moisture and cleared the well of emotion from her throat. "I know I said that our relationship pointed out my flaws, but that's not a bad thing, either." She moved her hand from his clasp and cupped his jaw. "I found all this peace and thought that my business was enough to bring me fulfillment, but being with you . . . I'd stopped dreaming of a future with love in it, you see. Which is stupid, because love is the most important thing in the whole world. Growth isn't always fun. It can be painful. But I grew up these last few months. I started dreaming again. Once I stopped freaking out about the baby, I started looking forward to the future. There was just one problem. I wanted a future with you in it, and you weren't here."

"I'm sorry . . ."

"No, don't. You're here now. I love you, Ethan. It scares the living hell out of me to say that, but it's true. I'm trusting you with it, which is also huge. The thing is, even when you were so angry and confused, I knew deep down that you are the best man I've ever known. You're strong and kind and brave, and an incredible father. Your heart calls to mine, Ethan. It calls and mine answers and that is something so rare it needs to be treasured."

He leaned forward and touched his forehead to hers. "Every time we've been together, you've humbled me somehow. It's your gift, Willow. You have a beautiful spirit. What I said the first night about you . . . I didn't know what to do with all your, I don't know, perfection. What I discovered is a complete lack of artifice and a heart that's so genuine it puts mine to shame." His lips touched hers briefly. "I resented you because you made me want to be a better man. And then before I knew what was happening, I loved you for it."

She closed her eyes and leaned her face closer to his, not quite kissing. "And the baby?"

"Of course I want to be a father to this baby. I just had to take my head out of my ass."

She laughed abruptly, so happy that Ethan sounded like his old self again. "And I want to be a mother. I don't know how it's all going to work out, but it will. I know it will."

"We don't have to decide right now. We just need to keep talking. Keep loving each other."

"And the boys. I love them too, Ethan. You must know that. I would never try to take Lisa's place, but I'll love them like my own, and hopefully they'll love me back."

"They already do," he said.

She kissed him then, a slow, lingering kiss that healed wounds and made promises. It wasn't until she tried to shift closer that the pain in her hip knifed into her.

"Here," he said gently, setting her back on the sofa. He got up and went to the freezer and took out an ice pack, then wrapped it in a little towel and brought it back to her, along with a glass of water. She drank, then he sat on the futon with the throw pillows at his back and eased her back against his chest. He tucked the ice pack against her hip and then stroked her hair away from her face as her head rested in the curve of his shoulder.

"Better?"

"Almost."

She reached around for his hand, and guided it to the tiny bubble that had begun to form at her belly. His palm was wide and warm, and she closed her eyes. "Now that's better."

"I love you, Willow."

"I love you, Ethan."

"Don't scare me like that again."

She smiled. "I'll try not to go to such drastic lengths if I need your attention."

He kissed her hair. "You won't need to," he assured her. "I'm here, and I'm not going anywhere."

CHAPTER 24

The Darling Elementary School held a Fall Frolic on the Green the last week of September. Willow had agreed to supply ten dozen cookies for the snack table, and she'd volunteered to do an hour at the face painting station. Presently she was painting a pink and purple butterfly on the crest of a little girl's cheek.

The boys weren't into face painting so much, so they were off to try their luck at the dunk tank. It was just their luck that the police force had sent two officers to take turns getting wet, and one of them was their uncle Aiden. Ethan was having far too much fun paying his quarters and taking aim.

The whole family was present to support the school, which was fundraising for renovating the library. Even Rory had come out, along with Oaklee from the town office, who was walking a strange dog . . . or rather, the dog was walking her. Rory was following her and laughing, which didn't seem to please Oaklee too much at all.

Throughout the afternoon the kids made their way

from one station to another. There was a cake walk, a
bouncy castle—which suited Ronan just fine—a game
of kickball, and food. Hot dogs and hamburgers sizzled on the grill, while another mom scooped up popcorn from a big popcorn maker, and someone's dad
swirled cotton candy onto sticks in lumpy mounds.
There would be tired kids and sore tummies later, but
it was the first time Willow had been included in anything like this and she loved every minute.

At one point during the afternoon, Ethan pulled her
aside. "Come with me for a minute."

She took his hand and let him lead her past the
perennial beds and toward the famed stone bridge. A
goofy smile lit her face as she realized where they were
going. "Really? I thought you didn't go for all this su-
perstitious crap."

"I have something to say, and this is where I want
to say it."

"Then I won't argue with you."

He guided her to the crest of the bridge. As they
looked down at the water, they noticed a family of
ducks floating lazily along. Willow rested her arms on
the stone railing and sighed. "This has been a great
day, don't you think?"

When she turned back, he was watching her with
such tenderness that her heart gave a leap. "You have
to stop looking at me like that. With all the hormones
running through my body, I'm not sure if it makes me
want to weep or jump your bones."

A grin flashed over his face. "We can discuss that
later. But really, I want to be serious for a minute." He
reached out and took her hand. "Willow, I made promises on this bridge before. You know I did. And I think
I need to be here, with you, to let them go. I felt for so

long that I'd been cheated out of my love of a lifetime. But I wasn't. I loved her for as long as she was on this earth, and she loved me. But she's gone. Our vows said until death separated us, and that was exactly what we had."

He twined his fingers with hers. "I love you, Willow. So I want to kiss you on this bridge and tell you that I love you and that I love our baby. That will never change."

He knelt down before her and pressed a kiss to her belly. She put her hands on his head, so overcome with love that she hardly knew what to do with it all.

When he stood up he kissed her, too, a soft, sweet kiss that said they had all the time in the world, and they were going to make the most of every second.

She met his gaze and smiled. "So should we tell them now? Are you ready?"

He nodded. "No rush, right? We do this on our terms, on our time."

"Well, one of us might have a schedule in mind, but yeah, that's the idea." Willow put her hand where his lips had just been, and he covered her hand with his.

"Okay, let's round up the family."

They found the boys, then Rory, Aiden and Laurel, and Moira and John. The girls were away at school, but they'd get filled in later. Hannah joined them at the last minute, and Willow and Ethan pulled the boys aside first and told them the news—both about the baby, and about Willow moving into their house.

Connor's eyes went wide. "A brother or sister? Does this mean Willow is going to be our mom?"

Ethan looked at Willow, and she patted her knee. Connor crawled up on it and she put her arms around him. Ronan plopped to the grass in front of them, but his tiny hand rested on her leg, a simple and genuine point of contact.

"You had a wonderful mom, Connor, and I would never want to replace her in your heart. But maybe you could make room for me in your heart, beside her somewhere? Because I love you, and Ronan, and your dad an awful lot. And we're going to have another baby that'll be your sister or brother. And I'll do what I can to make sure we're all happy."

Connor twisted around and hugged her fiercely, taking her utterly by surprise. "I miss my mommy," he whispered in her ear. "But if I can't have her, you're the next best thing. I'm glad." And he hugged her tight.

"We're going to get along just fine, aren't we?" she asked, grinning at him. "What about you, Ronan? Are you okay with another baby in the house?"

"Not a sister," he decreed. "No girls. 'Cept you, Wil-low."

She laughed. "No promises. Sorry, buster."

He stood up and put his hand on her shoulder. "Can I still have cuddles?"

"Every single day."

"Okay, then."

She looked up at Ethan. "Told ya," he said.

Once the boys were on board, they told the rest of the family. Laurel and Aiden and Hannah already knew about the baby, but Moira and John got a bit of a shock and Rory's eyebrows lifted so high they nearly disappeared into his hairline. "Willow's going to move into my place," Ethan said.

"It made the most sense. The kids are happy there, and there's the great backyard, and it means as little upheaval as possible," Willow added.

"Does this mean there's a wedding, then?" Moira looked hopeful, and Ethan laughed.

"We're trying to take things one step at a time, Mom. There are a lot of adjustments happening. Planning a wedding can be kind of stressful."

"Unless you make it a surprise," Aiden said, making everyone laugh. His impromptu wedding to Laurel was still a topic of town conversation.

"We have time to figure it out," Willow said, leaning against Ethan's chest. She'd never grow tired of being held securely in his arms. It was her favorite place in the world. "One of my things was that I won't have my yoga studio at the house. With the baby coming, the other bedroom will become a nursery. So, Hannah, Ethan had an idea that might pique your interest."

"Oooh, do I smell a deal?"

"So predictable." Willow nodded. "I've decided against expanding The Purple Pig. Emily's doing a great job managing it, and expanding would mean making structural changes to the building, and a lot of cost. Instead I want to open my own yoga studio. I've got my certification already, and I can teach until I'm quite far along. It won't take long to get the interior ready, and since I have the lease until next summer, it gives us lots of time to get things up and running. What do you say? Do you want in?"

Rory gave Hannah a nudge. "Just say yes. You know you want to."

Moira smiled. "You know the girls will be among your first clients."

Willow remembered. The first night she'd been at the Gallagher's for dinner, one of the twins had mentioned the dearth of available classes in Darling.

John came over and gave her a hug. "You and Hannah. Two very different girls, and equally ambitious."

"Motivated," Willow corrected him. "By happiness. And by wanting to spread it around." She looked up at Ethan, finding it hard to believe she could be this lucky. This content. "And I was nearly there, when Ethan came along. All I was missing was someone to love."

"Not anymore," Ethan said, and pulled her close.

Don't miss the next novel in the Darling series by
Donna Alward

Somebody's Baby

Coming soon from St. Martin's Paperbacks